# THE

# M · I · N · U · S

# MAN

ALSO BY LEW McCREARY

Mount's Mistake

# THE

# M·I·N·U·S

# MAN

### Lew McCreary

**GROVE PRESS**
*New York*

*To Marcy*

*First published in 1991 by Viking Penguin, a division of Penguin Books USA Inc.*
*Published simultaneously in Canada*
*Printed in the United States of America*

FIRST GROVE PRESS EDITION


Library of Congress Cataloging-in-Publication Data

McCreary, Lew.
The minus man : a novel/by Lew McCreary.
p.   cm.
ISBN 0-8021-3674-5
I. Title.
PS3563.C3526M56   1991
813'.54—dc20          90-23389


Grove Press
841 Broadway
New York, NY 10003

99 00 01 02   10 9 8 7 6 5 4 3 2 1

# THE

# M · I · N · U · S

# MAN

# ONE

.:.

I WILL MISS THE SEVEN RIVERS MOST. SEVEN rivers come together near where I once lived, and live no more. They turn into one solid river flowing east. Seven seems like a lot to me. I tell this to the postmaster and he says I'm such a fool, there aren't even four—what I see as seven is just nothing more than brooks broken off from the other main streams. But the post-master knows what he knows, and I know what I know. The waters all pour in together and roil. Seven rivers is seven rivers, turning to one. As in seven days become a week. I stare at the postmaster's daughter, a fair child, brown hair, shy. She looks away. I wonder what she's becoming. I reach ahead in time, imagining the incredible changes bursting within her.

"What do you say?" I ask her. "How old are you?"

"Seven," she says. On Saturdays the postmaster lets her be with him behind the grille.

"That's right," the postmaster says.

"That settles it, then," I say. "Seven rivers it is."

I put my pen to the form. I'm closing up my mailbox, Box 246. Almost nothing ever came to me. The Bible speaks of holding open a door to see what honors might come fill it. Shadows was all there were. I had no phone and came to the box three times a week, hoping for something. But I maintained no official relationships. Who knew me that might have sent a thing? When the truck was

*1*

fully paid for, which has been two years now, I would come and bend down at the box and see emptiness.

"Where to?" the postmaster says.

"Just east," I say, deliberately vague. This is Oregon. East covers a lot of territory. People ought to be warned, I think.

"Anything lined up?"

"No, nothing," I say.

"Place to live?"

"Nope."

"Where do I send your mail?"

"You don't," I say. "I leave no forwarding address."

"Okay."

"Just do whatever you do. Return to sender."

The girl eyes me when I say this. What does the young child, daughter of a postmaster, know? She knows that a man with no fixed address is interesting. I see the interest in her eyes. I smile. What will she be in five years? In ten?

" 'Bye, honey," I say. I hand the form across to the father. The left side is filled out, the right side is blank.

"Well, so long, Mr. Siegert," he says. "Good luck."

I smile at the daughter.

Before I set out I can't resist just one more trip to where I lived. I want to hear the rivers, walk in the deep ravine. I leave the truck running. First I peer in the cabin windows looking for whatever I might have forgotten. The cabin looks completely empty, but I can't see everything—there could be some old kettle left on the floor behind a door or a deck of cards up on a shelf. I half expect to see myself doing a normal act of living in the house, carrying an empty coffee cup to the sink. I won't ever come back.

I could go in, but I don't. Already this place is in the past. I'm moving. That fact takes hold. I turn from the cabin.

Birds are too high in the trees to be seen, but they cry out powerfully, and I can hear them even above the sound of the seven rivers joining.

The rivers always pulled at me. I was always able to hear the seven different voices rising out of the flowing together. Each had a personality and could not be trusted any more than it could be ignored. If I tried to ignore it, the voice got louder. Sometimes there was anger. I believed that they were angry leaving their seven smaller homes. I hoped that they would settle down in the new larger home. Seven individual voices. They were always polite to each other but hard on me. I had no special favorites. I'll miss them all the most.

The ravine is soft and damp. Underfoot the ground flexes as if the earth floats on a cushion of oil. I can almost see the thirteen bodies in the ground where I have left them, bathed in the cushion of oil and waiting for someone other than me to know they are there. But no one else will ever know. Finally I can see why I am sad to leave. I leave the thirteen bodies alone with the seven rivers. I envy the bodies, envy the rivers. I believe they will not even miss me.

I am like a comet that no one knows is falling. I obey certain laws of the universe, but I don't calculate it out ahead of time where I'm going to land. I am heading east, is all. I can't do anything about myself. I will just continue on. Sometimes, as I pull into a gas station, I think: People ought to be warned. I feel sorry for what I am. Should I go to the phone and call up a radio station?

"Can I have the key?" I say. The man doesn't answer but takes the key, attached to a big piece of plastic with the name of the brand of gas, and hands it to me.

"I'll pay when I bring the key back."

In the bathroom, it's bad. The toilet is full of everything. I turn on the faucet and listen to the water strike the basin. It surprises me: I hear voices rising from the sink. I turn the water off. I piss in the sink. The drain makes a whispering noise. The sound falls deeper into the earth, then the silence reigns—lonely. I'm almost afraid to move my feet. Who can stand the sound that breaks a good silence?

"Here's the key," I say. "It's dirty in there." He looks at me for a minute, like should he bother with me and what would it change?

"No kidding," he says.

I slide the money toward him. He places his fingers on one end of the bill and pulls it slowly out from under my three fingers at the other end. The bill sighs. The man plays the register like an instrument.

I spend an hour sitting in the truck at the side of the road debating: Will I look at maps or not? Inside the glove compartment there might be a map. I don't exactly recall; it could be that I never knew. But I will not open the glove compartment until the question is settled. If I decide to look at maps, I'll open it up to see if there is one. If I decide not to look at maps, I'll open it up to throw out whatever maps I might find inside. The hour takes too long. I feel weak and unhappy; it ought to be easier to decide a thing. But every time a car passes, at a speed that makes my pickup tremble, I am distracted and have to start over.

My decision is that I will not look at maps. Does a comet look at a map? To me, it won't matter. I'll find my way. One thing will lead to another.

But deliberately I decide not to check in the glove compartment. Who knows?

A woman named Kyra finds me.

"How do you spell that?" I ask her.

"Like it sounds," she says. "How should I know?"

I am seated with Kyra at a table near the door to a place called Hal's. A man who might be Hal and might not is at the bar carefully folding bar rags in the middle of the day. The pile grows. He does it in a certain way without looking. Instead of watching what he's doing, he pays close attention to Kyra and me. I don't even know what state we're in.

"What state is this?" I ask Kyra.

"Idaho. Listen, are you crazy?"

"No," I say.

Kyra watched me come in and got up and came over. It was boring. She was helpless because I had showed her my smile, which is like a charming hamster a boy might keep in his pocket and take out only to show on a special occasion to a special friend. When I smiled I saw that Kyra felt honored. She floated toward me above the surface of Hal's dark floor. I told her my name was Randolph and showed her one of the many driver's licenses I hold in reserve. "That's Randy, then," she said, looking hard at a picture that wasn't even me.

Now we're the best of friends.

"You don't know what *state?*" Her voice rises high and sharp.

"Well, now I do," I tell her. "But can I trust you? Probably not."

She doesn't smile. She pretends she takes this seriously. She looks deep down in her glass like Mr. Wizard is going to appear in the bottom, explaining something. Not even an ice cube is left. The glass is dry.

"Can I?" I show her the smile again, and I can just about tell that the smile is getting tired of being shown.

"Sure," she says.

I debate what to do. I can see how this is going. It is almost like Kyra was in here waiting for me during every minute of recorded history. She was the unhappy woman left waiting for the comet to fall, and there was only one of her on the planet, and only one of me. I watch the bartender quietly folding rags. He begins a second pile of them that for a while has an insignificant smallness to it. He looks straight at me and doesn't flinch when the phone rings. He just lets it go on ringing.

"Oh, for Pete's sake, Artis," says Kyra. But Artis doesn't move. The phone rings until it stops. I welcome back the silence. I imagine drugging Artis with a certain drug. Kyra lets go of her dry glass and reaches across to my hand.

"I'm empty, in case you were keeping track," she says.

I simply get up and go, not saying a word to Kyra or Artis. Outside, I start the engine and check to see if anyone has come to the window. The hanging neon seems to shudder and swing, but I see no faces. For the afternoon I roll across Idaho thinking I should have stayed and done something to Artis. And Artis will go on with his stupid life not knowing what a lucky man he was one day. And for two or three hours Kyra will miss me.

I find a lake in the middle of the night. The water calls me off the interstate highway, directs me south on a state road without light poles, then left on gravel. There is a ferocious moon that dances on the pocked surface of the road. The gravel glints. Sometimes a journey seems charmed. I go the whole way smiling like a slave, happy to be called. I need no maps to get to the lake. I vision the scene before I arrive, where the moon bends and waves upon the slow water, which hums like a song. And when I actually get there, that is exactly what I see. The gravel leads to slick hardpack, moist from a day-old rain. My tires whisper and ripple. The hardpack runs tight between crowding thickets. Leaves and brambles swoosh against the sides of the truck, squealing. Then everything opens up, and what does it matter what state I'm in? The lake lies singing in moonlight, and I am the only witness. The mouth of the water yawns wide and lets out the truth in front of my tired eyes. The water says to wait. I wait for someone to come from the water dripping, like a gift from it to me. I watch the still surface until my eyes ache. The moon slides lower. For half the night I hold my breath, and for the other half I gasp for air. My heart races and idles.

Finally, from the dark behind where I left the truck, I hear a noise that frightens me. What would anything else be doing here in this, the kind of place where a killer might loiter? I get to my knees and crawl to the truck and carefully place my hands on the chrome, whose coolness settles me and makes me just an odd-shaped part of the truck extending forward. My breathing stops. Twenty feet away—no more—I hear a whisper. I can't make out the particular words, but the sound is human, light, small. I hear a laugh that breaks my heart. With my back to the water I know the water to say to me, "See?" The word has the warmth of a grandfather smiling. The whisper now is as close as the back of the truck, and I am ready.

Later I will thank the lake.

Before sunrise I left the lake, and now it is a dream that hardly happened. I am driving with both my hands in my lap and the truck going straight of its own accord. No one else is here with me on this road. It must be Sunday. A peacefulness passes over me, and I am honored. I'll stop at the very first church, no matter what faith, and go in and say my thanks. Maybe it's Wyoming. Maybe Nebraska, South Dakota. The sun is in front of me, low and silver. Between me and it is some kind of weather, which might be the wintry future. I go a hundred miles before there comes a town. My truck sails through. I can sense the houses shudder in my wake. Then I see the church. Automatically my foot finds the brake, my hands take the wheel.

I am first in church. The padre is lighting candles. He speaks to me in Spanish, then English, smiling, but when I first opened the door he spun around and showed his fear.

I ask if I can help. He points to cardboard boxes of books and has me put them out in the pews. The books that are deepest in the boxes are the warmest. I let the dimpled covers slide in my hands; between the covers the paper squeaks when I squeeze.

"Thank you," the padre says. "I was falling behind."

The cars and trucks begin to come. I hear the doors slamming and the voices. I finish with the books.

"See? I wouldn't have made it," the padre says. "Sit wherever you want."

I drop to kneel in the aisle and dip my chin to my chest, pressing so hard that the glands in my jaw begin to ache. Then I drop some quarters into the wooden plate and leave the church. A man and woman brush past me in the doorway. I get my truck out before someone blocks it.

My sleep is never right. I seldom wake from it refreshed. Somewhere in Iowa I am stretched across the seat of the cab in a sleeping bag. I have driven off the main road and down another road, and another. This is the familiar process of disappearing from the face of the earth—beneath the skin of the face of the earth—which I have never had to be taught. Even when I was a boy I knew this much. Sometimes I went to school in the morning and did not arrive there at all. Instead I spent the day in the basement of an apartment building and hid in a place where I could hear the ladies doing laundry and talking in sharp voices or whispers. Or I would go to a certain store and help the Chinese man in back slice open boxes with a carpet knife, which he taught me how to use without damaging the goods inside. I always discovered the most undiscoverable places and people. But no one ever discovered me. A woman named Greta sometimes gave me lunch. Her house was near no other house, and all the blinds were drawn. I knocked on her door one day, smiled the smile and told her I was looking for my mother, who was mentally ill and not responsible and could have wandered anywhere. Greta listened as I described a person no one has ever seen before. Then she shook her head and invited me in. The air inside was sour. I gave her a false name. She prepared a sandwich—slices of thin white bread with a grainy pink spread smeared between them. Nothing to me ever tasted better than the sandwiches this Greta made, but by choice I have not eaten them anyplace else.

I can tell that there is something difficult about Iowa, something complicated that hangs in the air like pollen—as though the flat, low sun has cooked the dust all day and changed it into a deadly toxin. I lie with my eyes wide open and stare at the dim interior of the truck. My breathing comes hard. Sleep is the assailant that could be creeping toward me with a knife in its teeth. I sit up. The sleeping bag slumps down off my chest. Out the windows there isn't a thing in sight. Not a tree, not a house—just the usual dark, which makes me think that the truck is blind and I am caught inside it, as though in the ribs of a whale.

No one is ever happier to see daylight than me. The faces of the dead come by the truck all night and scare me, just like in a movie.

In Oregon, every six months or so there would be an article in the paper from Eugene saying how the police were mystified by the disappearances of certain people. They had a computer on it trying to uncover some pattern in what these people had in common. But the amazing thing was that they had almost nothing in common—they were men and women, old and young, white and black and Spanish, rich and poor—and this pointed to either no connection between the disappearances or else a very unusual killer. The police favored the view that there was no connection—probably because uncovering patterns is how they catch people, and they couldn't stand to think of all the work it was going to take to catch a killer who had no pattern. And since these were officially only disappearances and not yet murders—because you need a body to have a murder—the police kept saying that these were probably people like most other missing-persons cases: They wanted to disappear.

And who can say? Maybe they did. Because I swear I had no trouble at all in taking them. There was a readiness in them that drew me. Whether it had been inside of them for a week or a month or a year, or only just a minute or two, each one of them was susceptible to me. And I have spent a lifetime learning how to recognize and take advantage of susceptibility. I could teach a course to salesmen. I could make a tape for them to play while jogging. My first thing would be: When you smile at them, do they smile in return?

In Eugene, six months from now, will some detective scratch his head wondering why certain kinds of people have stopped disappearing? No. No one will even notice. The change will not be statistically measurable. My thirteen were just a drop in the bucket of official sadness. The scars will all be private and unanswered in homes I've never seen. The detective will forget and move on to other things. Only the seven rivers will continue to know; only the soft, damp earth.

Outside of Indianapolis I find a carnival. From a distance the lights almost sear the evening sky like a welding torch. There is no way for me not to get closer and closer. The carnival is a magnet, and the inside of the truck buzzes with the energy that reaches out from it. The light has a smell: perfume, tonic, popcorn balls, the dyed orange and blue fuzz of stuffed dolls whose necks are stuck through tarnished loops of wire at the sides of the booths.

The rides are parked on a dull field where the grass is trampled flat or buffed from the soil by foot traffic. I always believed it was pathetic that the carnival rides never seemed to belong to the ground they rested on. A carnival is a too temporary, indifferent and rootless thing. It comes and wastes the people's affection for it and gives them back nothing they can be sure of. The carnival workers are smart and mean and don't care a bit about the places they come to or the people who live there. They are like the members of an angry tribe.

After a short line I get on the flying teacups. Being alone, with no one to bump against, I fly around the teacup hitting my elbows and ribs and shoulders against the edges. I almost fly over the rim. I pay a second fare and ride again. Each time my teacup sweeps down past the operator, I hang my arm out and try to swat the top of his head, which is down a foot too low. I hear people laughing on the ground and see their faces turned up to watch my arm stretch down as far as it can.

I vow to make a friend. I walk the alleys looking for a possibility. I lean against a wagon and light a cigarette, letting the match glow deep in the cup of my palms so its warmth flickers on my face. Before the match burns me I blow it out. But without its light I feel empty. Moving here and there I light other matches, pulling their light from my hands to my face. Finally I meet Jody, a twenty-year-old boy—maybe younger—who says he wants a cigarette.

"Sure," I say. I crumple the empty pack and let it fall from my hand. I tell him to follow me out to my truck. "I got a carton under my seat."

Before we get there Jody attacks me with a rock. Suddenly I am on my back between two rows of parked cars and this boy is on top of me calling me faggot. He reaches back and cups his hand on my privates and squeezes so that pain ricochets down to my feet and up to my head. I feel blood matting in my hair. Jody smiles angrily on top of me until someone comes by and pulls him off, a big man who starts in on Jody.

"Never mind, mister," I say. "It was all my fault. Leave the boy alone."

The man has his hand drawn back, and I can see it's a struggle for him not to go ahead and do it. But he lets Jody sag away from him.

"Thanks a lot," I say. "I mean it."

"You're okay?" he asks.

"I think so. Yeah. Thanks. I mean it." Then he goes and leaves me to Jody, who is exactly the kind of thing you find at a carnival.

"Thanks for that," says Jody, pointing at the man walking away. "Did I hurt you bad?"

I reach to the bump at the back of my head and return my fingers covered with fresh sticky blood. "I'll have to get it stitched," I say. "Can you tell me where's the nearest hospital? Better yet, can you drive me there and back? I'm not some faggot."

Jody drives me in his Mustang. He takes a towel from the trunk and drapes it over the seat I sit in, but I'm careful not to get blood on the towel. As soon as we are out on the highway I lean forward and start to be sick.

"Pull over, man. I don't feel so hot. What was it you hit me with?"

Jody slows the car in the breakdown lane. I throw open the door and stagger out before he even stops rolling. Then I disappear down into the brush off the side of the road. I stay and wait, groaning. After a while I hear Jody calling. I don't answer. When he calls again I groan. Then I hear the undergrowth snapping, and Jody comes closer. I take him out fast with the palm of my hand. Once he's down I crush his windpipe with my foot.

I take his wallet and car keys and windbreaker. In five minutes I'm back at the carnival, putting the Mustang in the same exact spot. I wipe down the car with the towel and put the towel back in the trunk. Then I lock the keys in the car and leave.

My older brother died in Pennsylvania. I strongly suspect that he was slowly poisoned by the woman he was living with, but no one could prove a thing. She was unusually kind to everyone. At the funeral she wailed, and all of us were sad for her. She wanted to have his children. There was never a court case. It looked in all respects like a natural death—in the night his heart just stopped. She's probably still living there in the same apartment, probably with all of his clothes in cardboard boxes in the closets or the cellar. I would have taken the clothes for sure, but they didn't fit me. Instead I took his books and didn't read them. I returned them to the library in Oregon, a few at a time, pretending I'd borrowed them in the usual way. I just walked in and smiled at the ladies and left his books on the counter and turned around. One day I heard one of the ladies saying, "These aren't ours." But I pretended I didn't hear her.

As a result of the death of my brother, I hate the state of Pennsylvania. I cross the Ohio River into West Virginia and sense the great weight of Pennsylvania north of me. By comparison, West Virginia seems clean and sweet. I can almost imagine lingering here and there.

My first stop is at a roadside farm stand in front of an orchard. I want to buy some cider. A cat dashes out from under a chair and stops in front of me and stretches. I reach down and scratch its head. It slumps over sideways and curls up in a ball and starts to bat at my hand with its feet. From behind a wall of cider jugs a woman says, "That's Hank." I nod.

"We took out his claws," she says, "just so's he could do like that and not hurt people."

I buy the cider and open the jug and drink. The woman watches me. "Thirsty," she says. I keep on drinking. The cold cider buzzes deep in my throat and ears. Looking up through the jug I can see the sun. The cider itself is murky and thick. Behind me I hear the slow creak of my engine cooling. Information contained in the cider spreads out through my body from cell to cell. This is one of the best days I've had in years.

When I finally lower the empty jug the woman is smiling at me.

"We've got plenty more," she says.

My second stop is a movie at a mall. I buy popcorn and Cherry Coke and go into the dark in the middle of the day. The movie is foolish. It mixes cartoon characters with real people. I'm supposed to care what happens to this loud-mouth rabbit. It's really a kids' movie, but the handful of kids that are there don't like it any better than I do. After fifteen minutes I get up and go into one of the other theaters. Whatever this movie is, it seems to be raining in it all the time. All of the characters are wet and angry. I fall asleep with my hand in the popcorn and don't come to until the lights go on and people are trudging toward me up the aisle.

Outside, there's a cop standing next to my truck.

"Yours?" he says.

"Yep. Anything wrong?"

"No sir. It's just, I see you come from Oregon, and so do I."

"Is that right?"

"Near Klamath Falls," the cop says. "How about you?"

"Between Corvallis and Eugene. A place too small to be a place."

"Well, the reason I come over is I saw someone eyeing all this stuff in your truck." He points to the tarp stretched over my possessions. "I shooed him away, and then I saw the Oregon tags. You been here long?"

"About two hours. I went to the movies. I'm passing through."

"Then you don't live here?"

"No, sir. I'm moving out east."

"Whereabouts?"

"Philadelphia. I got a brother up there in Philly."

And all the while I'm asking myself has something unraveled back home in Oregon? Maybe some of the thirteen bodies bobbed up out of the oily loam and hunters found them. And so I'm waiting for a hundred other cruisers to come wailing into the mall and I'll be spread out against the car and patted down and cuffed. I think it through and say to myself that I'm ready to be stopped. And I can feel the soft smile getting ready to stretch across my face to greet the expected conditions of my captivity. My muscles go slack. I rehearse forgiveness. But the cop only smiles at me and says he hopes I "have a safe trip to Philly."

"Thank you," I say. "I mean it. Thanks a lot."

And that puts me on the road again, vowing not to stop for anything.

I stop for a beer in Maryland. I pretend to be unable to speak. I take my notebook inside the place and write my order on one of the pages. I rotate the notebook for the bartender to see.

"A beer," he says.

I nod.

"Any special kind?"

I shake my head. He pulls a bottle from the cold bin and cracks off the cap against a fixture without looking.

"Glass?"

I shake my head. He goes away and talks to a man three stools from me. A farmer.

"What's the matter with him?" the farmer says. "He can't talk?"

"No. But he can hear just fine," the bartender says.

"Oh," says the farmer. He turns his head and looks at me. He has a head as large as a big pale squash. He holds his gaze steady upon me as if he's memorizing something about my face. And then I suddenly don't interest him anymore, and he goes back to whatever he was thinking and doing. He sips his beer. I stand up and take my own beer by the neck and walk around the bar. There are framed photographs on the walls of various farms and farm events and people. Pigs and cows wear ribbons. Men and girls stand near the animals, smiling. A man holds an ear of corn up into the camera. The kernels are fat and shiny. There's a picture of a barn wall lined with hanging yokes and harnesses casting hard shadows in bright sunlight.

"I took every one of those," says the bartender. "You like them?"

I almost speak my reply, but then instead I turn to him and nod. I do like them, too.

"It's been forty years," he says. I get a glimpse of how a life can go on for forty years and be fully satisfying in ways that are nothing special. I looked at the bartender carefully, and I could tell that his wife was dead. Don't ask me how. I just knew it. She died a number of years ago. I looked at the hunched-over back of the farmer, and I could tell that he was a heart patient who went every week to the teaching hospital in Baltimore and allowed the doctors to do anything they wanted to him, and he was grateful for it.

The room is still and hot. I feel beads of sweat on my forehead. The beer almost disappears in my hand. When you hold a thing in one position long enough, your senses fool themselves into believing it isn't actually there. I could almost open my fingers and nothing would hit the floor.

"Go ahead," I say out loud. The farmer spins around and looks white as a ghost.

Just about nothing pleases me. Food has no taste. I eat new foods to see if they will be different, but they aren't. I eat the old familiar foods to see if something will change, but it doesn't. This has been this way for as long as I can remember. When I was a child in Spokane, I sat at the dinner table and stared at the plate with a deep concentration, summoning up a kind of appetite that I knew was only an approximation of the real thing. It didn't matter what was in front of me—what color it was, what texture, if it was hot or cold, spiced or bland. We were four in the family: my mother, father, brother and myself.

My father went ahead and ate, not waiting for my mother's grace. She would still be cutting the pink meat slowly into smallish bites by the time he was finished and pushing himself away. He would jerk his head to one side and then the other, hard, cracking the bones in his neck as though the exertion of eating had tightened him. The cracking echoed around the table.

My brother ate nearly as fast as my father, and sometimes I stopped in the middle of eating and watched him, believing that his appetite was real. One night he came to the side of my bed and said he thought he was a homosexual. I started to argue with him, saying "Oh, no, you're not," but then I decided I didn't care. I stopped on a dime.

"Suit yourself," I said. He said, "Pray for me," but he never mentioned it again. I think he completely forgot about it. He spent the rest of his life with girls and women. Until he was poisoned he seemed to take pleasure in their company. I was jealous of him. He could eat and enjoy the company of women and think about himself in a questioning way. I pretend to be like him.

If you saw me in a bar drinking a cold beer, you would swear I loved that beer as well as any man alive.

The closest I get to Pennsylvania is Delaware. I can almost feel the poisoned heat of the place. Off to the left the night sky glows from the lights of Philadelphia. I see the name "Philadelphia" in glass beads on the big green highway signs. My headlights make the beads burn hot before the truck passes under. The truck seems to have an eagerness of its own, and it sails up through New Jersey. I stop for gas and cigarettes and candy bars, and that's it. The engine never cools.

On the morning I cross from Connecticut into Rhode Island I hear on the radio they've executed three men—two in Florida and one in Texas. Three in one day is a modern record. The men have done mayhem on other men during robberies and on women during rapes. I consider the difference between me and them to be anger. I've never felt a moment's anger. I've never done mayhem on anyone, just the minimum that was necessary. And I think in their way they all knew that I would be like that. I remember the soft pleadings in countless eyes, and the pleadings always reached me. I felt privileged. The color of fear turns out to be gray—it floated above their faces like the aura of tang that hovers around a lemon. Soon I could hardly see their faces at all. The gray became part of me, part of them. Principally, I relied on drugs. It was never long before they were fast asleep; the fear cleared out like fog. I don't believe any one of them felt a thing.

I can't imagine being executed. I get stuck just short of the final instant. The newspapers reported that Ted Bundy became a coward at the end and had to be supported by two deputies on the way into the room. I was supposed to think less of him for that. I did. I expected him to show some curiosity. I believe about myself that I would be curious. I would go in slowly, without support, and walk the room thoroughly, absorbing every detail. I would memorize the witnesses' faces. I would watch the gray gas fill the rooms—my room and theirs, my fear and theirs. I would greet the officials and question them about the event, believing that they would have powerful thoughts to share with me. I would tell the witnesses exactly what I was feeling. I might liken all that I have done to what was being done to me. I would finish by offering them the pleadings of my eyes. I would honor them, feeling no anger.

I can bring myself as far as the chair. I can bring myself to the moment of hearing the last human voice, which might be mine. But I can't go any further. Are the last things dull or sharp? Ted Bundy probably learned and forgot all in the same half a second.

Toward the heart of Providence, the truck veers right and heads beneath the signs that say "Cape Cod." I think of the line in the song: "You're sure to fall in love with." I see far off a sign that says "Fall River." I shouldn't be able to read it at such a distance, but the two words balloon up large, growing off the sign cartoon-like, signifying. Something clicks. I am a comet falling to a river. I press the pedal deeper.

Off the highway I smell bacon cooking. It makes me almost hungry. In a vehicle, the feeling that you are inside of something, that's completely an illusion. As you drive, the environment flows through. You smell the smells, you taste the dust, you feel the dampness, dryness. You're not inside of anything at all. You are not safe from anyone. I drive down the next exit ramp, past two gas stations with signs turning slow atop hundred-foot poles. I find a small town with a restaurant where bacon is cooking—bacon, potatoes and onions join me in the cab. I sit idling with my eyes closed. Slowly my hand reaches out and turns the key. The engine halts. Water settles and sighs. I take an urge to meet new neighbors.

# TWO

.

I WASTE AN ENTIRE DAY DOING NOTHING. BY
the end of it, I still don't even know the name of the town I'm in.

I buy a New Bedford paper and sit in my truck drinking coffee.
People walk by and don't notice me there. I observe them, trying
to pick out something different about them that you wouldn't see
in Oregon. But this is just wasting time. What I am really doing is
getting over the long trip east. I'm probably not ready yet to stop
being in the truck and start actually living somewhere again. So I
let the place pass in front of me like a movie that I can't decide
whether I ought to walk out of or not. I would like something
special to occur in my line of sight that could help me decide. I tap
out rhythms on the steering wheel. I think of what the Bible says
about entering into a new house: If the house is sanctified you shall
surely know it. But if this place is, I don't know it yet. If something
special occurred even once in my line of sight all day, I missed it.

Oregon was dense and soft, a mystery that I had already solved.
But this is new. This is the devil I don't know.

I drive to the ocean and spend another night in the truck. Long
before dawn a policeman raps on the window and wakes me. I roll
the window down. The patch on his shoulder says "Town of
Bledsoe."

"No sleeping in your vehicle, sir. I'm sorry." The cop has a smooth, young face, and he says what he says as if he expects me to like him for it.

"Why not?"

"It's against town ordinances. You'll have to move on."

He's such a calm cop. His cruiser is empty. I look around and see he is alone. He might even be lonely, thankful for my being here to bother. His radio crackles with static.

"Okay," I say. I sit up and stretch. The way my father used to do, I roll my head sharp to one side then the other, cracking my neck bones. It isn't cold, but I cup my hands and blow into them, rubbing the warm air around. The cop steps back from my door, and I continue to shape myself up. I yawn and catch the terrible whiff of my breath.

"I'll swing back by here in fifteen minutes," the cop says, letting me know how much time I have. "Okay," I say. "I'll be gone by then." The cop gets in his cruiser and drives away, using his turn signals for the benefit of no one other than me.

I wriggle free of the sleeping bag and get out of the truck. I'm parked near a public boat ramp. I walk over to the ramp and then down to the edge of the water, where it surprises me that the ocean can meet the land in such a gentle seam. The toes of my shoes rest just above it. The water rises and falls an inch, darkening the ramp. I crouch and put my finger in it, then the palm of my right hand. I cup my hands in the water and bring some water to my face, splashing it on. The ocean buzzes in my pores and on the stubble of my cheeks. I run my tongue around my lips and taste the brine.

I answer the newspaper ad of Mr. and Mrs. Dean, who have two rooms and a bath to let. The rooms are clean and have a separate entrance and overlook the back of the house where the two Deans garden and park their cars. There is a tool shed and a garage. If I'm prepared to clean up after myself, I can have use of the Deans' kitchen at certain hours; I can have a shelf of my own in the fridge. To show me what she means, Mrs. Dean opens the fridge and begins moving things from my shelf to the others.

She tells me she prefers to be called Mrs. Dean, but that her husband will want me to call him Doug.

"He works in the postal service," she says. She sweeps her hand around the kitchen as if to prove by Mr. Dean's not being there that the postal service is exactly where he is at the present moment. "Before I say anything one way or the other about the rooms, I want him to meet you."

"Well, like I said," I say, "I like the rooms a lot."

"Don't worry, Mr. Siegert. Meeting Doug is just a formality, I'm sure. He ought to be home around five-thirty. Can you stop back at six?"

"You bet," I say. I show her the smile. She drops her eyes.

I stand in the yard with Doug. Doug leans against the fence and calls attention to the special properties of evening light in this season, in this part of the world. He's still wearing his postal service shirt and pants. He points between the sides of two houses behind his own. The sunset glows in this gap, beyond some distant trees. The land slopes down. Doug turns to me and smiles like a retired baseball player looking back across his career. He's about the right age for that, too.

"Mrs. D. tells me you come from Oregon."

"That's right."

"What made you want to come east?"

"I don't know," I say. "Sometimes you just get bored of a place, and there's nothing to keep you there, so you leave. I didn't really mind it, though, but I guess I'd been there just about long enough to wear it out."

Doug takes a pipe from his pocket and lights it with a special lighter that shoots a flame downward. He sucks the flame into the bowl; blue smoke curls out.

"We were thinking when we placed that ad that maybe there'd be a girl going to the junior college here. Something like that. Our own daughter started college in South Carolina this fall. We weren't exactly counting on a grown man."

"But here I am."

"That's right." Doug stands quiet and puffs up clouds around his head. I stare off into the pink sunset that glowers between the two neighbor houses. I can tell he is thinking it over, a fair-minded man. A pipe gives that impression to the world—of someone thinking something over carefully—and the impression carries back inside to the person and forces him to behave that way. I can see him coming around to taking me in.

"Well, it's okay with me, Mr. Siegert," says Doug. "If Mrs. D. doesn't mind."

I tell him I'm sorry, for his sake and Mrs. Dean's, that I'm not a young girl at the junior college. "I can't do anything about what I am," I say, "much as I might want to."

Doug smiles. He taps the pipe against the palm of his hand and points me toward the house.

"Okay," he says. "You can move in tomorrow."

I spread my stuff around the rooms. How it feels is that you deal yourself like cards into a new space, and the space gives up the ghost and takes you in. Then it's yours. It becomes as though the Deans no longer, and never did, own the place. Here is the high school picture of my brother, Neil, smiling and squinting at graduation. It rests on the pine dresser as if it always belonged there. And I can almost see the dust growing old in the shadows along the base of the gray metal frame. I set my chin on the dresser top and breathe across the grain of the wood. My breath fogs Neil's own chin and clears away. I open the top dresser drawer and inhale the dark, resinous air that has been alone, unmoving, inside for so long. I sort of hear Jane Dean downstairs. She might be a squirrel in a deep, distant wall, scratching along a stud, testing with claws the plastered underside of the lath. Below me in the house, she is not a person in the way we think of a person. Until I meet her on the stairs or in the yard, or coming and going in the kitchen, Jane Dean is just an idea with a Mrs. before it. To me she is the sound outside of my home.

I fill the drawer with socks and underwear and swirl my hand through, mixing white things and dark. Socks unball and separate, and the mess is unruly and makes me angry at myself for doing this. I close my eyes and breathe the dresser scent again, now made different by the addition of all my things. The closing of the eyes and the slow breathing calm me. I open my eyes again to see my brother in the picture, looking so much more pleased than he did when I saw him the last time, in a casket, poisoned. The casket was only half open, and I believed he was naked below the waist where none of us could see. I didn't check. We stood and watched him for a minute, saying nothing. Then my mother grabbed my wrist and shook it. We left the room in a hurry, I like a train following the engine of my mother. Neil was left behind with the pink lights shining down on him. New white shirt and blue tie. A death is theater for the living.

"Neil," I say to the silent picture.

I hear his voice say "Vann." The voice is perfect, exactly the way I recall it.

"Mr. Siegert?" Mrs. Dean. She is right behind the door that leads to the inside of the house, but she sounds loud enough to be in my head.

"Yes?"

"Here's something for you."

I go to the door and open it. She is standing with the kindest smile, holding a pan of macaroni casserole with hamburger and tomato. The smell is steamy and good.

"Thank you," I say.

"It's to welcome you."

"Thank you," I say. "You shouldn't go to the trouble."

"Oh, yes, I should," she says. She extends the pan forward. "Take it by the holder things. It's hot."

I take the pan from her and turn, looking for a place to put it. "There's nowhere to put it," I say. I keep turning until she's in front of me again. Her eyes are busy scanning the room, looking beyond the living area to the shadowed bedroom.

"You've got it so nice," she says. I look behind me at the room. The heat of the pan is coming through the hot pads. The way I have it, the room isn't nice at all.

"You're just saying that," I say.

"No, I mean it," says Mrs. D. "I don't like a lot of clutter. It just absorbs the light."

She reaches out and takes back the pan. "I'll put this on your shelf in the icebox, and you can heat it a little at a time in the microwave. But you ought to get one of those little ones that you'll like to keep some sodas and beers in. I'll bring you up a few glasses and plates. And I know there's a folding card table up in the attic."

"Thank you."

She nods and leaves, leaving the door for me to close. The smell of the macaroni hangs in the room along with the smell of her perfume, which is candylike, sharp as peppermint. Long after the macaroni fades, the perfume stays, dimming slowly through the rooms. I spend the rest of the afternoon walking around the new space, getting used to the number of steps it takes from here to there and back. I pick up a book and sit in the chair and read it. I hear Mrs. D. set plates and glasses outside my door. After a while the sun comes past the window sash and blasts me full in the face. I look up squinting. I go to the window and stare down onto the empty red bed of my pickup truck. Everything that came out of it is here around me. The silence makes me restless, and I wish there was a clock on the wall, one with a room-filling tick.

What am I waiting for?

I go out most nights. I drive into Fall River and park the truck and sit inside it for a while, watching the people on the streets in the nightlife section of town. During my years I could have grown a full white beard in all the time I spend sitting and watching. But this is me—patience and curiosity and fear combined. The pedestrians get closer to the truck, and the light from the vapor lamps hits their faces in a certain way and tells me something about them: how old, how many brothers and sisters, if they're happy or unhappy, Catholic or not Catholic. Something, never enough. Then they're gone, and I'm still there, ready for someone else.

But soon the sitting and watching wear out like a stick of gum. I get out of the truck and stretch my legs. I walk to a bar called Hobie's. The noise inside rings like a gong. By the time I get there—maybe ten o'clock—the memory of it ever being quieter, say at seven or eight (when I have never been in the place), is gone from whoever has been there that long. Waitresses smaller than the mostly male drinkers are threading through them with brown trays of empties or refills raised higher than their own heads. People two and three deep are leaning over and between and through the people seated at the bar, trying to order drinks from two bartenders who never smile and don't stop moving. Shards of ice fly away up their hands, liquefy and disappear. In corners above the bartenders' heads two televisions show a hockey game that no one seems to be watching.

I stand here at the edges of everything, feeling the warmth that oozes from this crush of people spread out in waves toward the windows and the street. In the midst of it I see the mouths of people moving and hear the sounds of laughter and shouting, but nothing that makes any sense—less words than something like the feeling of ore being melted in a foundry. People put their ears right next to the mouths of others and nod their heads. The crowd bobs and rises and stretches, like a boiling. If someone passed Hobie's right now on the outside, he might hear the noise and think that the large front windows were slowly dimpling in and out, ready to burst. When the door opens and people come or go, the commotion dims a fraction then grows again. I stand with a beer in my hand at the outside of it all, waiting to see something that welcomes me in.

Most nights I remain unwelcomed. I have my three slow beers and then leave, feeling like I've let my flesh be shot through with dangerous rays. In the street the sudden quiet is like cool water flowing over me. I feel saved from something. Walking back to the truck I say the prayer my mother taught me: "Dear God, you have left my side and returned to me. Thank you." I expect the truck to be locked, but it isn't. I might have forgotten. Slowly I scan the street to see if someone somewhere is watching me. Nothing registers. But on the seat of the truck is a dead starling, small and flat. The little sliding vent window behind the seat is open. The rearview mirror is cracked. This suggests an explanation. But someone also could have done these things. I pick up the bird and put it on the curb. Before getting in I stare at the spot on the seat where the bird has been. The spot seems to shine. In my mouth the lingering beer taste sours and chants.

In the dark I think of a girl named Charlotta. The bed that used to be the bed of the Deans' daughter spins. Charlotta tires easily.

She has come to Eugene from Spokane because of a hospital that treats serious asthmatics. She has nothing to do with her nights, and so she spends them drinking diet sodas in half a dozen bars. We talk at a table for hours. I smile her the smile. She smiles back. I tell her things I wouldn't tell the bare walls of the darkest, emptiest room. She presses her lips together tight and listens. She rubs her eyes—"allergy," she says. The catch in her breathing disappears and returns, disappears and returns. Past midnight she puts her head down on the table and closes her eyes. Her brown hair falls forward toward my folded hands. I feel the hairs on my knuckles rise; my joints ache. I imagine my drug is already inside of her, turning the switches off. Then she sits up quickly and tells me she has to go.

"Early day tomorrow." She smiles.

Before I can stop her or say a word she puts her hand on my hands and says good-bye.

"Thanks for a lovely evening, Neil." The words come out slowly, and she heaves her chest at the end as she says my brother's name, dragging her next breath in as though it doesn't want to go. She turns quickly and walks away from me into the rest of her life. I could have followed, but I didn't. And now I believe she is out for a drink somewhere in Spokane tonight, where it's three hours earlier. I close my eyes and think of her reaching across the continent, as though it were a table, to remind me of something I told her that I wished I hadn't.

Beneath me in the house I hear Doug cough. The spinning of the bed slows, stops.

Doug takes me to a high school football game. His nephew Gene is a star running back—short, built like a stump, but deceptively fast and shifty. Doug cheers and leaps up from his seat in the stands. Out of politeness, I leap up half a beat after Doug does. Over and over Doug turns and puts his face in my face and smiles crazily, saying nothing. Gene breaks a school record for most yards gained in a single game. Tacklers fall away from him like dolls—their heads snap back. He scores five touchdowns rushing and one catching a pass. And this isn't even a record for Gene. Three weeks earlier he scored eight rushing touchdowns, the most in the state in at least a decade. Doug points out the men he believes are college scouts. I nod, telling him he's probably right.

After the game we wait outside the locker rooms. Gene comes out and gets mobbed by fans. People squash in around him and slap his back and muss his hair. He smiles, he's used to it. But now he just looks like a boy. Playing football he looked like an eager brute. Doug hangs back, waiting. I watch him watch this Gene, and there are almost tears in his eyes. Gene finds his mother and father, and his mother and father find Doug. I fade down the hall and let this family meeting happen without me. On the walls are pictures of past teams and stars. I slide sideways back in time along the wall until I get to the year that would have been mine if I'd gone to Bledsoe Memorial High. The big drum of the marching band has a snarling badger painted on it. Staring at the picture of the football team, I imagine myself in the middle of the second row—a row above Neil, the captain, who sits with the football in his lap and the numbers of the perfect record painted on the ball. I would have wanted to be a linebacker, staring into the eyes of asshole quarterbacks.

"Vann," says Doug, "come meet some people."

I turn and see four people staring at me, smiling, waiting for me to come to them. So I do.

"This is Vann Siegert, Paul," says Doug. "My brother-in-law Paul Fowler, my sister Lois. And this is Gene Fowler."

"Great game," I say. I grab Gene's hand.

"Thanks," Gene says. His hand in mine is dead and strange. His voice is flat. I search for the football player in the thick bones, but there is nothing to find. His eyes are gray, empty. Surrounding him, his family shines in football pride. But Gene is a dead star, orbited by fast, happy others. I let go the hand. It hangs in the air and regains its coolness. I think of the plans I could make for Gene. Doug says his sister's name twice. Gene slowly looks up at the low ceiling. People passing in the hall call out to Gene, his name and nothing more.

On a Monday morning, I get up out of bed and faint. It's as if the floor turns into a cloud and slowly I slip right through it. The vapor rises to my chin and chills me. Some time later I open my eyes and am staring up at the living-room ceiling, white as powder. My head is in the living room and my legs are in the bedroom. In my mouth is the sour taste of aluminum. The surface of my stomach itches, tingles. This is only the second time in my life this has happened.

On the first occasion a man named Galen was drinking my dangerous coffee. I stared at his back from the front window of the cabin, counting the seconds. He gently slumped forward. I heard the coffee mug clunk to the floor. Then my knees disappeared beneath me and I feared that I had done to myself accidentally what I had done to this Galen on purpose. But when I woke up Galen was sleeping the way he would always sleep. His cheek was smeared against the tabletop. His mouth was open and his eyes were shut. I carried him out and buried him like that. Birds sang. I recited the words I always recite. Galen's back was to me; his face was deep in the earth. "Dear God, take Galen unto your protection. Cherish him the way he needs it. Listen to his grief and let him empty it upon you, for you are unbreakable and can bear it. Hear too my sorrow and my remorse, and I vow you will have no cause to ever hear them again. All this in your name I pray. Amen."

Galen lay motionless in the hole and waited for the dirt to fall. His back was ready for it. The ravine was cool. Air currents flowed through carrying water from the seven rivers. As the moisture landed gently, blessing my cheeks, I believed I could tell which droplets came from which rivers. As on all such past occasions, I sensed the rivers' approval. They whispered not to shut the hole. "Don't be so quick." Staring down, I watched the damp invade Galen's shirt and hair, darkening him. The sun fell lower, dimming the ravine. I waited for permission.

"Please," I said.

I waited. The breaks of gray between the dark trunks grew as dark as the trunks themselves. Shadows were everywhere. I looked down upon Galen and could scarcely see him, as though the hole had deepened far down.

"Now," the rivers said.

I spaded in the dirt. It fell forever and could not be heard hitting

Galen's back. In the darkness I imagined the hole was empty, but I finished filling it and walked upon the mound until it compressed below the level of the edges. Then I arranged the fallen trees to conceal the place. Chunks of spongy wood fractured softly. When finished I leaned against a tree nearby and replayed in my mind everything I recalled about Galen. The rivers sighed. Soon I had his image floating in the ravine like the head of the Wizard of Oz, coming nearer to me then drifting off, his lips moving words around the edges of a smile. Galen was my seventh. He was a carpet salesman who had a flat tire, and then I stopped to help.

Lying on the floor in the Deans' house, I retell the story of Galen Skyles in the delicate whisper that absolutely cannot be overheard, even if people are near me in the room.

Because I have some savings I do not need to work for money right away. But I listen carefully when Doug tells me there are temporary seasonal opportunities at the post office.

"Christmas is coming," he says. The smoke curls up from his pipe. He looks off across the yard at the fence. I imagine Christmas getting ready to climb over it into Doug's yard.

"I know," I say. But I don't know. I haven't been anywhere for Christmas or observed it in even the smallest ways for years. It is something that swirls around other people and comes from the speakers overhead in the stores and streets, and out of the television. I pass beneath Christmas and near to it, but it doesn't enter or touch me. If it has a telltale smell, I couldn't say. One day, just for a second, I couldn't remember if it was the birth or the death. That's how far away I had gotten. I might as well have been a Jew, except even Jews must know more than that.

"We need delivery help. We need sorting help. Volume triples. We break down the routes into smaller units."

"It isn't even November yet," I say.

"But the volume starts building in October. A lot of catalogues. Magazines get thicker. Think about it."

"Okay."

"I could put in a word."

It's late on a Saturday afternoon. When I came outside Doug

was mowing the lawn. The grass smell hangs in the air. The manual push mower lies with its wooden handle thrown forward over the rotary blades. It appears to be napping. Mrs. Dean is pruning roses at the side of the yard. Doug points at her as though he's about to say something, but his hand falls back down and all he does is puff on the pipe.

"That's nice of you," I say. "I think I might like to deliver the mail."

"Well, you understand there's no guarantee of that. They might put you back in the office sorting or out in a truck on collections. They put you wherever they think they need you. You're not civil service, you've got no say. And you don't make the same as the lifers."

"That's okay."

"About seven dollars now, maybe six."

"Uh-huh."

"No, I guess this year it's seven. Last year it was six."

"Sounds okay."

"Think it over."

"I will."

Doug points at Mrs. Dean again, and she turns around and says "What?" She's holding a wide-open salmon-pink rose in one white-gloved hand.

"Nothing," says Doug. She squints at him and goes back to work. Doug puffs on his pipe.

The unusual thing about this scene is that Mrs. D. had her back to Doug when he pointed. She felt his finger on her, she must have. I turn and look at the side of Doug's head. The pipe sticks straight out and the muscles clench in his jaw. Slowly I get the idea that Doug wants to kill her. He turns his head to me.

So I go to the post office and fill out an application for provisional employment. The application asks about my service record. I tap the pencil point on the counter. Sometimes I lie and tell people that I am a Vietnam veteran. (In some situations I will show a fictitious wound and call it shrapnel.) But not this time. I leave the boxes unchecked. I use the name that I am known by and the

history that belongs to it. Vann Dothan Siegert. Born 8–13–55 in
Bellingham, Washington. Mother's maiden name: Estelle Dothan.
Father: Henry Neil Siegert (deceased). My hands sweat. My fingers
slide down the shaft of the pencil. In school I was called Dotie
because of my middle name. My brother Neil was a year ahead of
me and sometimes volunteered information about me that was used
unkindly. I didn't hold this against Neil. Walking home from school
he draped his arm across my shoulders. At school I never fought
with anyone. I walked away and listened to the hurtful things said
louder and louder behind me. You could not make me fight. Neil
tried to advise me on this issue. He would show me ways in which
a fight could be quickly won. Some of them were amazing and
cruel.

"I'm not like that," I said. As I got older I spent less and less
time at school. Instead I wandered around Spokane. Whenever I
returned to the classroom, I arrived there like an exotic guest. I
possessed mysterious new knowledge that frightened my class-
mates. They didn't even have to hear what it was—they saw it in
my eyes and the way I moved. They kept their distance, most of
them. By the time I was eleven a girl asked if she could mastur-
bate me.

Where it says "education," I write in "11th grade." Where it
says "List any relatives working for the U.S.P.S.," I write "None."

"Here." I hand the application to the shift supervisor. "I'm a
friend of Doug Dean's. I rent rooms in his house." The supervisor
looks me up and down and nods. "Okay," he says, staring at the
application. "When could you start?"

"Tomorrow," I say.

"Good deal. We'll start you inside. Seven A.M. sharp."

I nod. Early mornings have never been a problem for me.

"Thanks," I say.

I spend the afternoon at the beach. It's an Indian summer day,
temperatures in the mild seventies and only a rustling breeze. It's
a wonder I know what to do at a beach in the East. The ocean
beaches I've been to in the Northwest are rocky and unswimmable;
the river beaches are muddy, slick, alive with bugs that buzz in

your ears and hang like motes just inches in front of your eyes. But this is a beach where you might see families picnic the way you have seen it done in movies. The woman lies flat on a towel on her stomach and undoes the straps, and the man reads a magazine, facing the water, sitting on a sawed-off folding aluminum seat. Two children turn pails upside down and arrange the sand into cities, go down and mix seawater into pails of sand until they have made a drooling type of cement that they drip down over everything. The picnic cooler is near the woman, ready. At some point she slips her straps back in place and rises on one arm as though her body is just now waking up to whatever has been happening while she was lying on her stomach doing nothing. She finds out where everyone is. She puts on big sunglasses with white frames and looks at her kids and her husband. Then she reaches for the cooler and says something. The children stop playing and look at her. The pails hang from small hands. The husband puts the magazine aside. Everybody turns to the woman and moves in closer. She opens the cooler lid. The family looks down inside. They stare at the food without expression, as though they don't know what to think of it. I've seen this on television a hundred times. I could close my eyes and see their faces.

I wait for this family to come to the beach today, but it does not. On the stretch of sand where I am there are only myself and a middle-aged woman who is stooping down by the waterline at a point where the foam rushes up and sinks away to nothing. She goes back and forth a hundred yards in either direction in front of where I am sitting on a towel that Mrs. Dean insisted I had to take if I was going to any beach. The towel is wider and longer than a normal towel. In the middle of it is a big red whale smiling above a set of big blue compass points. The West arrow points like a spear at my right calf muscle. The whale is between my legs. I have my jeans rolled up to my knees and my shirt off. The shirt lies in a clump on the sand beside me.

The woman picks things up and looks at them before throwing them back in the water. Sometimes she pauses and looks up the beach at me from wherever she happens to be. Let her look. I try the smile, but she's too far away. Some of the things she picks up she holds at arm's length and brings slowly closer to her, slowly away, then back again. Then she pitches them into the water. She doesn't collect a single thing. They might be shells or stones or any piece of junk—I can't see what they are. She stoops, picks up an object, straightens herself, examines the thing, discards it, moves a few more paces down the beach and repeats the process. Sometimes she holds a thing up to her ear and shakes it. She pauses and looks at me. I try the smile again. She doesn't respond. I watch her stoop.

Finally I lie back on the towel, carefully, making sure my head is still on it. I close my eyes. The sun feels good on my face. I imagine this stooping woman eventually coming up quietly and standing over me, looking down at me like the family looking down into the picnic cooler. I imagine reaching out and touching her sandy ankle. The waves flop in and hiss, flop in and hiss.

Later I get up and do what the woman was doing. I go along the water's edge bending down and picking things up. This is how I learn exactly what she was doing and what she was picking up. I am almost sure I am finding some of the same things she picked up and discarded. Every now and then I stop and look higher up the beach to where the woman now sits on a large towel reading. I wait for her to notice me. She continues reading. I go another few paces along the sand. The surf runs up across my feet and sinks down into the sand. The hundreds of bubbles break silently. Holes form in the sand and seal themselves. The woman takes off her sunglasses and runs both hands through her hair. She holds the glasses in her teeth by one of the bows. She tightens something at the back of her head, and the gray-blond hair lies flatter, closer to the bone. She puts the glasses back on again. I pick up a smooth black stone just inches before the bubbling surf runs across it. The stone is warm, shiny. It fits in the palm of my hand. I close my hand and feel the stone tremble and speak. I hold my closed fist to my ear and shake it. The stone rattles and slides. The words of the stone leak out from inside my fist.

I pocket the stone. I walk up the beach, away from the waves, to meet the woman.

She looks up at me and takes her glasses off. She squints. I smile the smile. "Hello," she says, waiting for something from me that is more than a smile.

"Great day," I say.

"It is," she agrees. Cautious. She waits for more.

"I just moved east from California," I tell her. I hold out my hand. "Galen Deane. With an E at the end." She reaches up and shakes it. "I represent a line of carpets made in Sacramento. Synthetics and natural fibers. Both." I nod. She squints.

"I don't need any carpets, Galen," she says. "I've got all the carpets I need."

"Oh, no," I say. "I didn't mean that. That was just to say what I do. And besides, I don't sell residential accounts. I mostly do business with institutions—offices, schools, hospitals. Like that."

"Uh-huh."

"The weather today really reminds me of home."

Her book is folded across her knee. She taps the spine with her glasses.

"Look, mister . . ."

"Deane, with an E."

"Mr. Deane. I was just enjoying myself here alone. And don't take this the wrong way. But I'd like to go back to that. To being alone here. By myself. I'm sorry. I'm sure you're nice and all that. But sometimes you just want some privacy. Okay?"

I shake my head and shrug. "Hey, look . . ."

"Okay?"

"No problem," I tell her. "Really. Sorry to bother you."

"No, it isn't a bother . . . But."

"It's okay." I'm backing up. I reach down and brush some sand from my shin. I feel bumps along the edge of the bone there. I do the other shin. Same kind of bumps.

"What's the name of your book?"

She stares at me. I feel the stone cooling deep in my pocket. She doesn't answer me.

"I'm sorry," I tell her again.

"Never mind," she says. "Don't worry about it."

Sometimes people just aren't ready for me. You can't accomplish everything that crosses your mind. Only what seems right at the time.

I go back and lie on the towel awhile longer. The sun sinks and cools. Soon my flesh gets chicken skin. I stand up and walk back to my truck. It's parked near a low Japanese car. Silver, new. I brush myself off. I take my notebook out of the glove compartment and copy the license number of the Japanese car. I draw an arrow from the number to a question mark. Then I draw the face of a woman and make the hair tight against her head. I draw an arrow from her head to the license number. I put the notebook back in the glove compartment and throw the stone in, too. I drive home. I shut off the truck. Doug comes up to the side of the truck and tells me I got the job.

"I know," I say.

Doug smiles. Pipe smoke curls out from the rim of the smile.


The first thing I do is separate the coupon books and supermarket circulars into routes. Over and over I see a package of bacon and a jar of mayonnaise. If I close my eyes the bacon stays there, the lid of the mayonnaise floats like an egg. I see a clown face shouting "Big Savings!"

"This country is two-hundred-and-forty-some-thousand neighborhoods," a girl named Ferrin tells me.

"Uh-huh."

"And you're?"

It takes me a second to see she wants my name. "I'm Vann," I say.

"I'm Ferrin."

Nobody in authority has actually told me what to do. But Ferrin has me fall in beside her at a long counter. She shares with me her stacks of circulars and coupon books. This Ferrin has yellow hair and red, red lips and a face with cratered skin. Everyone around us wears a shiny blue shirt and gray post office pants with a dull blue stripe. But Ferrin wears jeans, and I'm in khakis and a sweatshirt from the U. of Oregon. This is work for fools, whatever it is. Ferrin smiles down at the circulars. She has a rubber thing on her thumb the color of a flower pot that flips the circulars up one at a time to where she can snap them out of the air with the other hand.

"This doesn't even matter," she says. "I could just take so many for every route and stick 'em in the carrier bins. But then it wouldn't be mail. So look . . ."

She points to a label and reads it out loud. " 'Mrs. D. H. Slobey or Current Resident, Eighty-one Eastern Point Avenue, Bledsoe, Mass.' That's what makes it mail. Otherwise they could just hire a kid to drop 'em on the front steps. That's what some places do."

I don't know what she's talking about. I don't even know what I'm doing here. Then Doug comes up behind me and slaps my back.

"Hi, Ferrin," says Doug. Ferrin's thumb keeps flipping the circulars up where the other hand snatches them out of the air. Then she sends them down various slides into the route bins.

"Hi, Doug," I say. Ferrin smiles softly down upon the business of her hands.

"Here comes Dan Shames, Vann," says Doug. "He'll get you doing something."

"He can do any fucking thing he wants," says Ferrin, still flipping. "If he wants, he can hide out in Duffy's truck for years." It takes me a week and a half to figure out that Duffy's truck is what a Bledsoe postal worker calls the toilet.

"You're Siegert?" says Dan Shames. Doug melts away but leaves his pipe smoke hanging.

"Yeah," I say.

"C'mere." Dan Shames hooks his finger in front of my nose and leads me out to the loading dock to the back of a truck full of dead gray bags.

"As fast as you can. Up to the plywood divider. The bags in the truck go here . . ." He points to a wooden trolley. "Then the truck leaves and we never see it again. Okay?"

I nod. He goes back inside. The engine of the long truck idles far in front of me. Who knows where the driver is? I begin to fill the trolley.

Ferrin asks me to the lunch truck and recommends the clam roll. I walk behind her and watch her body twist as she tries to see where I am, how close to her, if I am looking at her. Steam rises from the coffee urn. The line at the truck curves. Ferrin whispers up at me that there are people here from the courthouse, people from the library, people who come up just because they like buying their lunch from a truck.

"The clam roll's best," she says, but when we get to the front she buys a tuna sandwich squeezed thin in plastic. The gray tuna filling spreads sideways under the clear wrapping. The crust would have to be damp.

"Clam roll," I say to the man. He takes a plastic-wrapped sandwich out of the bin and puts it in the microwave.

"How much for a truck like this?" I ask. He looks at me.

"You're new."

"That's right," I say. He nods his head.

"It's not the truck," he says. "It's all the licenses. It's building up the goddamn business. That takes time. It's cutthroat."

"How much?"

"Thirty-five, forty thou. Then you gotta stock it."

The bell rings on the microwave. He pops it open without looking. He stares beyond me down the line. "Hey, Vinnie," he says, greeting someone. He reaches in and gets the clam roll without looking. "Let it sit a minute and evaporate with the plastic off. You don't want the clams too moist. Three ninety-five, plus twenty tax . . . You want anything to drink?"

I can't think of anything. I can't see what there is. The drinks are out of sight in a bin. I shake my head.

"Get a Mountain Dew," says Ferrin. "They're great. Just don't look at the color."

"C'mon," says someone in line behind me. "Let's move it. I'm hungry."

"Nothing," I say. I pay the money. He gives me change. His name is sewn in red thread over his shirt pocket: "Monte." On the other side is an oval patch: "Suburban Catering."

"Thanks, Monte," I say.

"Who's next," he says.

On the way back to the post office we walk around the other side of the truck. I see my face split into diamonds, reflected in the quilted, polished steel of the lowered panel. "Look at that," I say. Ferrin turns as if she heard a bird sing.

Ferrin takes an immediate interest. When we get off at four, she says, "Let's go for a beer." I tell her I don't drink.

"On account of what?"

"I don't know," I say. "On account of nothing."

"Then come along and watch," she says. "It's interesting."

I sit with her in a place called Peter Garrett's. Inside, it could be any year. There's a big jar of pickled eggs and no TV. The ceiling is dirty. The man behind the bar is reading the paper. The beer that comes from the tap flows so clear it looks warm. Ferrin has a draft. I order one, too.

"You said you didn't drink."

I shrug. The bartender carefully lowers the mugs onto cardboard disks.

"A mystery," says Ferrin. I don't have to look to know she's smiling, all red, red lips and her pale, powdery face. The beer tastes like nothing—not warm, not cold, not anything. I wait for the flavor to reach the very back of my tongue, where for an instant after I've swallowed there seems to be a sourness resting there, thicker than the beer itself.

"Let's grab a table," Ferrin says.

We get up and go to a table Ferrin picks in a darker area near the glowing jukebox. Ferrin asks me for quarters and goes to pick tunes.

"What do you like?" she says.

"Fats Domino," I tell her. "Charley Rich. Little Richard. Jerry Lee. Chuck Berry."

"Time warp," she says. She picks other things. Between songs I close my eyes and listen to the slow arms moving inside the jukebox, putting the record back, taking another, turning it, lowering it down. You could think of a hell where that might be your job. Or maybe you might think it would be heaven. She taps a nail on the side of her mug. The sound of it makes the music better.

"So. Oregon," she says. She's making conversation.

"I lived there once," I say.

"What did you do?"

"I sold stereos. Televisions. I stood in a store in Eugene all day and waited for people to come in and look like they needed help. Everybody who comes into a store like that looks like they need help. They can't help it." I wonder if this is true.

Ferrin smiles and tilts her head like a dog. I feel sorry for her skin. It looks like the moon. I can imagine a surgeon taking a special skin-colored putty and smearing it across. Then he would shine a surgical lamp on the putty that bonds it to the rest of the face. Ferrin would wake up perfect. She has good hair that falls thickly in loose yellow waves.

"Do you like dogs?" she says. The question surprises me because I was just thinking of a particular dog.

"I'm not sure," I say. "Some of them are okay, I guess."

"I've got a dog named The General that I inherited from an old boyfriend. It's only about this big . . ." She cups her hands so that they would hold a small dog. "And I don't know how old, except that it smells old. I've had it three years."

"I was just thinking of a dog," I say.

"Well, there you go. What kind?"

"My brother's dog. A hunting dog. Black. It would sit and hold a doll in its mouth all day without hurting that doll. You could take the doll from its mouth and the dog wouldn't care. Heidi. Then you could put the doll back, and it was like putting it on a shelf. The dog would just hold it for you."

"It was trained."

"My brother loved that dog. Heidi."

"That's a pretty name."

"She's dead though now."

Ferrin finishes her beer and orders another. Both of us do. Not long after, Doug comes in with two other letter carriers. He waves, and the three of them settle at a larger table far across the room. Soon I smell the smoke of his pipe.

"Doug's a nice guy," Ferrin says.

"Yeah."

"You live in his house, right?"

"Yeah."

"I've seen it. It's a big house."

"Big enough," I say.

"Would you like to see where I live?" Ferrin says.

"Maybe sometime."

"But not today?"

"No. Not right now."

"Okay," she says. "Here's a rain check." She passes something invisible across the table to me and sets it by my wrist. I find myself staring at it, the space it takes up.

"Thanks," I tell her. My eyes are still on it. She drains her mug.

On the way home I drive past the high school. It isn't dark yet, but the lights are on at the football practice field. I stop the truck and watch. Three squads are running plays half-speed. Only one group runs its plays against a defense, and this is probably the defense meant to look like the team's next opponent. It's easy to spot Gene Fowler. The first thing to see is his balance. He could run along the edge of a razor blade and not fall off. His legs bow out when he walks to the huddle. I hear a sound from inside the glove compartment. Maybe there's a mouse in it. I reach over to the latch.

"Break!" The players shout when they leave the huddle. I open the glove compartment, waiting for the mouse to tumble out or at least be scrambling around inside. But all that's there are my notebook, a pen, a map and the stone I got at the beach yesterday. I take them all out and look at the remaining emptiness.

"Hut! . . . Hut! . . . Hut! . . ."

A play begins. I see the ball go first into Gene Fowler's gut and the quarterback take it back and roll to the short side to throw a pass. The pass sails high, across to the wide side of the field and into Gene Fowler's gut again. On this team the football knows where home is. A defender slaps the top of Gene's shoulder pads, but Gene runs slowly into the end zone anyway.

I hold the smooth black stone in the palm of my hand. I stare at it, and it seems to move like a mouse, quivering, sniffing. All I can think is "Gene Fowler. Gene Fowler. Gene Fowler." I close my hand around the stone and hold my fist to my ear. "Gene Fowler," the stone says. "Gene Fowler." Between my fist and my ear, the stone is whispering. I am whispering, too.

"Break!" The players shout when they leave the huddle. On the now darker field the lights take hold, shining down yellow like candles. You can see the heavy breath of all these boys. The coaches stand to the side with their clipboards and their arms crossed. They kick the turf and talk to each other with their heads down. Nodding. When practice doesn't end soon enough I leave. I am still thinking *Gene Fowler*.

My father gave me a leather suitcase when I was ten. I still have it. He brought it up out of the cellar and into the kitchen and said, "I'll never use this again." My mother looked at him. He seemed unhappy about something. "I want to give it to Vann."

"Is Vann going somewhere?" my mother said.

"I might," I said.

My father opened the suitcase on the kitchen floor. Inside of it were books.

"I'm giving the books to Neil and the suitcase to Vann."

Neil said, "I don't want the books, I want the suitcase."

"But I've decided," said my father. "You get the books, your brother gets the bag. It's final. Believe me."

He stressed the point by jerking his head from side to side like a rung bell, cracking the neck bones. He made a pile of the books on the kitchen floor, but the pile got too high and my mother told him to make two. The two piles sat where he left them for almost a week. Neil refused to take custody of them. But I took the suitcase right away. My father stared at the books off and on all week. If my mother offered to move them, my father wouldn't let her.

"Those're Neil's," he'd say. "Let Neil move them."

One night I crept down and took the books upstairs a pile at a time. I hid them behind a table in the hallway, inside of a hole in the wall that the table was meant to conceal, a place where a foot square of plaster and baseboard were missing. I sat beneath the table and put the books in the hole one by one. It was like feeding something. I heard a deep wind moving through the walls, the sound of it coming from far below—hundreds of feet, thousands of feet. With each book I put inside the wall, the sound of the wind adjusted slightly. I could smell the odor of cold earth rising up from somewhere. Then the door from my father and mother's room opened, and I heard someone standing there looking out into the hallway, breathing. In one of my ears was the sound of the wind in the walls, and in the other ear was the sound of my mother breathing. A dim light leaked from their bedroom halfway past the table. But I stayed absolutely still and wasn't seen.

The next day no one said anything about the books. Neil stopped complaining that the suitcase was given to me and not to him. The books are probably still in the wall.

The suitcase is high in the closet in my bedroom. I look up and see the initials H.N.S. in gold that has nearly rubbed out of the deep impressions in the brown leather. When the suitcase first became mine, Neil had to show me how to use it. He took it from me roughly and laid it on his bed and showed me how the latches worked. He told me what clothing belonged in which spaces inside. I stood and listened politely, waiting for there to be a secret compartment. Neil couldn't find it. He stopped at all of the things you could see right away and explained their use. He used his own clothes to show me how to pack. When he had filled it and strapped things in as they ought to be strapped, he closed the suitcase and secured the latches.

"Now," I said.

I took the suitcase from him and put it over on my bed and slowly unpacked it until it was bare inside. I put my face down to it, closed my eyes and breathed in the soft, toasted-leather smell. Neil had his hands on his hips.

"Now, look," I said. And I went straight to the secret compartment, unsnapping a mesh shoe holder and finding behind it the zipper concealed beneath a stitched leather seam. I unzipped the zipper and stuck my fingers inside until they touched something that felt like money.

"It's empty," I said. "Too bad."

Neil stared at the secret compartment, amazed.

And that's where I keep the drug I use.

In the bathroom, wearing rubber surgical gloves, I mix maybe a hundred grains of the powder into a flask of Southern Comfort, whose sweet orange flavor is believed to hide the taste of the drug. Within the shadows of the mouth of the flask, the amber powder lies on the surface of the liquor briefly, then sinks, disappears. What I hold in my hands could kill the Deans and me a hundred times. I put the black rubber stopper back in the vial of powder, and seal the vial in a slim steel canister lined with cotton batting. The mixing is a test of nerves. No single grain of the stuff can go unaccounted for. Imagine it floating down unseen onto the bristle of my toothbrush, waiting. Because of this danger, I move everything out of the way. I do my mixing in the nude (except for the gloves), using the small chrome measuring spoon from a chemistry set. I wait for my hand to tremble, but it never does. I screw the cap of the flask down tight; upend the flask a few times to mix the drug; run hot water over the sealed flask, the steel canister, the small spoon and the rubber gloves; return the canister to the secret compartment in the suitcase; take the gloves off, by turning them inside out, and drop them in the toilet. I flush the toilet.

Then I take a hot shower, staying in until the water temperature begins to fall.

When I get in my truck to go to work, I open the glove compartment. I stare at the smooth black stone. I put the flask inside the glove compartment. I close it, lock it.


Ferrin keeps her distance, but she doesn't have much choice. Dan Shames puts me out on the loading dock all day.

"Whatever comes in full, you empty it," he says. "Whatever's empty, you fill it."

"How will I know with what?" I ask him.

"You won't. But the driver will. Plus, he ought to have a bill of lading on him. If the driver doesn't know, you come and find me. Okay? But you won't meet too many assholes. You won't meet too many people of any kind, period. Today's your first vacation day."

I nod. They must have hired me before they really truly needed me. Otherwise they wouldn't have stuck me out of sight with nothing much to do. So I stay where I'm put. I organize the equipment. I line up the trolleys side by side. I smooth out the empty gray bags and make a stack of them, alternating the open ends so the stack doesn't start to lean. I listen for the sound of approaching trucks. When I hear a truck I stop what I'm doing and look out from the back of the dock. Most often the sound first gets louder and then slowly fades away. But sometimes a truck arrives and backs in, beeping. The brakes hiss. The truck settles hard against the black rubber pads of the dock. I hear the door open and slam, and suddenly the driver is climbing up around the back of the truck onto the dock where I am standing.

"Take it off straight back to the plywood," he says.

"Okay."

"Can I buy you a Coke?"

"No thanks."

It's the same driver as yesterday, and yesterday he also offered to buy me a Coke, which I also said no to. The first bags are deep in the trailer. I push a trolley inside, swing it sideways and kick down the brakes on two of the wheels. I start stacking full bags on the trolley. The driver returns and stands at the back of the trailer drinking his Coke. He just watches. Exactly like yesterday. I hear my own breath fill the trailer, and I smell the strong piney plywood scent of the inside walls. When the trolley is full, I step back and look. It's like a cord of wood.

"Lotsa mail," says the driver. He said exactly the same thing yesterday. I kick up the brakes and wheel the trolley out past the driver and in off the dock. I get another trolley and return. I fill three and a half before I get to the next plywood barrier.

"That's it," I say.

"Okay. I'm outta here," says the driver.

Incoming mail goes on red trolleys. Outgoing mail goes on blue trolleys. Ferrin is suddenly standing beside me watching the truck pull out. She smells like a Hare Krishna.

I go with her again for a beer after work. We sit at the same table and drink drafts. Ferrin plays the same music again. After half an hour or so she asks if I would like to go see where she lives. I say, "Maybe tomorrow." She smiles. She has clear blue eyes.

"How old are you?" she says. I was thinking of asking her the exact same thing.

"Thirty-four."

"I'm ten years less," she says. She smiles again. It's like those ten years younger are a special gift she would think of giving me if I asked her to.

"You don't look it," I say.

"I look older. I always did. I always felt older, too. I think I look about thirty."

I can see the childhood Ferrin looking about the same as she does today. She isn't tall. She could play the part of a child who looks older than she is. But she stretches back in her seat, which makes her breasts push forward. She looks older still.

"I do," she says again, as though I've argued with her.

"No you don't," I say.

Slowly Ferrin is drawing out the kindness in me. I remember how I stopped in a church one time and helped the pastor put out the prayer books. Just doing that one small thing drew forth my kindness. I sit with my cold hand wrapped around the glass and feel something stirring.

"You really don't," I say. Her face blurs, and the cratered skin seems right as rain.

"I do," she says. And I can see that she is sad now.

"No," I say.

After football practice I wait in the truck. The lights on the practice field go out. Soon the big steel door on the side of the gym begins opening and closing. Boys come out in the flood of yellow light that slants through the door. They come in ones and twos and threes. I wait for Gene Fowler, looking for his bowlegged walk. He's one of the last to leave. He comes out the door with a coach, who stands and talks to him for a minute. They separate. The coach goes to his car. He honks as he drives past Gene, who waves. Gene is alone now, walking. When he gets off the grounds of the school he crosses the street and stands there by the curb as though he's waiting for a ride. I start the truck. The flask is up on the flat of the dashboard. I circle around the block where the school is situated so that I'll come out on the street where Gene is standing, with my truck headed in Gene's direction. At the corner, before I make my last turn, a car goes past me. In its lights I see Gene with his thumb stuck out. The car brakes and slows but doesn't stop. Gene looks after it. I turn the corner. My headlights flash across Gene's face as he turns back. He's still standing there with his thumb out. I slow and stop. He looks in the window before opening the door. Then he opens the door.

"Hi, Gene," I say. "Remember me? Vann Siegert? I live in your uncle Doug's house."

"Yeah, right," he says. "That's right. Hi."

"Need a lift home?"

"Yep. That'd be great."

"Okay," I say. "Just tell me where to go."

He gets in, pulls the door shut. I start to drive. I don't say a word. Some people don't need to be nudged, they go right to the danger. If you need it proved to you beyond a shadow of a doubt that someone is ready for trouble, if they go right to the danger, that's proof enough.

"What's in the flask?" says Gene.

"Uh, Southern Comfort," I say. "At least I think it is. It's been a while since I had a taste."

"You want some now?"

"No thanks," I say. "But help yourself."

"Turn right at the light," says Gene. He points. "Then through the center and take the first left after the commuter tracks." His pointing hand hangs over the flask.

"You sure?" he says, picking the flask up.

"Yeah. Go ahead, help yourself."

He unscrews the cap and drinks. I feel the cold thrill of a perfect event. I take the right.

"Must be old," says Gene. "It tastes old." He drinks again to make sure. "Yeah, really."

We roll through the center. The truck bounces on patched streets that need repaving. Gene's head lolls forward. Across the commuter tracks. I take the left. I hear his shoulder hit the door. The switches are going off one by one. There is nothing faster.

"Shit," says Gene. The word echoes and breathes.

"Where next?" I say.

I reach over and take the flask from his hand. The emptied hand keeps the shape of the held flask.

"Where next?"

No answer. The power of speech goes first. The rest follows quickly. I look. He turns his face to mine. I pull the truck over to the side, shut the engine off. I want to capture this perfectly. Slower and slower he shakes his head, until the shaking turns to nothing, not even a quiver. He just looks at me. Gradually he closes his eyes, like the moon going down. But his mouth stays open. It looks like "What's going on here?" The muscles in my legs are trembling uncontrollably. This is the way joy travels in the body, visiting here and there. The air in the cab vibrates. I roll the window down. The quiet of the street joins in. A car honks in the distance, and I wonder if this is the last thing Gene Fowler hears. I stare at the face of the boy. I lean close and put my ear by the mouth. Nothing. Maybe just the dimmest echo of faraway thunder after a storm has passed. I can sit here and think: He was lucky he met me.

When I turn the key I am almost surprised that the engine starts. It rolls over the silence like an eager wave.

# THREE

·-·

PEOPLE GIVE UP HOPE SO EASILY. NOT EVEN a month goes by before they hold a memorial service for the disappeared Gene Fowler on the Saturday before Thanksgiving. Doug asks me if I want to go. I tell him it doesn't feel right to me to have a funeral when the body hasn't been found.

"But this is what Paul and Lois want," says Doug.

"Maybe so. But what if Gene just ran away," I say. "I think it's a little too soon to declare him dead. He could come strolling back."

Doug scratches the top of his head with the stem of his pipe. "I doubt it," he says. "Besides, no harm in putting things to rest."

"Too little faith," I say. I think of the fishermen going out to catch what they cannot see.

Doug shrugs. He wears a dark gray suit, a white carnation in the buttonhole. "Then you won't be coming?" He stares at me sadly from the landing outside my door.

"I'll come," I say. "Give me five minutes."

He nods. Mrs. D. calls up to him. "What, honey?" he answers. I close the door as he turns away.

"We'll be late," I hear her say from below.

"Vann's coming," Doug tells her.

I go to get my suit on.

I helped them search for Gene. There were over four hundred of us, including all of the members and coaches of the high school football team. There were also two players from the Boston Red Sox, two from the Celtics and two from the Patriots. We started at the high school and went in a line deep into the woods behind. Five feet apart, and a state police for every ten volunteers. In my opinion, you could not miss a body in a search like this. We started at the parking lot of the school. The local Dunkin' Donuts served free coffee and donuts from the back of a station wagon. Paul and Lois Fowler were standing with the Bledsoe police chief and a captain from the state police, and there were television news cameras and still photographers out from New Bedford, down from Boston and up from Providence. The police chief introduced Lois and Paul Fowler, and both of them thanked everyone for coming. They looked shocked and tired, and you could tell that they didn't say enough, or didn't say it in exactly the right way, to please the television cameras. Then the police chief gave a short explanation of how the search would be conducted and turned it over to the state police captain, who had us count off by tens and assigned each of the ten groups to a handful of state police, who divided us up even more.

The search was simple. We walked through the woods and looked down at the ground and, now and then, up in the trees. The state policeman in charge of our group was careful to describe to us the kinds of things we ought to be looking for without naming exactly what they were or suggesting how they could have come to pass. The reason he told us to look up in the trees was in case Gene Fowler had hanged himself. But what he said was, "Don't always keep your heads down. There could be visible evidence up in the air above you. The rule of thumb is sixty percent down, twenty percent straight ahead, and twenty percent up in the air. What you're looking for is anything that doesn't look right, where the leaves are disturbed or it looks like people have been there. You're looking for signs of digging in the ground, for signs of the leaves being moved to cover something up or hide it. You're looking for an item of clothing or a wallet, or a belt or hat. Anything that doesn't look right. Something that might have been dropped or lost."

All through this, behind me, I could hear a girl crying quietly, the sniffing and the sharp, delicate breathing. I wanted to turn around and see her. I could tell that others in front of me also wanted to turn and look—I watched a number of heads start to move and then stop. They couldn't do it either. What if she was a sister or a girlfriend? In fact, you didn't want to look too closely at any of the people here. They could be anyone. That was why they were here.

When we fanned out in a line, we ended up being wider than the woods we were searching. The state police captain used a bullhorn to order us to close ranks until everyone was in the woods. With our arms spread, we were close enough to overlap hands. Because of the counting off by tens, no one ended up being in the same group as the people he or she had come with—I was a four; Jane Dean was a five; Doug was a six.

Ahead of us, the woods were empty. The police communicated with walkie-talkies. They stayed ten yards out in front of their groups and kept the line straight, either slowing us or moving us along faster, depending on what was needed. It was important to the search that the line stay solid and straight. But I've never walked so slowly. The air was filled with the swish of kicked brown leaves and the gassy static of the walkie-talkies. Other than that, nobody near me talked.

I looked at everything carefully. My eyes almost ached. For a while I even forgot that I knew what had happened to Gene Fowler. Whenever I remembered, I would imagine that someone was looking at me. But the heads of the people around me were either down or up or straight ahead. Nobody cared who I was or what I knew.

We reached the edge of the woods, at a high cyclone fence that bounded the interstate highway. The sound of the leaves stopped, and you could feel the sadness spreading along the line—nothing had been found, and the place to search had been exhausted. We watched the cars go by. Some people laced their fingers through the fence. Then the bullhorn turned us around and marched us back. We searched in the opposite direction with the same result.

We searched four other woods in town that day. The groups got smaller and smaller, and we were made to spread out farther from each other. There was a kind of loneliness. The swish of the leaves became the swish of the leaves in front of you only, and not the sound of all the leaves together. Once when a shoe was found, Paul and Lois Fowler were brought to the scene and asked if they recognized it. This happened far down the line from me, but I heard it through the trooper's walkie-talkie. There was a silence, and then a voice came over: "That's a negative on the object." And we started moving again.

Between finishing at one woods and going to the next, I stood with Doug and watched a television reporter tape part of his story. He was tense and in a hurry, and he stumbled over some of the words. "Damn! Okay. Again. Keep rolling." It took him three tries to finish. "As the shadows lengthened in Bledsoe on a sunny but in other ways grim autumn afternoon, there was no good news to report. In fact, no news of any kind. According to Bledsoe police chief Charles Fitch, after nearly a full day of hundreds of volunteers searching acres of woods and meadows in this south coast town, there is still no trace of vanished high school football star Gene Fowler." Then the reporter stopped and changed his orientation so that a dozen or so searchers could be seen behind him walking out of the woods to their cars. "And you can tell by looking at the faces of the volunteers that the disappointment of finding nothing is taking its toll." He turned and gestured. I looked at the faces of the volunteers and saw what I guessed was the disappointment of finding nothing.

"What an asshole," said Doug. "C'mon."

We drive to the largest church in town. Catholic. Doug drives. The church has the shape of an old church, the kind you could see in Europe—two thick towers side by side and a circular stained-glass window between them, lower, showing the passion of Christ. But instead of dark stone, the church is built out of red-orange bricks that a school might have, and the bricks are washed with a donuty glaze that makes them shine, even in the gray November afternoon light. I feel the tightness of the necktie beneath my Adam's apple as I look straight up at the towers. Doug is parking the car, and Mrs. D. is beside me waiting. People are in front of the church in family- and friend-type knots. Some of them I recognize from the post office, some from the search. I feel myself wanting to nod at people.

"Pardon me," says Mrs. D. She leaves me alone and goes to one of the knots and touches her hands to another woman's forearm and wrist. I watch the woman both nod and shake her head, her lips tight and thin. My heart races. I caused this. All of this action belongs to me deeply, just as if I'd written where everyone should stand. The nodding and shaking, the clothes they all are wearing, the sounds the cars make arriving, parking, shutting off, knocking in the crisp chill. The distant, deep organ chords escaping out the open oak door. If I had not come to Bledsoe, Massachusetts, these people would all be somewhere else, home wrapping thick plastic sheeting around their tender shrubs for the winter, watching college football, or maybe out shopping. Who can say? At any moment inside of the church—soon—I could spring up and create the deepest silence and awe by speaking a single sentence. I could make it so that, years from now, people would still remember exactly what they were wearing and what they had for lunch. I think of myself slowly rising to speak, and I shiver. It feels like watching the whirling blade of a millyard saw. The teeth blur, and the wind of the turning seems to draw you in closer, like a vacuum. You wonder and wonder and wonder. Time gets larger until you breathe again.

"Hi, Vann."

I turn my face down to Ferrin.

"Ferrin," I say.

"This is so sad," Ferrin says.

I nod. Doug comes up behind her and puts his hand on Ferrin's shoulder. She turns.

"Hi, Doug." Ferrin is wearing a wine-red knitted dress under a black raincoat.

"Should we go in?" Doug asks. I take a step forward and everyone joins me. Jane Dean sees us heading inside, disengages from her knot and arrives next to Doug by the time we get to the door. Going through it she whispers hello to Ferrin.

The back of the church is dark. Boys in blue or black or dark gray suits—probably teammates of Gene's—are handing out memorial programs. I take one from a boy who looks angry. But this is probably what grief looks like in a boy of seventeen, eighteen. I stare down at the program, which is light gray bordered in a red that matches Ferrin's dress—the colors of Bledsoe Memorial High School. Printed on the cover in deathly black script is "Eugene Kerrigan Fowler, 1972–1989." Without Gene, the football season ended in a loss.

The Mass for the Dead is long and sleepy. The droning song of the priest rolls out across the stone floor, up and down the walls, vibrating. A small bone trembles in the depths of my left ear, tickling me. I shake my head. The sideways spread of Ferrin's thigh touches mine. The song rolls on and on. My eyes narrow helplessly to a squint. I remember the funeral mass for my father, who died in the cellar in the middle of the night. In the morning the dog found him lying by the furnace. The dog barked and moaned. I went down to see what the matter was and found her licking my father's face. He was on his back. His eyes were open. In Bledsoe I close my eyes and see the Catholic church in Spokane where along the walls were pictures of soldiers serving in Vietnam. Some of the pictures had black ribbons on them. I was seventeen. Neil was nineteen. This was the year Gene Fowler was born. We sat on either side of my mother and felt her lean this way and that against us. She was drunk. The smell of liquor hung around the three of us. She kept saying she had no idea what he was doing down there in the cellar. She couldn't stop asking: "What was he *doing* down there?" I wanted to slap her, but she couldn't help herself. The organ music shuddered, deep tones from the thickest pipes. I believed I could see the lead-colored coffin shaking. When the last notes died in the air, the priest looked up at the high ceiling as though there was a leak. Then the song of the mass began.

I never wondered what my father did in the cellar. He was my father. At night he wandered through the house, still asleep, doing things he would never remember in the morning. I sat up in bed when I heard the stairs creak. I heard his bare feet slipping down. He cleared his throat at the bottom of the stairs, standing for a minute in the dark until his eyes adjusted. He cracked his neck. The wallpaper rattled. I heard my mother cough dimly under the covers. I heard the radio go on in the kitchen, playing soft Spanish music, a soft voice talking between the melodies that sounded all the same to me. Sometimes I sat on the floor in the hallway and listened. Sometimes I crept down the stairs, and around the corner at the bottom and through the living room, and stood in the kitchen doorway and watched him sitting at the porcelain table with the lights out, the dial of the radio glowing orange and trickling amber light out onto his large, stiff hands. Sometimes I came into the kitchen and stood right beside him and stared, and he never knew that I was there. I saw the light from the radio glow in his eyes. He looked like a spy waiting to hear a message in code. He looked like a stranded alien waiting to hear that the spaceship was on its way back to fetch him. He looked hypnotized. Sometimes I stayed in the living room and fell asleep on the rug or on the couch, where my mother would find me in the morning. Meanwhile, my father would have gone back up to bed, never to know that he'd been anyplace else. Once I overheard my mother telling my father she feared that I would grow up to be like him, a sleepwalker.

"He could do worse," my father said. Then he laughed.

There is suddenly a vast silence in the mass for Gene Fowler. Does a priest run out of words? I look up. He stares at his hands, which are tented before his eyes. His lips are pushed out, exposing the soft, shining wet of whatever lives customarily inside his mouth. I feel my own hands forming the same steeplelike tent in front of my eyes. I can't help it. I stare at my hands, imitating the priest. My lips push outward. If someone looked at me—even carefully— they would not know what I was doing; they would not automatically think that I was imitating the priest. But here I am. I lower my head slightly. Perfect. Out of the corner of my eye I see Ferrin looking straight ahead, waiting, punished by her cratered skin. I feel the silence of the priest aimed at my own heart, my thoughts, my voice, my private knowledge. The church yawns open for me. I could leap into it and fly; I could fall. My heart beats fast. If this were the school play and I was standing in the wings watching, someone would whisper urgently to me to go onstage: "Your cue!" I would stagger into the light, trying to remember my opening lines.

The priest's hands fly apart explosively and turn palms outward.

The song of the mass begins again and we are on our feet, responding. I mutter softly. My lips move without knowing what the words are—anything. The words are sound only. We all stop speaking and sit. Our voices and bodies stutter. The palms of the priest shine whitely; they might be wet with sweat. His song continues. His eyes are closed as if he doesn't care that we are there with him in the church—doesn't care if we stand or sit, speak or stay silent, laugh or read the paper. He would be here doing this no matter what. Like a truck on the interstate, he hums straight through the sobbing in the front pew. I strain my ears to hear it, but the only evidence is the sight of Lois Fowler's shoulders shaking. We stand. Somehow we know to stand. Suddenly Lois Fowler is as silent as the full dead church itself. No one even breathes. We stare past the altar at the empty cross. The emptiness symbolizes the still-unfound Gene Fowler. I remember what my mother would say when someone died: "God fills up the empty space where the person once was." She would say such things in a flat, worried voice, as though she didn't believe them herself or was still deciding.

I keep my eye on the cross.


Gene Fowler was the first time I broke these rules: Don't do someone you know; don't do someone who lives in the place where you live. No one can question the wisdom of such rules. Break one, and the risk goes up. Break both, and the risk goes off the scale. Why did I do it? I don't know. I'm not one who believes that killers cry out to be caught. I admit that I scare myself with the possibility of being caught, but only in the same way as people driving at night might scare themselves with the thought that the oncoming headlights will suddenly veer hard across the broken white lines— the arrival of helplessness. This isn't me. I am not a snake nursing secret hopes that someone will come along and beat this snake to death. But there is the fact in front of me as plain as day: I broke two rules at once.

I sat in the truck with the window open and stared at Gene Fowler. He was what he was. The music of the street poured in the open window. Television. The buzz of street lamps. Cars two streets away, tread hissing. I saw a pumpkin glowing on a stoop.

I breathed the air of life and death. Events went on. I was what I was. I put my hand in Gene's and shook it, and felt that it was the same as it had felt when I first met him: dead, cold, empty. I shook it harder. I looked down the street and guessed Gene's house—a white porch lamp above a black iron eagle, wings spread.

"Gene?"

No answer.

"Gene? Where should I take you?"

I drove him west, into Rhode Island, then south along the coast. I found a beach. In October, no one cares about the beaches of Rhode Island. In the swale of a dune I dug a hole in the sand. Gene sat in the truck. I finished the hole quickly. Deep and dark. Sand is perfect. It reminded me of the loam in Oregon—damp, easy to dig. The ocean percolates through. I counted my emotions: magic, loneliness, Gene Fowler, me. My heart beat fast. With my feet down deep in the sand, I placed a finger on the vein in my neck and counted the strokes of my heart: twenty-eight in ten seconds. I multiplied. The number was beyond imagining. Beyond the dune the waves flopped in.

"Gene?" I called in the direction of the truck, imagining that I could get him to walk to me.

My father's mass was shorter than Gene's. The crowd was small, and the weather was cold and wet. The season was winter. My mother never looked behind her to see who was there. "We don't know anyone," she said. "He didn't know anyone either." I turned around and saw thirty or forty people. I recognized maybe five of them, people from the neighborhood. I wondered who the rest were. My father was a salesman of hydraulic hoses and couplings. "With a tiny pump and a good, strong hose, you can move a mountain," he told me once. He also told me, "A man's own pecker is just a small hydraulic system." Then he put his curled index finger in front of my eyes and smiled behind it as it straightened up slowly. He sold the hoses that were used eventually on the cargo-deck doors of some of the Puget Sound ferries. He sold hoses and couplings direct to trucking company maintenance departments. I looked at the faces I didn't know and thought they must have been his customers. The church behind them was empty and deep. The chant of the priest spread like ripples on water. The weight of my mother shifted hard onto my shoulder. I swam in the smell of her perfume and her sour, stinging breath.

"Jesus, Mother," Neil whispered desperately. I put my arm around her shoulders and squeezed. I heard her breath rush out.

"Oh," she said, surprised. I continued squeezing steadily.

The priest, chanting, stared at the three of us. I bowed my head until my mother passed out. Then Neil and I carried her down the aisle, away from the priest and the casket. Some of the people gasped or stared. Mrs. Giese followed with her daughter Anna.

"She's all right?" said Mrs. Giese.

"Yes, I think so," said Neil. We laid her on a long, low bench with a pale green cushion. Neil bent over her and held her hand until her eyes fluttered open.

"Goodness," she said. She lifted her head from the cushion. "I think I might be sick." I reached for a wooden collection plate and held it by her head. But she wasn't. She looked at the waiting plate. You could see her deciding not to. Neil ran the back of his hand across her forehead.

"Nice," she said. She smiled. "Thanks."

"You're all right, dear?" Mrs. Giese said.

"I'm fine, dear," said my mother. She wore a plain black hat with a simple veil that lay across the fleshy part of her nose. Mrs. Giese lifted the veil and kissed my mother's cheek. Her daughter Anna slipped her hand in mine and whispered in my ear a word I could not understand—all it amounted to was warm breath and vowels. She stood back from me, smiling, and waited for an answer. I shook my head. She was fourteen and tall for her age.

"Anything we can do, Neil," Mrs. Giese said to my brother, putting her hands on his shoulders. "Please. Just call." Anna nodded and looked at me carefully.

"Okay, Mrs. Giese," said Neil. "Thanks."

"I'm fine," my mother said. She sat up with a moan and put her head in her hands.

Mrs. Giese returned with Anna to the singing of the mass.

"What happened to me?" my mother said.

"I don't know," said Neil. "You drank too much?"

"Maybe," she said. "I might have." She shook her head. "My God," she said. "Your father."

She stood up and we walked back in, all the way down the aisle to the very front pew, where we had been sitting before. I could swear that the place where I sat back down was still warm; something about us had lingered there. My mother laid her head on my shoulder. I made the muscle hard against her ear. She pretended she didn't notice. The priest spoke the cue for communion. People stood slowly and began to file up past the bier to kneel at the railing and wait to be served.

I took an instant liking to Rhode Island. Already, even after so short a time, Massachusetts was confining, strict. You could know a person five minutes, and they would give the air of expecting something more from you than you'd think they ought to. One afternoon I was sitting on the steps in front of the Deans', and a well-dressed couple came up the walk and began to talk to me about whether it would be all right to talk to me. A conversation like that can make your head spin.

"No, not really," I said. But they wouldn't turn and walk away. They opened up a brochure about the dangers of electromagnetic radiation. They pointed at wires in the street.

"These ought to be buried," the woman said. The man shoved a paper in my face. "Would you sign this?"

"I'm not interested," I said.

"You have to be interested," said the woman.

It went on like this for more than five minutes. Then Doug stuck his head out the front door and said my tea was ready. I told him, "Oh, thanks," and started to get up.

The couple wouldn't stop lecturing me. "We're telling you something important," said the woman. "You ought to know this."

"We'll be back again around five," said the man. "Do you know what this does to cows?" He pointed to a picture of starved-looking cows eating grass in the shadows of power stanchions.

"I'm sorry," I said. I went inside the house, where Doug was standing by a window laughing. The tea was just a story.

That first night in Rhode Island I stood in the bowl of the dune. Even though there wasn't a moon of any kind, the sand glowed blond around me, tapering down to the dark of the hole at my feet. I felt like a roulette ball. My eyesight rolled around the edges and finally into the hole. A voice from inside the hole called up that it wanted something.

"I'll get it," I said.

"Right now," said the voice.

"I will."

But I was turned around. I climbed the wrong side of the dune and couldn't see the truck over the rim. I thought it was stolen. But then, without looking—just by quieting myself in a disciplined way—I felt the truck behind me. If it was an animal, it would have been gently scraping the sand with its hoof, signaling to me. I turned and saw not the fullness of its shape, but the general outline of its character—a truck takes up only a certain amount of space. Instead of the truck in its fullness, I believed I saw the eyes of Gene Fowler waiting for me, floating in a patch of darkness above the blond sand. I went and got him.

Every one is different. The air smells the way it smells; the light spreads out in a particular way. I hoist the weight up onto my shoulder and buck it around to settle it right. The fireman's carry. But the weight is always different. With the life subtracted, the body can seem to float above my shoulder, sometimes like a balloon. I carried Gene Fowler toward the rim of sand. The rough beach grass sawed at my socks, catching and stinging. The ocean called steadily from over the dune, calling also up from the bottom of the new hole. I heard a choir of wanting, everywhere. Gene's hip was by my right ear, blocking the sound of the water, and yet I heard the ocean roaring in his body. The ocean roared in his body.

My heart beat like a factory. I walked concealed in an extra depth of darkness, and knew I was unseen. I took him over the rim and into the bowl of the dune. Slowly I knelt. My knees felt the chill of the sand through my pants. I bowed forward and slumped Gene Fowler into the hole. He landed facing me, his arms stretched up the sides of the hole. His hands were in what light there was, but his face was gone. From the elbows down, he was missing.

I stared at the fingers. Finally, I reached down the hole and gently pushed the two hands into darkness. The fingers were stiff and cold.

"Now," the voice said.

I began to shove the heaped sand in. It wasn't long before the hole was gone, and I was just a lone man kneeling in a dune, the sand glowing blond around him. With my hands I made the surface smooth. Then rain started to fall, falling on me and on the sand, which it pitted almost without a sound.

Ferrin weeps. She puts her hand in my hand. My hand feels trapped. Hers is warm around mine, almost hot. I feel the heat of her face and tears radiating to me. It seems like an endless hour before the communion call arrives. I am ready to go to the railing. Ferrin lets go of my hand. We all get up. I follow behind her and Doug and Mrs. Dean. The railing fills. A line begins to stretch back. The priest moves slowly across the railing, giving body and blood. People stand and are replaced. A space opens up. I go forward and kneel at the railing. Ferrin is beside me; we are hip to hip. The priest returns. In his shadow is the acolyte, carrying the cup. From one to the next the priest repeats the same words in the same way, pressing the wafer into the palm with his thumb. I hold my palm out. The thumb and wafer descend; I feel the weight on my palm. He wipes the gold cup with a wad of linen. I shoot the wafer into my mouth as the rim comes closer. I sip, close my eyes. I imagine the wine is poisoned. My head spins and my legs grow weak.

During the mass the sun has come out. We leave the dark church and go into the sunlight, squinting. Doug and Jane Dean are going to a gathering at the Fowlers' house. I tell Doug I think I'll skip it. Doug asks me how I'm going to get home. Ferrin pipes up and says she'll give me a ride. Doug nods and goes off to find Jane. Ferrin puts her arm through mine and squeezes. I turn and look down at her face and am almost ready to ask her what she thinks she's doing. This is what I have found in Massachusetts: People take hold of other people easily, without asking first, without even knowing them well. She smiles. Her eyes are puffed and red. I hold my tongue.

"I'll show you where I live," she says. She smiles.

I let myself be led. Ferrin drives us down to the Bledsoe marsh, which is khaki-colored and smells sweetly of decay, even in the chill of November.

"There," she says. She points to a thick clump of trees that rises out of the marsh. A dirt road trails into the clump. You can just make out a low, small house. She turns down the rough road. The car bumps along. I have the feeling of disappearing. My excitement grows. When the car makes the clump of trees and enters it, I think we have been swallowed.

"Here we are," she says. A tiny rat-sized dog runs yipping up to the car and seems to disappear beneath the wheels, except that the yipping goes on instead of suddenly stopping.

"That's the dog I was telling you about," she says. "The General."

She shuts off the engine and opens the door. The dog shoots into the car and across her lap to me. It crawls up my chest and puts its hairy black face to my chin. The quick pink tongue goes in and out like a snake's.

"Hey," says Ferrin. She snatches the dog around its ribs and tosses it lightly out the door. But it comes right back. This time she catches it in flight like a ball and holds it. She gets out of the car. The dog squirms and laps at the air; it makes a sound like a baby.

"Hey, you," Ferrin says. She holds the dog straight up at arm's length and shakes it. The dog goes limp. "That's better."

She swings her arm down like a bowler, roundhouse, and lets go of the dog just above the ground. The dog hits the dirt running and heads straight for the door of the house, leaping against the screen and falling back.

"Nice dog," I tell her. "It's even smaller than it looks."

"Yeah, it hardly weighs anything," she says. "I feed it cat food."

She opens the front door, which isn't even locked. The dog races in.

"You don't lock your door?"

"Out here? Why bother? Besides. There's not a thing in this place I couldn't live without."

Inside of Ferrin's house it's dark—oak-brown wood stained with pink light. Red-and-white-checked curtains hang over the windows. She goes around the room—the house is just one big open room— and spreads the curtains apart. The afternoon light seeps in.

"Have a seat," she says. She points at the only chair, an old overstuffed heap of faded red cloth with a frayed cushion. She puts on a shiny fireproof mitt and opens the door of a wood-burning stove. She throws in a couple of fresh pieces and pokes them around with a poker.

"Go on," she says. I still haven't sat. She closes up the stove.

"This is nice," I tell her. What I don't say is how much it looks like my cabin in Oregon. I couldn't have imagined two places that were so much alike. I could almost go to her shelves and find the salt carton hiding behind the green canister of flour. The smell is the same.

"It's not mine," she says. "Meaning, I don't own it. But I've been here now three years. I feel like it's mine."

"You ought to," I say. But I don't know why she ought to. A person could live in the same place for decades without it ever getting to feel like theirs. On the other hand, I spent an hour in Akron between buses once, and I would swear to this day that I had the place down cold—it just poured into me through the skin, to the point where I would know what total strangers' voices were going to sound like seconds before they spoke. But in Bledsoe I can't even spit on the sidewalk and know for sure if it will land. Everywhere I go here feels like the first time, whether it is or not.

"Drink?" she says.

"Okay."

"I've got beer and scotch," she says. "And some Southern Comfort."

"Beer's good," I say.

She gets one out of the fridge and brings it, along with a glass. While the door is still open, I take a good look at the shelves. Every jar and carton on them is as bright as if the fridge had a small sun inside it. It's like a sudden theater set springing up in the room. She kicks backwards at the white door to close it. She puts the beer in my hand slowly, letting the brown bottle ease into my palm, cold to hot. But she leaves it to me to twist the cap. Then she goes and pours herself some scotch in a glass without ice. She holds it up to the light and watches the liquid swirl. I watch, too. My evaluation of this is she thinks she's pretty hot. She saw someone do this on TV.

She goes slowly to the bed and sits on the edge of it, elbows on the knees, glass tilted carelessly but not spilling. She looks at me.

"Well, so," she says. "It's Vann."

"I guess."

My father watched me having sex. He watched the whole thing without saying a word. He didn't mention it for a couple of weeks. In fact, he might never have confessed at all if he hadn't been watching me do it again when I caught him at it. I saw his pants and the top of his hair. He was hiding behind the car. I was in the narrow strip of patchy yellow grass between the pine-board fence and the side of the garage. The car was out in the gravel driveway. I think I heard the grit sound of his feet adjusting. Then I saw one cuff of his pants in the shadow beyond the left rear tire and the shiny light brown of his hair sticking out around the rear bumper. It was the hair that I truly recognized, butched up eager and straight. I wasn't undressed—I was only fourteen—just my pants pulled halfway down. I stopped moving and stared right at that hair, waiting for his eyes to show. The girl didn't say anything. She was older. She always kept her face squeezed tight and breathed in a fast rhythm that seemed to never change, no matter what happened to me or her. I slid backwards out of her and into my pants. She sat up slowly and looked at me.

"Thanks," I whispered.

"Sure," she said. "Don't go." Her hand reached out. But I beckoned her with my finger and then put it to my lips to say be quiet. We crawled to the end of the garage and then both went over the fence and into the yard of the house behind. We found a deep, full bush and lay quiet inside of it. I heard my father cough and start to sing a song in German. Soon he was cutting the grass between the garage and the pine-board fence. The blades of the rotary mower spun musically over the spot where he had seen us. The girl didn't care. She stuck her hand in my pants and tried to find me again.

"You're soft," she said. "You're just a boy."

When I got home my father asked to see me in the cellar.

"I need a hand with something," he said loudly, to keep my mother from guessing anything.

I followed him down. The hairs on the back of his neck were gray, growing out of thick creases.

"This isn't the first time," he said. "I saw you doing this before." He waited for me to react in some way, but I chose to stay silent. I just leaned against the laundry sink and watched his face.

"Who is the girl?"

I shrugged.

"Don't you know the girl? Where does she live? How old is she?"

All he did was ask me questions until I almost had him in tears. I wouldn't tell him anything. I only shrugged or shook my head or looked down at my feet, or at his. He wouldn't hit me. He never got closer than five feet away. While he was waiting for my answers, the only sound was the noise I made sucking dashes of air back through my teeth. I watched his eyes get red.

Finally I told him, "You enjoyed it." He ran his hand back across the top of his hair and stared at me. "I don't mind," I said. "Anytime you want."

The next day he brought home a package of Trojans. "Here," he whispered, pressing them into my palm. "Don't let your mother find these."

The dog is spinning around the room, batting a dirty yellow tennis ball with its nose. Then the dog gets out ahead of the ball and turns to confront it. The ball collides with the nose and rolls back in the other direction. The dog goes after it again. Then I see that Ferrin has her clothes off. She steps in front of me almost from out of thin air. I am watching the dog and then suddenly there she is, white and thin. I shiver to see her. She has drunk her three scotches and I have drunk my two beers, and the sun is almost down. Two kerosene lamps are popping, and the red-checked curtains are drawn again. I feel tired and dull. She hardly moves, waiting for me to smile at the sight of her. My mouth is sour from the beer. The dog runs fast between Ferrin and me, skids and turns and makes another pass. The dog continues going back and forth between us, and my eyes are easily drawn down to it, the way it slides and turns and reaches top speed again so quickly.

"Please," I say without even looking up at her. "Get dressed."

And she seems to disappear in that thin white condition and reappear not much later in her clothing. She doesn't mention it. She sits again at the edge of the bed.

"Beer?" she offers.

"Okay."

She gets me one and makes herself another scotch. It seems that we hardly look at each other for an hour or so. We just sit and sip and swish our drinks around, staring at the liquid as though something important will slowly appear in it—a message. Then she drives me home.

"I had a good time," she says. The car idles at the curb in front of the Deans'. I reach my lips across to her and kiss her cheek, which is cool.

"I did, too," I say.

# FOUR

--

EARLY IN THE MORNING I HEAR DOUG SHOV-
eling out from the first snow of the season, ten days before Christmas. I don't have to stir from bed to know it's Doug. There is
something like him in the soft, dull scrape of aluminum on concrete.
I close my eyes and imagine the driveway appearing slowly beneath
his exertions. He pauses every dozen strokes or so, and I picture
him leaning on the handle, with his hands cupped at the top of it,
tucked in the shadow of his chin, tight against his breastbone.

Snow started falling last night when I was driving home from
Fall River. Ordinarily I am alone, and the drive is silent, automatic.
The truck moans and the cool green signs float overhead like ghosts.
But last night I had a person with me who wanted me to take drugs
with her. She curled her legs up underneath her on the seat and
cradled the drugs and set of works in her lap with both hands, like
all of it was a cat. I still don't know her name. What she told me
was "Casper."

"Turn off here," she said, pointing to a sign for a rest stop.
"This'll be empty as shit." She said this almost too late, and I
fishtailed making the exit.

"Just pull over anywhere."

I did. It was dark. I found the darkest place.

"Lights out," she said. "But leave the engine run. Keep it warm
in here."

We sat in the idling truck with the heat on full blast, and I watched her put her works together, tie off her bicep with a rubber tube, cook the dope with a Bic, suck the yellow liquid up and put the needle in her arm. She closed her eyes and held her breath. I started counting backwards from a hundred. I got to eighty-three. She sighed.

"Now you." She smiled; she hummed. The remaining poison swam in the lid of a peanut butter jar in her lap.

"Okay," I said. I untied her tube. Carefully I took the works and the jar lid from her lap and put them on top of the dash. Then I opened the glove compartment, reached into the shadows and pulled out my flask. I put it into her hands. "Try this," I said.

"What is it?" Her hands didn't quite close around it.

"You'll see," I said. I took back the flask, unscrewed the cap and held it to her lips. "You'll like it."

She swallowed. "Unh-uh," she said and pushed it away. "I hate that sweet shit."

"It doesn't matter," I said. "This is different." She shook her head, but she didn't know what I was talking about. I waited until she understood. Soon everything inside her slowed and stopped, the way it must.

"Snow," I said. She was silent. I rolled the window down and stuck my hand out and let the flakes fall on my palm and disappear. Later, after sitting with her for a while and pulling the hair back off her forehead, tucking it close behind her ears, I carried her down to the second in a row of four outdoor toilet cabinets and sat her on the seat inside. I arranged her exactly the way she would have arranged herself if she'd done this alone. I went back to the truck. Behind me the cabinet door swung shut on strong springs. At the truck I put my gloves on and took a chamois and wiped down the set of works and anything she might have touched. I wiped the flask and shut it up inside the glove compartment. Then I returned to her and tied the tubing tight around her bicep. I refilled the syringe and slid the needle back in. I set the peanut butter lid beside her.

"Casper," I said. I closed the door gently and shivered outside it.

Then I drove home slowly, carefully. The snow was just beginning to stick to the roads.

In the morning, hearing the steady chuff of Doug Dean shoveling, I doubt my memory of anything I have ever done. It seems as far away as the farthest place I've never been to. I see the face beside me in my truck—not a full face seen head on, but out of the corner of my eye, indistinct, a paleness—and the truck becomes a familiar dream, a small space alive with funny thoughts. In childhood I would ride the Spokane bus and see a woman with a grocery bag, and I would think of her skull split open, a neat white fracture, half an inch of ragged bone showing like a treasure beneath the blooded roots of black hair. I thought of her loved by someone, so I put her in loneliness, undiscovered, with rats sniffing and gnawing. These were only thoughts. The bus went on its way with me and her sitting across from each other, across the rubber aisle, staring at nothing, thinking. She had the bag at her feet, between her feet. Then someone else got on, and I forgot the woman—her fracture went together and healed as if it never happened. I examined the man coming closer . . .

Doug stops. A minute goes by, more than a minute. The world is snow-silent. I think that he is lying beside the shovel dead, his cheek in the deep snow, melting it. I get out of bed and go to the window. The driveway is empty, cleaned of snow. The edge between snow and no snow is sharp, what you would expect from a Doug Dean. Deep in the house I hear his feet stamp hard. For a moment the snow will lie on the mat outlining the shape of the boots. But slowly it will disappear, like a thought, and the mat will only be blank and damp. Everything will have happened exactly the way it happened, except there will not be a trace.

Some days I get to deliver the mail. They shrink the routes at Christmas. If they didn't, the routes would take the letter carriers half again as long, or longer, to complete. The normal route is three hundred addresses in a thickly settled neighborhood. But at Christmastime, the normal route becomes a hundred and eighty. If Bledsoe has ten carriers who normally do three thousand total addresses, for the holidays they need an extra seven or eight bodies. In addition, Bledsoe is the depot and collection point for six smaller nearby towns that hardly even deserve their zip codes. When Dan Shames doesn't put me in Bledsoe, he sends me out to Harding sometimes, or Pimmaccasset or Oak Bay, where I drive the right-handed Jeep from one lonely, leaning rural mailbox to the next. I stick my hand into their shadows and deliver, imagining a rattle-snake coiled at the back. Sometimes I speak into the hollow box and take pleasure at the richer sound of my voice and at the way my breath accumulates inside and slowly turns back to me.

Harding is my favorite town. You would never know there was an ocean near it. You would never take it for Massachusetts proper. Harding is just a typical country environs that could be anywhere. The houses are farmish, mostly white with green or black shutters, some with tin roofing—red or green. Today the snow has its way with everything. The roofs are covered. Slender streams of snow blow from the edges and peaks. Going from box to box, I have to bang sharp on their sides to break the seal of ice that locks their doors. Sometimes I hit the name itself. "Wheeler" is one of the names. "Kandinsky" is a name. "Hodges." Snow shakes from the tops of the boxes and dances down in sweet veils. In the country, in the snow, the sound carries—sometimes so loudly that I stare at the windows to see if anyone appears.

Nobody in Harding seems to be young. I don't think there's even a school. Sometimes an old man or woman—smiling, tired look-ing—comes out of the house to meet me. Even if I am just about ready to drive off, I change my plans and wait for them to get to me. I take the mail back out of the box and hand it to them directly. They seem to like this. I give them the smile.

"Thank you, young man."

But today, with the fresh snowfall, I wait in vain for the sight of a single soul. The town is dead. I am the one who makes the first tracks in the snow-covered streets. Mysteriously, no one passes me in either direction all morning. I think of the scenes in movies where a killer virus has deliberately been let out of a vial. People are suddenly frozen in the act of shaving, or with the coffee cup an inch from their lips. Someone pulls the newspaper in through the mail slot and brings the germs in too, and now he's stuck in a crouch forever with the still-folded newspaper underneath his nose. His eggs are burning up on the stove. The coffee boils away to a smoky sludge.

At the mailbox belonging to "Goldblum," I put today's mail in on top of yesterday's. In the postal manual it instructs that unexpected accumulations of mail can be a sign of trouble. Letter carriers are encouraged to "notify the local authorities" when this occurs. Instead I get out of the Jeep and trudge across the yard. I go up on the porch and ring the bell. I hear it ring in the house, so I know that it works. I peer through the slender glass panels on either side of the door, waiting for someone to come. But nothing moves, not even a cat or dog.

"Hello?" I call. I bang on the door. Nothing happens.

I go around to the side of the house. I look in the windows. All I see are emptiness, stillness, order. I circle the house. Behind is a garage with the door down. I look in the side window of the garage. The car is there, black in shadows, as still as a sleeping horse, shining dully. I go back toward the house through the snow. I lift a lean-to cellar door. The ice breaks; the snow slides off. I descend the half dozen steps. I reach for the handle as I let the lean-to lid fall shut behind me, leaving me in the dark. I turn the porcelain handle and open the inner door. I step into the cellar. I hear the furnace and feel its warmth.

"Hello?" Nothing.

I stand in the cellar and breathe the smell of heating oil, sweet like coal, a thick smell that clings to the raw lining of my chilled nose. My eyes adjust. I make out rows of jars along low shelves. The half light shines on old tomatoes hanging in amber liquid like biology objects. There are pickled things, and peaches and pears. Some of the jars are dusty and impenetrable by the light. You can put anything in a jar. A squat freezer hums in a corner. I go to lift the lid but find it locked. This angers me unexpectedly. I have come here to offer help in case something is wrong, and yet I find important information is barred to me. This suddenly makes me feel unwanted, strange. I walk quickly to the inside steps and climb them. At the top I turn the handle and go through into the main house. And it becomes like *The Wizard of Oz* when the film turns to color. The kitchen tile is fiery red. The dining room rug is red and blue, with gold swimming through it. The chairs have seats of deep blue velvet, and the table is brown wood polished like the finish of a new car. I stand at the head of the table and stare out the window at my Jeep. A car goes by, the first of the day. I climb all the way to the top of the house, slowly, finding no one. Each room is perfect, clean. The dressers have combs and other items aligned as if for inspection—and I am the one inspecting. The beds are flat and taut, and their spreads hang exactly right. I could go down to my hands and knees and shop closely for dirt and still not find some. Everyone in the photographs smiles—people who are already dead, people who are still children. From the attic windows I stare out at nearby Harding, feeling the house beneath me like something conquered.

The Goldblums are not home.

I like to work alone. Not everyone does. The world could probably split into those who do and those who don't. Ferrin, for instance, likes to have plenty of company when she works. She would hate to be put out here in the Jeep, where there isn't even a radio. But if I had a radio on board, I would probably refuse to play it; and if that radio ever tempted me, I would pretend that it was broken, and in my head I would just play colorful thoughts. I have always been able to entertain myself, not needing others. So, in reality, I was made for a job like this. In silence I do it uncomplaining. At the end of the day, the Jeep is as hollow and empty as the frozen mailboxes were at the start of the day.

An hour after the gloomy winter sunset, I drive back into Bledsoe, last Jeep in. The other letter carriers are gathered inside the post office, in the warmth, loud and joking. I walk straight into their midst, wary, squinting. Doug Dean is in front of me wreathed in pipe smoke, a smile inside of a cloud.

"Vann the man," he says.

Ferrin hops off a bench and heads my way. I tighten inside.

On Christmas Day I get up early and drive up north. This way I won't be asked by Doug to join in with them in anything. There's hardly a lick of traffic on the roads. Christmas falls on a Monday. I go up into southern Maine and park at a mall. For a time I am the only vehicle there. Then another car comes in and circles the lot slowly, like something swimming after prey. The car swoops by close to my truck. I see a man looking hard at me. He is bearded, large. I stare back at him. The car goes around my truck in a widening arc until it is far away. Then he leaves the lot and is gone. I think to myself that in some manner I have been visited by Christmas.

I find a church in Maine. Saint Dominic's, Catholic. People are filing out of it. I go in against the tide. The weather is warm. The people are joyously dressed. The children seem unhappy. Inside I light a votive candle and leave a dollar in the box. I cross myself in the aisle, enter the last pew and kneel. At the altar the curate is putting things away. I take a moment to clear my thoughts. I close my eyes and hear nothing but a low humming sound in the space where my own voice otherwise would have been. I imagine myself joining into a Latin chant, taking a low drone as far as I can, to the edges of losing consciousness. Behind me I hear the priest clear his throat.

"Merry Christmas," he says to me.

"Merry Christmas, father," I say to him without looking back. And knowing that he will turn me down, I also say to him, "Hear my confession."

"Not on Christmas, son," he says. "We don't on Christmas day." I nod, still facing the altar. "You ought to know that."

The curate sweeps from side to side, putting things down, picking things up, his skirts floating and swaying. When my knees begin to ache I stand and leave.

I drive to the ocean. On a wide, flat beach with black-flecked sand, families and couples, lone people with dogs, walk on the firmer parts and stare out at the water, which is far away. The wind is cold, but the sun is warm. There are at least a hundred people out walking here. Two hundred. To the north and south they intersect, form knots, seem to mingle, separate. From the cab of the truck I watch them.

Once my father drove me down to California with him. It was a business trip. He stopped as often as a dozen times a day and made sales calls at trucking companies and local and regional public transit authorities in cities along the coast. Sometimes I sat in the

car and waited, reading magazines with my feet up on the dashboard or stuck out the window. Sometimes he took me in with
him and had me shake hands with someone who didn't care if he
met me or not. I was ten. One afternoon, between calls, we went
to a broad, flat beach like the beach in Maine. I can't remember
the town, except it was probably part of the sprawl around Los
Angeles. The waves came in unending, one after the other in a
roar. A portion of the frenzied water vaporized and gassed the air,
making a cloud. I breathed it eagerly; it had a taste. We walked
the sand with our pants rolled. My father slung his suitcoat over
his shoulder. His bluestone cufflinks winked at me. I kept up with
him even though he walked rapidly. We were a boy and a man in
a suit. The beach was crowded with walkers. I remember how
people looked at us carefully, but without expression. They looked
at us and seemed to be thinking something unkind about us. At
some point I stepped out in front of my father, walking faster and
faster. Soon I heard him call my name, and his voice seemed far
away, muffled in the sound of the surf and the cloud of seaspray.
I stopped suddenly and turned to look at him, and saw a fool
coming toward me smiling.

It was about that time that I began to think there was something
wrong with my father. In the motel at night he would get up and
go into the bathroom, shut the door behind him and disappear.
When I followed on tiptoe and listened at the bathroom door, there
wasn't a sound from inside. At first I believed he simply stayed in
the bathroom all night, working on his accounts or reading. But
one night I tried the door and found the bathroom empty, the light
still on. The window was closed, but unlocked. In the morning he
was sometimes back in his bed, sometimes not. If he was, he would
wake me by throwing his pillow, which always landed on my face
like the fist of a dream.

"Vann," he would say. "Shake a leg, kid . . ."

But other mornings he woke me coming through the door with
the newspaper, whistling. He dropped the paper on my bed and
told me to read to him from it.

"Show me what you can do," he said.

"Which story?"

"Any story. I don't care. Pick one."

So I read to him while he buffed his shoes until the vein on his forehead bulged, or while he readied his pants on a hanger, just so, and hung them from the shower rod for the hot steam to refresh the creases and make the wrinkles vanish. It was summertime. He had one tan suit and one of blue poplin, both easy to wrinkle and both cut full in the old-fashioned style. This fit with other facts about him. He brushed his teeth with powder from a can, like his father before him. I was used to this side of my father, but yet I could not understand it. We lived in a world of amazing progress. So, why was my father among the small number of people who were bound to ignore it? I favored a brand of toothpaste that had a cap so broad you could stand the tube on end, taking up less space on the windowsill by the sink.

"Don't stop," he yelled from the bathroom.

I read him a story about a woman finding her cat hiding in a charred wooden box in the cellar three weeks after a fire that she thought the cat had died in.

My father came out of the bathroom with lather on his face and the shaving brush in his hand. "I'm real glad we don't have cats," he said, and went back in to shave. "Read the story about the riots," he yelled. "Page one."

We were actually in Los Angeles at the time of the Watts riots. I remember the smell of smoke hanging thick in the air. We got into the car one morning, and my father pointed to the gray-black blot in the sky that seemed to float, not too far off, like an angry blimp. "Those people are burning their neighborhood down. What do you think of that?"

I shrugged. I always wanted to know where my father was headed in a thought before I joined him.

"You can't blame them, can you?" he said. "If you and I were there, we'd have a bottle of gas. You'd light the rag and I'd throw it. We wouldn't care what happened. Would we?"

"I don't know," I said.

All day long we drove where we could. Sometimes we came up against police or National Guard barricades and had to turn back and try to find another way. Military trucks and Jeeps were everywhere, speeding in twos and threes, and the sound of sirens was so commonplace that it virtually disappeared from our hearing. Out of seven appointments my father had scheduled, he was able to keep only three. He refused to let me stay in the car because, he said, there was danger no matter what part of the city you were in. In all of the offices we visited there were people crowded around the windows watching the smoke spread, cursing blacks, telling racial jokes. My father joined right in, but he winked at me. At a trucking company he made a big sale. His forehead sweated and I could see his hands shake holding the purchase order. Then the purchasing agent asked him if he knew the difference between an L.A. nigger and a dead cockroach. Before my father answered the man he handed the purchase order to me and told me to wait outside the office. I stood beyond the closed glass door, feeling I had my hands on something important. Then I heard the two of them laughing and heard the handle of the door turning.

I can't remember exactly which afternoon it was that we went to the beach, but it might have been on one of the riot days. The two facts—the riots and the beach—seem widely separated in my recollection because they were so different, but it's not impossible they happened on the same day. At the beach, the way the waves rolled in with a steady, powerful sound, I had to shout to be heard. All of my attention was drawn to the water. There were boys not much older than I paddling out through the rollers on surfboards or else riding in fast, some of them flying off their boards, legs and arms flung apart, cartwheeling into the foam. The beach was wide open, straightforward, direct. But the riot was something hidden trying to break out and be seen. Everyone outside of it strained to see in, but no one my father and I encountered ever got closer than we did—one of those barricades where police cars and National Guard trucks were spread across the street like a tourniquet, holding the damage to a certain point. I tried to look beyond and see something, but all I saw were police cars and fire trucks idling, National Guardsmen slouching against storefronts smoking cigarettes, looking jumpy. The big gray-black blimp of soot hung close above us. The sound of sirens was nearer. But there were no flames to see, there was no anger. In a way, the riot was motionless, serene, deep in hiding. As we turned and drove back from the barricade, my father asked me what I thought of it. But I couldn't answer him truthfully, so I just stared out the window. At the age of ten I looked into the flesh of a riot and believed I was looking into myself.

Then, possibly, my father drove us out to the beach.

On Christmas day in Maine I decide that the ocean is best in winter—hard to love, easy to fear. I get out of the truck and walk the beach with the others. I squint. The vastness of the blue-green water is weakening. I could never go in. I would disappear like a crumb into a pot of broth.

The cold wind causes tears to form at the corners of my eyes; the wind then smears them back into the hair at my temples. I could walk like this for days. But suddenly, unexpectedly, I meet Irene. She is walking twenty yards in front of me when the wind takes her hat and blows it back. The hat skids along the sand, coming closer, flipping and spinning. It hits my shin and sticks there, pushing back against me, not falling. I reach down and grab it.

"Here," I say. I hold up the hat. It's a West Coast type of hat, red felt, what they used to call a crusher. You can stick it upside-down in a crystal stream and capture a dome full of water for yourself. I think I used to have one, a dull green one. Irene's is better.

"Thank you so much," she says, running up. She smiles. I'd say she's forty-five or so, maybe older, maybe younger. She has a face that's used to sun. Creased and brown. I think of the bumper sticker: "If you don't have wrinkles, then you haven't laughed enough."

She takes back the hat and pushes it down on her head. The wind starts to lift it again.

"Oh, my," she says, catching it.

"You better just hold it," I tell her.

"Yes . . . I guess." She folds it in quarters and shoves it into a pocket of her parka. "Thank you . . ."

"David."

"I beg your pardon?"

"David," I say. "My name is David."

"Oh, yes. I see. Well, I'm Irene. Thank you, David."

"Irene what?"

"Uh, Lilly. Irene Lilly."

"Pleased to meet you, Irene." I reach out to shake her hand. She takes off a wool knit glove. The offered hand is warm and moist.

I can see by her face that she's having the usual complicated thoughts about how such an encounter is supposed to conclude: Normally she takes back the hat and thanks the man, and then she turns and is on her solitary way again. The fact that this is different throws her off balance. The man isn't letting the encounter end as it should. But what can be wrong with that? The man—David— is just the first person her hat found. The hat might have blown right past him to someone else, or into the water. This is a random thing. The event has just sprung up by accident. David is alone. He might be lonely. He's making conversation exactly the way a lonely person might. After all, it's Christmas day. How do people spend Christmas alone?

"Merry Christmas," Irene says.

"Likewise," I say. I give her the smile. We go into town for coffee at Dinah's Donut Dugout. Irene drives an old blue Honda with her name on the license plates. I follow in the truck, staring at the name. A woman's name on a license plate conveys a certain impression. She is not cautious; she isn't afraid to be well-known. The world is not for her a dangerous place. She will stop at a light and a car full of men will pull up beside her and start the "Hey Irene" thing, and she will have to smile. Even if she forgets for a day or a week that it says her name on the back of her car, someone will always oblige to remind her. She would be the kind to smile and not to say fuck off. The busy Irene-ing season must come in the summer. I think of this as a younger woman's thing, having the name on the license plate. But everyone gets older—all of these women are aging inside of their cars. Irene is older now. What is she supposed to do? Does she ask to trade in her name for number plates? No. It becomes a habit.

She parks head-in. I park beside her. The Donut Dugout isn't busy, but the windows are steamed inside and the coffee smells good. Dinah, or someone who might be Dinah, is standing on a chair to reach the stereo to change a tape. The place is tiny, and it's painted a kind of blue that I would call silly blue—the perfect shade of blue to paint a donut place or an amusement park. I follow Irene to a booth. Dinah gets down off the chair and turns around to see us.

"Irene," she says.

"Hi, Di."

The tape comes on. Brenda Lee, rockin' 'round the Christmas tree.

"Didja get that . . . did whatsisname get in touch with you about that approval thing . . . ?"

"Yeah," says Irene. "Thanks. I finally did go to the planning board meeting, and those people are just so stupid."

"Tell me about it," says Dinah. "Coffee?"

"Please."

Dinah comes around the counter with a glass pot in one hand and the index finger of the other looped through the handles of two mugs. She clunks down the mugs.

"Beach is crowded, believe it or not," says Irene. "That's where I found David here." She points at me. "He rescued my hat from the wind."

Dinah nods hello. She pours.

I like Dinah. Her top lip sticks to her large front teeth as she smiles. The lipstick is cracked and thick, and stains the teeth. Also, she doesn't automatically bring you those plastic cream things. I always drink mine black. Dinah recommends a special holiday donut, a regular fried cake decorated with icing to be a green wreath with a red ribbon.

"No thanks," Irene says. The music changes—a black quartet singing "White Christmas." Then Irene and Dinah continue talking about town business in a kind of code that I can hardly make any sense of. No one else is in the place, so Dinah plops down in the booth beside Irene and sets the coffee pot on the table. Both of them sound importantly involved in stopping development and getting some kind of arts school started, but that's about as much of it as I can understand. It's "committee" this and "board" that, and writing a lot of letters to the local newspaper—all mixed in with a cascade of names that make me sorry the crusher ever hit me. I sit there staring down at the steam coming up from the coffee, or else I glance across at the two of them. Irene smiles at me in an "I'll get to you later" way, and Dinah almost erases me from the table. The music changes and changes. All of them are pop song Christmas tunes: Elvis Presley, Bruce Springsteen, Nat King Cole, Loretta Lynn, the Chipmunks, and so forth. I become quieter and quieter inside of myself until the heartbeat almost dies in my chest. I could close my eyes and be nowhere at all, hearing nothing, feeling like nothing, disappearing completely from wherever it is I am on Earth. Then the door opens behind me, ringing a small, sweet bell, and Dinah gets up and goes away.

Irene leans across the table and invites me to see her home.

"I've got a tree up," she says. "It's really something."

I follow her again, keeping my eyes on the "IRENE." It's left and right and left, and then straight for half a mile or so, heading away from town, away from the beach. Then she signals left and into a driveway, and on past a big house to a little house in the same old architectural style as the big one, as though it's the child of the big one.

Irene holds the door for me.

"Thank you," I say.

I have no idea what I'm going to do. The house is bright. There are paintings everywhere. Eerie landscapes, depressing portraits. There is one on an easel that looks to be almost finished. A smiling boy is holding a gun to his head. In the background are sailboats in full sun. A hand reaches into the painting from the side farthest away from the gun. The hammer of the gun is a blur.

On a card table near the easel there are twisted tubes of paints that look beaten. Some ooze tongues of color onto the table. The surface of the table would make a better picture than the painting itself. I stare at the tabletop. How did I get here? Irene bends over in a corner and lights the Christmas tree. It fills the room with a jolt of colors. For the millionth time I recognize that I don't have an actual life of my own. I enter and leave the lives of others like a virus, coming to know these people in the strangest ways. Who are they? Afterwards, I would not be able to answer even the simplest questions—height, weight, color of eyes and hair. Whoever they are, either they give me strength or else they fight me off in some secret way. Staring at the tree and the tubes of paint and the strange painting of the boy who is about to die, suddenly I feel fought off.

Irene says, "I'll be right back," and goes into the bathroom. I take this golden opportunity to leave quickly, feeling clean. The air outside hits my lungs freshly. I could almost sing. I run to the truck and start the engine. I turn the truck around and drive off. In the mirror I see her coming fast out the front door of the small house. Her face has a funny expression. Surprised. She gets much smaller—much smaller, and not moving—until I make the hard right turn onto the street. I retrace my steps back to the donut place looking for Dinah, imagining the soft red stain of lipstick shooting like a star across her two biggest teeth. But the place is already closed—and the clock isn't even at noon yet.

I point the truck south and go. On Route One outside of town someone stands at the edge of the road with his thumb out, holding in the other hand a cardboard sign that says "Boston." He stamps his feet and squints. My foot finds the brake. I stop just past him. He runs up and opens the door.

"Merry Christmas," he says, smiling through a young man's beard. I look up the road ahead and then behind me in the mirror. The road is empty enough.

"Merry Christmas to you," I say. He slams the door shut. I begin to run up through the gears. Everything seems simple.

"Going to Boston?" I say to the man.

"Uh-huh," he says. I see him nod in the corner of my eye. This all seems familiar. Familiarity fills the cab like an old smell. The man feels it too.

"Can I turn on the radio?" he asks. I nod without looking at him.

"Go ahead," I say. "But you're on your own. I don't know any of the stations around here. I'm from Oregon."

He reaches out his hand and turns the radio on. Then he tunes it. The red needle slides across brief, senseless slices of sound and comes to rest where the hitchhiker wants it. Foolish music fills the cab, music that rushes ahead of itself, that hates itself, that is sung by a voice like aluminum foil, a voice achieved electrically. I turn up the heat to fight a chill that has crept to my hands. The forced air whooshes out and softens me. I breathe in and out slowly and wait for the passenger to start the conversation. But all he does is sit. His foot jitters rapidly up in the shadows beneath the dash. I hold tight to the wheel and watch the road.

"There's a flask in the glove compartment," I say.

His hand shoots forward and works the latch. The flask slides out on its own, and he catches it. He offers it to me.

I shake my head. "Go ahead and help yourself," I say.

A headwind strikes the cab and causes the familiar whine of vibration in some part of the hood or the grille. I refuse to watch. I hear the cap turn, the threads scraping. The music ends, replaced by Morse code beeps that signal news to come.

"*Coast Radio 101 news time is twelve o'clock noon on this sunny and snowless Christmas day,*" says the voice of a woman. "*Here are the stories we've been watching for you.*"

All of this has happened before. The hitchhiker does what anyone would do—what others have already done. He drinks from the flask and slowly becomes the silent thing beside me. He joins my life. We ride down the road together. I try to feel the drama of this and to grasp the size of the loss. But it only feels small and unbelievably easy, and he is nothing—he could be anyone. He continues to hold the uncapped flask in his hand. I imagine the morbid liquor trembling in the near-total darkness. I weigh in my mind how to make the process work less simply and be more difficult. But slowly the strength flows out of him and into me, like a surf rolling invisibly across the vinyl seat. And finally I reach the place where it doesn't matter to me how much or how little is required to achieve what I have. I am nothing but energy. Beams could shine forth from my eyes.

His foot is the last thing moving. I turn the radio up until it hurts my ears. I reach over and cap the flask.

--

Christmas wears away. The truck goes left and right, left and right, searching for a place to leave the passenger. I wait for the familiar gentle voice, knowing it will come. Hardly anyone is on the roads. We hit a bump and he pitches forward. I grab the back of his denim jacket and pull him aright. A soft hissing escapes the body. Venting. This too has happened before. Nothing is truly different.

On both sides of the road are unbroken woods. Here, the voice tells me. My eyes race ahead and find a dirt turning on the right. I slow the truck and take it. I go deep in, slowly. The road bumps; the leaf springs groan. I hold his collar, my knuckles hard against the back of his cooling neck. I turn from the dirt road and drive between two trees straight into the forest, where the sunlight dies. I weave between trees. Soon the voice says, Here. It means a particular tree. I stop the truck. I take the flask and put it away. I get out and go around to the passenger's side. I pull him out backwards by the collar and the waist. I empty his pockets of wallet and papers. I sit him on the ground and lean him back against the tree.

It will be spring before anyone finds him. When the snow comes, it will bind him to the tree. When the snow melts, there will be nothing left. A magic trick.

Good, says the voice. Merry Christmas, says the voice.

I know exactly how grateful I am supposed to be. I expect there will be a price to pay someday, but so far I haven't been asked.

Good, says the voice again.

# FIVE

I IMAGINE A TIME WHEN I WILL BE CAUGHT and questioned by detectives, and I will not lie to them. I will not wait for the lawyer and sit there mutely, drinking the coffee they offer me, smoking the cigarettes, knowing that saying nothing is saving myself. They will want more from me than that; they will have greater overall expectations. With what I have done come certain responsibilities. I can hear them tell me this; I can see me believing it. I can feel how the energy gathers inside me to go on an honest search with them, leading them on through everything that I have ever done and been and thought about. Beginnings. I will want their fascination.

I will tell them first about the quiet, distant, cool, sad loneliness of the earliest times. I will want them to look with me among the thousands of hard early moments to find the hardest ones of all, the ones that began me on the certain path that led to this room, to them—these bitter, determined men. We will all need to show our commitment. This will be a process, not an interrogation. I will need to be given some latitude.

But they will naturally be most curious about my method. Skipping far ahead, they will want to know first about the crimes. There is truly no patience for an earnest explanation. They will hear the mysterious past offered up and drum their fingers or look at their watches. They will get out of their chairs or up off the corners of the table and walk to the windows and sigh, leaning hard on the sills and letting me know in every possible way that I am a deep disappointment of a killer.

"What about the murders?" one will say. "Tell us about this poison."

And I will be stopped in the midst of my very first memory: my father holding me out over the rail of a ferry boat so that I float face down in the wind like a gull, the water hissing three decks below me, whispering fast, the soft words speeding up to me out of small mouthlike whorls of wake that survive for only a second. In the telling I emphasize not my fear, but my connectedness to the water that will come to play a role later on. I try to create a thread. The detectives are uninterested.

"Yeah. But what about the poison?"

So I stop immediately, feeling the large hands of my father disappear from around my ribcage, and I begin to tell them a story about Tim Jackson.

On certain kinds of late fall or early winter days I think of Tim. Oregon had plenty of days like these, when even the rivers were silent, when the sky was low—so low it almost touched your hair, skin, clothing. The air was thick with mist. The mist went through you, became you—you became it, there was no difference. Nothing had any depth. On days like these I think of Tim, who found me in a hospital bed and conquered me with medicines.

Sometimes I will see a man who looks like Tim—a shining mahogany face and helpless smile—and I will almost feel one of Tim's medicines recall itself from my cells and spin me a certain way, lifting me from the ground and making my heart beat fast or my groin tingle or my muscles weep and bend. This lasts a small fraction of a minute, only long enough to let me form the small word: Tim. And hear it echo.

I can never remember how I got to where Tim could find me. An important piece of time has disappeared forever, the way it has for people who say they were taken aboard an alien craft and studied carefully. I laid there in bed in restraints, like something prepared for mailing. The window by my head was uncurtained, vast, its glass old and wavy. I had my head turned watching through the window. Fog erased the world. I tried to cut through this fog. Something would come into view, but hardly long enough to be recognized as a distinct object, or a person or a car or a distant white building. Just dim motes, floating out of reach.

While trying to see through the fog, I could break out sweating from the pure exertion of it. I recall my tears rolling slowly across the bridge of my nose, mixing with sweat. Sometimes I believed the fog was not the world's, but mine. But then I would see the dew forming on the aluminum shade of the lamp by my bed, the drops enlarging, sliding, falling in an unrhythmic way.

Tim Jackson first came to me as a voice. My head was turned to the window. I was far out through it, deep in the distance. So his voice seemed to be inside of me.

"You're Siegert," he said. I thought, Yes I am.

Slowly my eyes came back to the room, searching for the room. When you find yourself in restraints, you can defeat them by enacting in your body a stillness even more pronounced than the stillness compelled by the restraints. Gradually they loosen; your garments float away from your flesh, and you can spin rapidly inside of the clothing, becoming a gas and spreading evenly through the atmosphere of the room—an exactly measurable number of atoms per cubic centimeter, not simply an average. In restraints the body begins to mean nothing. You can go anywhere you want.

"Mr. Siegert . . ."

"Yes," I said.

"My name is Tim. I have your medicine."

On January second at the post office, just as I'm about to go buy lunch from the canteen truck, Dan Shames puts his hand on my shoulder and tells me I'm through, the season's over. He holds my gaze with his sad eyes, something he must have learned to do. There is no reason for me to regret this news, but it aches in my head just the same.

"Dan," I say.

"I'm sorry, Vann. But provisional means temporary. You knew it. I knew it. We said it to you right up front."

"Yeah, but . . ."

"I know. I know what happens, how it happens. Everybody just puts it out of their mind. Look . . ."

"It's okay. Forget it. I know the score . . . As of when?"

"As of end of the week."

"Okay."

"We'll pay you through then. But you don't even have to come in if you don't want. Just don't say I told you so."

"Thanks. I'll be coming in, though."

"Whatever."

"It's only a few days."

"Anyhow, I'm sorry."

"Okay."

I walk out to the loading dock. The weather is gray like Oregon, foggy, temperature in the middle fifties. On the weather map on television, a surprising bulge of warm air has risen from the south, and no one knows how far north it will creep or how long it will stay. But it lingers, hanging the wrong season across most of New England. This southern air has ushered the dense fog in off the ocean. From where I stand I can't even see the top of the Unitarian church, two blocks away. I am thinking of Tim when Ferrin comes up behind me and says how sorry she is.

"I hate this part," she says. She puts her arms around my waist. She can't help it. I look down and see her knuckles laced above my belt. I feel her cheek against my spine, her chin moving slowly— chewing gum.

"Let's go for a ride," I say.

"Okay," says Ferrin.

The fog lets me not even think about where we're going. Ferrin doesn't ask—which is good, because I don't have a clue. She sits quietly on her side of the cab and stares out the window. We are just driving. First we go slowly through town, the way you do when you want to be ready to see someone you know. We bump across the railroad tracks. Then town dissolves in the familiar way. Leon's Superette, the Dunkin' Donuts, the auto supply, the pet-grooming place.

"Let's take off the rest of the day," Ferrin says.

"Okay."

"I feel like something to drink," she says.

"Okay. We can stop at the package store." I signal left and pull in at Romie's Liquors.

"Leave it running," Ferrin says. She goes inside and comes back in a minute with a pint of Johnnie Walker's.

"That's better," she says. She cracks the seal. We drive off.

There are low-lying places just outside of town where the road dives down and the fog is so thick the truck billows it to either side in slow motion. If I didn't look at the speedometer, I wouldn't have any idea how fast we're going. Then we come up out of the dive and the air half clears. I turn the lights on.

Somewhere along the way I begin to have knowledge of where we might be heading. My driving decisions have the dim familiarity of decisions I might have made before, in the past—not that I am dead certain about it, but maybe . . . The fog confuses me, though. These could, after all, be new decisions, only similar.

"This is something else," I say, pointing up ahead at the fog. Ferrin passes me the bottle. I put its mouth to mine and taste something moist of Ferrin still left on the threads. We pass a sign that welcomes us to Rhode Island.

"I hate Rhode Island," Ferrin says. "A couple of cities, some beaches, a bunch of rich people with sailboats."

"We could turn around," I say.

"No, go ahead," she says. "How bad can it be? We're not gonna end up living here."

"No," I say.

It wasn't long before I figured out that Tim was dispensing medicine outside of official channels. I would sip a clear blue liquid from a tiny paper cup he held in the thumb and forefinger of his delicate hand. Minutes later, I was light and perfect, floating in the midst of wise thoughts and deep, generous feelings. Anyone could have said any terrible thing to me, and it wouldn't have mattered.

Soon Tim stuck his head back in the door and asked me how it was. "You high yet?"

The three words scampered like small dogs, chasing the question mark through the crystal air of the room.

"Yes," I said. I heard the amazement in my voice—the word hissed with happiness. I watched the smile break across his face, the finest, most perfect teeth glowing like lights.

"Thank you," I said.

This was how Tim became my amusement park.

Sometimes he sat in my room and watched me. I would be high and floating, and Tim would be anchored in a chair, sitting straight and still like a lighthouse, shining up at me, approving, now and then speaking softly—words that were hardly words at all, just a deep vibration mixed with breath.

"Damn . . ."

I knew how much he enjoyed me. I was Tim's amusement park, too. I could feel the pleasure of observing me come off of him like heat. Others might believe that Tim was not healthy in his interests, but I thought I understood him. And he acted toward me as if he believed I did. In return for my understanding, Tim favored me with the best pharmacology he could offer. Not everyone was so fortunate. Tim would return to me from another patient's room and chew his lip, listening, until the man began crying out.

"Poor Tucker," Tim might say, and shake his head. "But he's a fucking Klansman"—which was what Tim called any white man who was too crazy to talk to him politely. I always knew that Tim could hurt me, and this was an important part of understanding him. Almost anyone can hurt anyone. They just have to know how to wait for the moment, how to be calm, what to use. You take the momentum of the person and draw it toward you. Everyone's momentum can be tapped and used like electricity, and added to your own. Tim is a perfect example of my belief in this.

"Life is a martial art," he said. "Everything in life is a weapon."

The detectives will now be drawn up close around the table. This is what they want. It's what they live for: to be in a room with a lawyerless perp, the tiny reels of tape turning slowly—the clean side emptying, the other side filling with words. I am setting the stage to tell them what they think they already know. As hard as they try to hide it, the excitement shows in their eyes. They have no trouble connecting me to Tim Jackson, no trouble connecting Tim Jackson to certain future criminal acts of mine that they might

just come to believe were inspired by this highly experimental orderly, Tim Jackson. They are ready to regard poor Tim as the
switch that gets thrown in my past and dooms double figures to
death by poisoning. One of the detectives too eagerly pushes the
nearer of two tape recorders even closer to me. Deliberately I stop
speaking and look up, showing everyone in the room that this
detective has distracted me. I don't have to say a word. The detectives freeze. The room dies to a sudden stillness.

Ferrin falls asleep with the open bottle braced in her crotch. I reach
across and screw the cap on gently, quietly. She shifts, and the
mouth of the bottle moves. I finish, still driving.

Soon we are at the beach where Gene Fowler is buried. At least I
think we are. One beach in Rhode Island is probably very much
like another, but right away I think I recognize it. When I turn off
the engine Ferrin wakes up.
    "Where are we?"
    "A beach."
From the spot where the truck rests on semi-firm ground the
sand rises before sloping down to the water. Sitting in the cab we
can only hear the waves without seeing them. After a minute of
listening, Ferrin gets out and walks up and over the rise, out of
sight. Then she reappears and waves at me to follow her. I do.
    The sand is deep and soft. My feet sink in, and sand packs tight
around them, into the shoes. Each step is a pulling out and sliding
back until, closer to the water, the beach solidifies and supports
my weight. It takes a long while to reach Ferrin, who doesn't stop
but walks more slowly.
    "Hey," she says when I catch up.
    Ferrin has a long jaw and crooked teeth. She draws me into her
clumsiness, which feels ordinary and good. She acts like she expects
something from me, as though I could give it to her easily. And
yet, whatever she gets from me, which is almost nothing, it's enough
for her. I have no trouble believing that I am always succeeding
with her. She would never complain about anything.
    She points up and down the empty beach. "All to ourselves,"

she says. She rushes up to me and throws her hands around my neck and chokes me lightly, until I cough. I stagger backwards, surprised. She races away from me, up toward the dunes. She goes quickly over the top of one and then down, disappearing. I stand with my back to the water hearing the bubbles foam into the sand behind my heels. I wait for her to reappear like some dog crazily chasing after nothing, suddenly changing directions, leaning in circles. But she doesn't. She stays out of sight. I hear the voice—a voice that often sounds like Tim's voice—saying "What if she finds him?" The words sink in like the bubbles into the sand. She's up in a dune that looks like the dune where Gene is buried. I imagine her finding the tips of his shoes jutting through where the wind has shifted the bowl of the dune from one place to another. I walk slowly toward the rim of the dune.

Tim mostly worked at night, like a dream. In the morning I would wake up to the faces of the resident doctors, men who I thought would have shaved themselves better—more carefully or more often—if they had been working in more important institutions. A carelessness came through in the way they asked their questions and then hardly noticed that the patient wasn't answering. They left a space for the answer and then moved on to the next question.

"Are the headaches better?"

Silence for twenty seconds.

"Do you believe you can control your thoughts now?"

Silence for half a minute.

Sometimes I imagined that the mouths of the doctors would move without any sounds coming out. Their white coats were not clean. When they leaned close to check the eyes, I smelled the rancid breath of old food caught unyieldingly in back teeth. The mornings were heavy with the remorse that I was no longer in the firm grip of Tim. I had no objections to being controlled, but Tim was so much better at it than the doctors. I would shut my eyes to blot out the morning and summon Tim's voice from the back of my mind. If I held a fingernail to my ear, the voice came from the enamel.

If I asked the voice of Tim why I was there in the hospital, it would say, "For me."

--

Ferrin kneels in the bowl of the dune undressing.

"Stop," I say, "don't," but she doesn't stop. I stand on the rim. I can see the goose flesh rise on her back. The jacket and shirt lie together on the sand. She half turns, and the low pout of her breast hangs in the fog. I go down to her.

"It's cold," she says, squeezing her shoulders together. She lies back slowly in the sand and undoes the snap of her gray postal trousers. Gulls circle and cry.

"Here. Pull at the ankles," she says. I yank her cuffs. The legs are pale and shivery underneath. I ball up the pants and throw them on the other clothes.

"Hurry up," she says. All she has on are the underpants, blue and shiny, but I'm soft as a baby. I lean down and kiss her breast. The flesh is cold and tight. She moans. I stir in my jeans.

"Hurry up," she says. I start to unzip myself.

"Wait," she says. She puts her four fingers on herself and frigs away through the underpants for twenty seconds. Her eyes and mouth open and close.

"Okay," she says. She hooks her thumbs in my pants and shorts and pushes them off my hips. "Okay, come on." I settle on top of her, but too low. The tip of my penis slaps straight down into the cold sand. It aches. Ferrin grabs it back and twists it into position. I follow along. She arches up and moves her hips and takes me in. I feel the grains of sand inside of her, between us, rubbing. The fog thickens. I hear the gulls flapping above, breathing with half a cry.

Somewhere beneath us, two feet, three feet down, is Gene Fowler. Ferrin's spine presses into the sand, warming it. Can she feel the strangeness of where she lies without knowing why? I push myself up and spread my hands beside her shoulders. I look down on her face and see the tears flow out the corners of her squeezed-shut eyes. Already I'm soft again, and nothing's happened. Ferrin moves slower and slower. Hope dies. I roll away.

One night Tim came to my room and whispered that he was slowly killing Evan Tyrer, the man three rooms away who was unable to stop combing his hair. He could appear to be normal and fine until he began combing his hair, and then he would pathologically be forced to continue on with it—wetting the hair, combing it straight forward hundreds of swipes, eventually scraping raw the pale scalp underneath to the point that it bled and scabbed. He would lean in close to the mirror as if he was finished, then step back to regard himself and, finally, mess it up and begin again, splashing on the water. Thus could his time be filled. Some days he never even got to part it; something would always be wrong with the earliest phases of the combing, and he would be stuck there, never progressing. Other days he would breeze through all of it until his head was a perfect finished product. He could go forward and eat his lunch on a good day such as that. But after lunch he would go to the mirror and see that it wasn't exactly right.

"He'll be gone by the end of the week," said Tim. "Fact. I make him a minus. And nobody knows but me and you."

I lay flat on my back like a dead pope. My nose stretched up to the ceiling—I could smell the ancient plaster. Tim's breath warmed my cool ear. A soft brown capsule he had given me was spreading paralysis across the bed like frost.

"Don't talk," he said—he knew I couldn't. "Just listen."

Tim hated Evan Tyrer, and many times he had spoken of stealing his combs or taking the mirror off the bathroom wall. But he had never said before that he would kill him. I began to wonder if Tim would soon kill me or others, the sad dozens who didn't know what we were doing there. For a minute longer I heard Tim whispering in my ear. The fear of helplessness was exciting. I tried to open my jaw or turn my head, but none of the signals from the brain got through. Tim's voice spread out inside me like a drug—the deep whisper, cottony and certain.

"This is my first," he said. "I know exactly how to do it. No one will even know it was murder."

I couldn't move my eyes. They stared straight up. Tim was unseeable beside me, except that sometimes the top of his hair rose into the corner of my eye. He spoke rapidly about how he hadn't realized at first that his work with medicines would progress to this point; but slowly it dawned on him that his activities would someday have to include murder, and that he would be unable to stop himself.

"But I promise I won't hurt you," he said. He put his hand on my forehead; it felt heavy and cold as a slab of steel. But I heard him smiling. "Don't thank me," he said.

Then I drifted off into a place that was red and damp, and filled with furnishings that had the texture of nougat, and with people whose faces were saucelike and who ran from me. In the morning I opened my eyes to see the soft face of Dr. Rosengarten, who looked down upon me the way a deer in Montana once had done.

"Evan Tyrer died last night in his sleep," said Dr. Rosengarten. "How are *you* feeling?"

It took me the longest time to remember what Tim had told me. But it came back to me in a messy clump while Dr. Rosengarten held his bright light to my eyes, first one then the other.

"Fine," I said.

Some of the detectives, not trusting the tape, are writing down everything furiously in skinny notepads, hard blue waves of scribbling that wrinkle and dimple the narrow paper, making it suddenly seem old and worn. I vary the pace of my speech, becoming excruciatingly slow for a while, then speeding up for no apparent reason and leaving them all behind. This helps them to learn that the story belongs to me and that I'll tell it in my own way. I need to take every opportunity to set some limits.

Ferrin rises to a sitting position. Her face is puffy from crying. She looks like she's been beaten up. I imagine beating her, and believe that she would let me do it—she would lend herself to my desires in a way that enabled me to continue succeeding with her.

"That was nice," she says. She wraps her arms around her breasts.

"I agree," I say. I pull up my pants and fasten them and tuck myself in. Then I reach over and put my hand on her shoulder. She leans away and gets her bra and shirt. She puts them on slowly, as though she is not thinking about what she is doing. Carelessly she buttons the shirt.

"Let's lie here side by side," I say.

"Okay."

We both lie back on the sand, staring up into the fog, not speaking. The fog thins and thickens, causing the low sun to brighten and dim strangely.

"Do you like me?" Ferrin asks.

"Yes, I do," I say.

"It's hard to tell sometimes."

"But I do."

She waits for a second. Then she says, "Okay, I believe you."

The matter is settled and I can't think of anything else to say. So I just lie quietly and let my thoughts drift along with the patches of fog above. Ferrin, too, lies still for a while, but then she is up on her elbow staring down at my face, smiling.

When Evan Tyrer died I waited for the agitation to spread up and down the wing. I waited for the sounds of people moaning and beating their fists against the beds and walls. I imagined that the nurses and orderlies would be running all over the place to contain a flood of upset bursting out. But nothing like that happened. The peace and quiet were unbroken and grand. The peace of God that passeth all understanding. You would hardly have known there was a death in the place. I turned my head and saw the empty gurney pass my door on its way to him. Ten minutes later the gurney returned full. That was all. Silence on soft rubber wheels. Later on, two orderlies went by sharing the weight of a trunk containing Evan Tyrer's possessions.

On that morning I was taken out of restraints. Dr. Rosengarten entered with an orderly named Mr. Day, and together they unstrapped me so that I became disconnected officially from the bed for the first time in as long as I could remember having been there.

"Don't thank us," said Dr. Rosengarten, smiling. "You are making progress."

"Why was I in them in the first place?" I said.

"Because you were decompensating. See?" He held up my chart so that I could see it but not read it, and pointed at several scribbled entries. "But drugs are a blessing. Applied properly by people who know what they're doing. The sick are made well now where, before, they never would have seen the light of day again. Your mother will be pleased."

"My mother."

"She is here to visit you," said Dr. Rosengarten. "All the way from Spokane."

"Great," says one of the imagined detectives. "Here comes Mom." I reach out and place my finger on the tape-recorder STOP button, pressing down until it clicks.

"I'm tired," I say. "I'm running out of smokes."

"Will somebody go get Mr. Siegert some cigarettes," one of the older, calmer detectives says. And someone immediately leaves the room like magic, the door opening and closing almost without stirring the air. Then a hand reaches into the center of the table and gently presses both the PLAY and RECORD buttons.

Ferrin insists that we take a walk. We go first in one direction and then in the other. After fifty yards the physical landmarks of where we started disappear in the fog. Ferrin worries that we will be lost in Rhode Island. So she runs back and scratches my name in the sand with a long stick, high above the tide line. I see the stick slant the hard angles of my four letters sharply in the sand.

"There," she calls from where she stands looking down at the name. "*V-A-N-N.*" At times I can barely see her, and her voice comes down the beach as thick as syrup. She runs toward me, becoming clearer. Everything about her is undone. Her shirt flaps. She is short, and her hair snaps from side to side behind her, done up in a ponytail. Closer and closer. She drives straight into me, smiling, almost knocking me to the sand. She could be seven.

I yell. My arms fling out. She rebounds from me and laughs. She comes forward again and takes my hand, pulling me around in the direction of walking away from the scratched name, swinging our hands between us.

We walk for half an hour, encountering no one.

--

My mother sat in the visiting chair and I sat in the patient chair, which was larger and softer and harder to remove from the room. The bed was freshly made up as though I'd never once occupied it, and the restraints were tastefully folded underneath, out of sight but accessible in an instant.

"You scared us so," she said. "We had to do it."

"Who is we?" I asked.

"Your brother and I. Neil."

"I can't remember a thing."

"That's good. I can't even talk about it. I don't want to."

She opened and closed her purse, shiny blue-black with a clasp that clicked. I had an urge to reach over and take it from her and click the clasp myself.

"You said there were hundreds of people you wanted to kill, and you started to name them. You said for each one exactly how you wanted to do it. I couldn't believe it. Neil cried and tried to hug you. You pushed him down."

"I don't remember any of that. I was sick. I must have been."

"I couldn't believe it."

"No. I'm sure."

I sat quietly with my head down, wishing Tim would deliver me something sweet but knowing that Tim was hours away from punching in. I thought back to visiting my mother in a clinic on Puget Sound where she was treated for her drinking. I went with Neil. She came out into the bright sun wearing a yellow dress and smiling, looking like Nanette Fabray, spinning in front of us while we still sat in Neil's convertible. He'd only just turned the engine off. She must have been watching the road for us.

"Let's go for a ride," she said. The day was hot. Even with the top down, my back was sweated stuck against the plastic seat. I wanted to get out and stretch, but Neil said, "Okay, Mom. Hop in," and our mother demanded the front seat.

"I'll stay here," I said, getting out. "The two of you go. I'll find some shade."

"Oh, Vann, come on," my mother said. "A drive'll do you good." She didn't seem to understand we'd just had one. But I walked off toward a tree at the edge of the gravel drive. As soon as I got there

I turned and waved. Neil started the car and drove off, hollering that they'd be back in twenty minutes. Just then a woman came running out of the clinic building and watched the car disappear. I saw her shake her head and go back inside.

Neil returned with my mother at sunset. She was drunk as a skunk. Neil yelled for me to help him. I came down off the porch, where I had been sitting on a glider reading the *Reader's Digest*. We took an arm each and brought her inside and sat her on a couch in the lobby. Other residents were then filing out of the dining room after dinner, talking quietly. A woman from this group came over and knelt in front of my mother.

"Estelle?" she said. "You've had some trouble?"

"Hmmmm," my mother said. She threw her arms around this woman's neck. Soon after, a counselor rushed up with two orderlies and took her off our hands.

"Nice going, you guys," the counselor said to us over her shoulder. "Real swift."

Ferrin doesn't want to leave the beach. She decides she likes Rhode Island after all.

"Let's turn around," I say. We've walked to Connecticut, for all I know. The light is fading beyond the fog, and the tide is creeping up the slope of the beach. I look behind us and see the high wash of the waves blurring our footprints. Soon the *V-A-N-N* of my name will blur, too, and we will be as lost as Ferrin feared, exhausting ourselves in the vagueness.

"No," she says. She sits heavily in the sand. I reach down under her armpit and pull her up. My fingers go deep into the soft dark tissues beneath the shirt, and she squeals in pain.

"Yes," I say. "This bus is leaving."

She looks at me like I'm crazy, but she is on her feet, and her feet are moving back in the direction of my name in the sand, of the truck.

We take a track just up the slope from the farthest reach of the surging water. Our former footprints are the merest dents.

"Tide's coming in," I say, liking the sound of the words even though I don't know the first thing about the tides. But any idiot could tell. The water seems eager and happy, conquering the beach. Ferrin doesn't say a thing. My eyes probe ahead through the fog, looking for the dozens of clumps of stuff I tried to memorize. Some of the clumps seem familiar, yes, but I have lost the reference points of where I memorized them in relation to anything else, and so it doesn't do us any good.

Suddenly I see a man and a dog.

"Hello," the man says to Ferrin. The dog comes up and sniffs her thighs. Ferrin bends at the waist and rubs the dog's back.

"He likes that," says the man. And then the dog suddenly breaks away and races on ahead, and the man follows the dog, shouting and waving a stick. And they are gone again.

"Your father disagreed with me," said my mother, "but you were always well behaved as a baby boy. You were perfect. Anything was all right with you. Anything and everything. I could dangle you over the porch rail on Cinnamon Street, and it didn't make a damn bit of difference. You just smiled and laughed. You looked at the sky."

Outside the door to my room the orderly named Bryce stood guard. He was large and unsmiling, like a bouncer, and he was apparently there to persuade me that strangling my mother was not in the cards as long as he possessed breath enough to protect her. He stayed where his massive shoulder was sure to be visible to me, a shoulder that stretched the usually dull tan khaki of his short-sleeved shirt into a high shine. A soft blue tattoo descended below the shirt, the hearty tines of an anchor—an ex-marine.

My mother had obviously had a couple of jolts before visiting. I could tell by her thoughtless narrative that bounced along without caring if I was listening or not. She smiled down at her hands, in which she clutched the purse that I was sure held a pint of something—Old Crow or a Hiram Walker fruit brandy.

"Why are you here?" I said.

She looked up and the smile remained.

"Poor Vann," she said. "You stripped your gears. The question you ought to be asking isn't why am *I* here, but why are *you* here. And the answer is I signed some papers, with Neil as witness—and he absolutely saw exactly what he said he saw and heard. I couldn't believe it. Neither one of us. You were out of control, Vann. You *assaulted* your brother."

"I don't remember," I said. "How is he?"

I remembered a turkey cooking, the overpowering smell growing dense and acrid in the small cabin. But I had no memory at all of Neil and my mother being present in the cabin.

"Neil? He's fine. He's back in Philadelphia with that slut. What is it? Naomi? Is Naomi a Jewish girl?"

Bryce turned and peered around the edge of the door, into the room. He looked at my mother and then at me, expressionless, like a security camera sweeping the grounds.

"We just had to see how you were doing. Neil came west to me for Thanksgiving, and I didn't even let him bring his bags in the house. I put a finger in his chest and said stop right there. I took him and the turkey and packed the three of us off to Oregon in the Plymouth. I said, Neil, what's a reunion when there's a body missing? Neil drove us most of the way. He has a kind of a heavy foot, but he has never said no to me as long as I can remember. As boys, you were identical. You were both perfect. We put the turkey in the trunk to keep it cool.

"And this is how it ends up."

She opened her purse and took out the pint of brandy. "Do you think they'd mind?" she whispered. I shrugged and closed my eyes. I wanted to lie in bed by myself and stare out the window.

"Please leave," I said. "I like to think that maybe this is the last time we see each other."

She looked slapped. She screwed the cap on the brandy and put it back in her purse like a treasure.

"The police asked me a lot of questions about you, and I told them you grew up to become an unhappy and restless youth. I told them about your wanderings and such. They looked around the cabin, and one of them said he'd go crazy, too, living in a place like that. We never even got to eat the turkey. Its skin was nut brown and shiny, like one of your daddy's old shoes. I looked through a window and saw you in the backseat of the police car, out cold, with your head thrown back and your Adam's apple bulging. There was nothing at all to give thanks for. Neil had broken a finger. We packed it in ice."

"I'm sorry," I said.

"How many times have I heard that?"

She shook her head. I began to remember the two policemen taking me down expertly, working together like brothers who knew each other's every move. Their similar faces bobbed in and out, serious and careful—it was their work. I felt completely helpless. I wanted to throw up my hands and tell them I surrendered, but my body kept moving and raging; my heart roared like an ocean in my ears. I fought them off and let them hurt me until they moved in together—one stick at the throat and one at the back of the neck—and squeezed me senseless. The blood stopped moving to the brain. The next thing I knew I was in the hospital, lying in bed and staring out into the mist, waiting for Tim but not knowing it.

My mother stood up quickly and left without saying good-bye. I suddenly wanted her back. I sat in the chair and listened to her heels click against the linoleum, disappearing. I smelled her in the air.

"Nice fucking mother," said the orderly Bryce, as he closed and locked my door. What did Bryce know? For the rest of the day I sat in my chair without moving, waiting for Tim.

We walk as high on the beach as we can, up by the grass, so as not to miss the truck. I let Ferrin continue believing that we could actually become lost, but what I really think is that Gene Fowler, the buried minus, transmits a signal of steadily increasing volume, drawing us back.

Ferrin's chin juts out and up, penetrating the fog. Her neck elongates and she stands on her toes.

"Relax," I say. "We'll find it."

Because I hurt her she isn't talking to me. She is thinking it through independently. It could take her a full half hour to completely like me again, and she will do this all on her own. I won't have to say a single word, apologize, explain or charm her. We are not linked in any way that requires an exchange. She simply has this need that I am the answer to. If I were to hurt her again, she would only need fifteen minutes, and so forth, until my hurting her became part of the answer to the need she sees me filling.

Sometimes—especially when her back is turned—I think I could easily begin to train her in this way. I imagine jamming my fist up hard into the fulcrum between her legs as she stands in front of me searching the dunes. I imagine shocking and scaring and hurting her repeatedly until I have turned her devotion to me into something perfect and unbreakable.

"All we have to do is just keep walking," I say. "So relax."

Tim took me for a walk one late afternoon before dinner. He gave me two green-banded capsules and got me into my leather jacket. He strapped me in a wheelchair and wheeled me down the shining corridors and through the lobby, then out the double doors and down the switchback ramp to the grounds. The sun was setting, thick and orange.

"Where to?" said Tim.

"How should I know?" I said. My words formed soft white cubes in the air which floated and changed positions with one another. Then the cubes raced on ahead to four different destinations and clamored for me to choose one.

"How should I know?" I said again, and the business with the cubes repeated.

"Then I'll just pick a spot myself," said Tim.

He steered us along a flagstone sidewalk toward the sunset. The orange color deepened to red and oozed across the sky, sharpening the edges of the clouds. Beyond a white, two-story clapboard building that Tim said was a staff dormitory—"where the doctors fuck their nurses"—he suddenly turned us left onto a gravel path that led into a woods. The trees darkened around us; the red sky leaked in between them from the horizon.

We went in deeper and deeper. The wheelchair bounced along and the trees blurred past. Whatever medicine Tim had given me had made me floppy and dim. I felt the flesh of my face sag down to my chest like lifeless putty. Closing my eyes was like closing the gigantic doors of a church. In my lungs I could taste the piney air I breathed, as harsh as Christmas, prickling deep inside.

Then the wheelchair slowed and stopped on the path, and Tim was swiftly around in front of me kneeling, taking my hands in his hands and squeezing them hard.

"I'll miss you, buddy," he said.

Then he threw his arms up around my neck and hugged me dearly. The wheelchair trembled beneath his leaning.

"I'll miss you, too," I said. I could feel his weight shift slowly off my shoulders. He smelled like Mennen's and pipe smoke mixed. I couldn't stand the thought of him leaving.

"Where are you going?" I said. He pushed himself away.

"I'm going nowhere, buddy. It's *you*," he said. "They're cutting you loose tomorrow. I've seen the damn paperwork. You're cured. I *cured* your ass."

Then he put his hand on top of my head and said he'd draw the devil straight up from inside me in the style of a Catholic priest. And I felt the unholy smoke shoot out of me with a puff and smelled for an instant the scorched air. He rubbed his palm in a circle, twisting the long hair around upon itself until it was tight and hurtful. Then he let it loose to spin itself out.

"There. I did what I could," he said. Then he took a thin steel cigar-sized canister out of his jacket pocket and put it in mine.

"What's that?" I said.

"Listen close." Tim widened his eyes. "I'll say it slow, and I'll say it twice." Then he pulled the canister back out of my pocket, held it before my eyes and said, "This is yours, for whatever you might want to do with it—you can pitch it in a river for all I know." And he slowly explained what the poison was called, how it worked, how much of it there was in the vial, how many it could kill, how carefully it had to be handled. When he was finished, he walked away from the wheelchair and seemed to study the darkening red flush of sun that hung between the black trees. Then he came back and said it all again slowly. And when he was finished the second time he asked me questions to satisfy himself that I had heard him.

"I don't tell you what to do with the shit," he said. "I just pass it along. It's a gift, a going-away present. But I know that you know that you never give a person anything they can't use in their own way. The best thing to mix it with is liquor. And the best liquor to mix it with is sweet."

Then he slid the canister back in my pocket and patted it gently. "Do what you want," he said. "Throw it in the trash if you want."

He turned the wheelchair around and rolled me back out of the woods to my room.

Around noon the next day they discharged me. "Without a full-blown commitment proceeding, we can only keep you the two weeks," the doctor said. "And that's up today. And, besides, I don't think there's anything seriously wrong with you anyway. What you experienced was a kind of mental tachycardia—your thoughts just raced a little out of control. You skidded on wet pavement. This happens to people sometimes. There was family pressure, the holiday . . . Believe me, you're not that sick. You're in fact not sick enough. You're like a fish that's below the legal size to keep. We throw you back . . . You look disappointed."

A plain white van took me into Eugene and dropped me off at the bus station. I went to a pay phone right away to look up Tim's number, but there wasn't any Tim Jackson listed. There was an Edward Jackson who hung up on me, and a Niles T. Jackson who wasn't home. Mabel Jackson said she didn't know any Tim. John Jackson and Paul Jackson were white, judging by their voices. That cost me all of the change I had. Then I heard the Corvallis bus announced and went to board it. I took off my jacket and put it on the overhead rack. The top of the slim steel canister stuck out an inch. But after that, I forgot about the poison inside it for a long, long time. My awareness of the purpose of the thing went dormant in me like a virus.

I lived my life. Then one day, sitting in the shade outside the cabin, scraping with my fingernail at a crusty stain on the knee of my pants, I heard the seven rivers chanting. The background hiss of rushing water slowly skinned away and left me hearing only the different voices, the voices of seven angry brothers. It took me a while to hear them all, but in the end I counted seven. I experimented with this. I got up out of my chair and went down the ravine. The voices got louder. I walked back up from the ravine, and the voices got softer. I followed a single river back from where the seven of them joined, and that river's voice remained strong while the voices of the others weakened. I went out and bought a half gallon of Southern Comfort and a box of rubber surgical gloves. I sat outside all night one night and listened, sipping the Southern Comfort from a jelly jar. It was the kind of night the stars might have been shooting, but I was in the woods and could not tell. By morning I knew the rivers were talking to me. At first I believed they talked only among themselves. But slowly I came to believe that I was important to them, with a necessary part to play in some scheme that connected me into the wider nature of the region.

At the sink inside the cabin Tim's voice came back to me and stood over my shoulder for the mixing. I smelled his cinnamon breath and felt his smile expanding. I screwed the lid on the silver flask.

"Good," he said. "Now shake it."

I ask my detectives for a glass of water. They look around the table at each other, pleased with themselves and pleased with me. They are armed to begin connecting things. I can see they are more relaxed now, and that some doubt that might have plagued them is dispelled. They have in me a criminal they can believe in. They have the dangerous recipe. They have what they think they need and will now be content to let me tell the absolute truth.

Ferrin sits in the truck and drains the pint of Johnnie Walker. I start the engine. The sky is dark. I switch on the lights. Fog swirls in the high beams as though it's been startled. Ferrin slides across the seat and rests her head on my shoulder. I reach my arm around her and squeeze her shoulders.

"I'm sorry," she says. I don't know what for, but Ferrin is the kind of person who hates to feel out of tune with any affectionate goal that she sets for herself.

"That's all right," I say. "We're here now. We found it."

She kisses my chin with the hot breath of the scotch. She scrapes her teeth along the stubble, making a sound like a thousand tiny clicks.

"Light me a smoke," I say. She reaches up into my pocket and takes out the pack of Luckies and lights me one. She puts it between my lips and leaves it there. We cruise away from the beach, rolling gently over waves of hard-packed sand. She puts her hand down between my legs and kneads the softness there. I keep my eyes straight ahead and wait for her to stop.

"You don't like that?" she says.

"Not right now," I say.

She slides away slowly. She stares out the window and hums.

I hear a voice—the voice of Tim—instructing me: Not her. In the dark of the cab I nod. We are in agreement. Not Ferrin. Ferrin is safe as can be.

# SIX

--

I PICTURE DYING THIS WAY: I STAND IN THE prison shower room, alone the way I always am. The water echoes, hisses, bounces off my shoulders, neck and upper back. The warm beads are large, heavy, soft, pattering against me. I slide the large cake of new soap everywhere, saving my face for last. My thumb feels the chiseled letters of the soap, which slips back and forth in my hand. I do my armpits, dick and balls, and crack—three times to be sure. The lather foams and billows. I bend at the waist to do my lower legs and feet, lifting the feet. First left, then right. I straighten up and throw my head back into the full stream of water. The water surges through my hair, around my head. I breathe beyond it, like a veil. I turn slowly beneath the shower head. My eyes are closed. My hands rub together around the soap, lathering. I drop the soap; it slaps the tile. I bring my hands to my face, rubbing even before they touch the skin, the hands to either side of my nose. Rubbing. I feel the sudden heat in my lower back, to the left of my spine, blooming, deepening, aching—the tissues dividing, layer upon layer. Lunatic heat. I move forward and down, and feel the pinning of it, the strength of the stabber's wish to put the blade in past the hilt. Deep. The blade wags hard inside me. The soap is in my eyes. I reach for the wall. I slap it and slide. The knife comes out and clatters on the tile. I go to my knees and look behind me. Blood thins in the patter of water. I see my brother

Neil going fast around the corner, looking back at the wound, looking scared. Neil, my brother.

I wake from this when the phone rings downstairs at the Deans'. I snort and twist in the fitted sheet that has popped off both of the top corners. I swing my legs down. My feet hit the floor with a bang. I reach around to feel the smooth spot just above my kidney where the wound would be. The room is quiet and calm. My heart slows gradually to match it. I breathe deeply and roll my head around three hundred and sixty degrees, letting the neck crack the way my father used to do it, like knuckles, sharp and loud against the close walls of the small room. I go to the window and stare out at the empty bed of my truck, the metal veined with frost. It's morning, and the light is rising.

I stand at the window. The cold comes through the glass like a ghost. I smell a skunk in the air. From below me at the Deans' I hear the phone slam down. Jane starts to sob. Her voice rises and falls, but the words are indistinct—just the troubled feeling percolating up through the floor. I feel the vibration in the soles of my feet. Doug speaks up after Jane falls silent. Then he stops, and the silence continues.

Something is wrong.

For me, Neil died on the telephone. It woke me early one morning. The cabin was deeply chilled. I dragged the covers off the bed with me and crawled across the floor to answer. A telephone rings louder in the cold for some reason.

"Hello?" I sat like an Indian with the covers around me. My dick slumped down to the floor.

"Your brother died in his sleep last night in Philadelphia," my mother said. "I'm going back there now. I've got a flight. That Hebrew bitch'll meet me at the airport, and I'll slap her shitty little face . . . Are you there? Did you hear me?"

"Yes."

"Hold on. The goddamn coffee's boiling." I heard the phone clunk hard against something, the kitchen counter probably. Then she got back on.

"She called. Naomi called. She said they said—the doctors said—

it was probably a heart attack of some kind. But they don't really know. Until they do a post-mortem. Personally, I think this was maybe some kind of a sleep-disorder thing—being his father's son. The heart just stops in the night. This is much more common than we think. Hundreds of thousands of people. Ninety-nine times in a hundred the person starts it up again. Neil didn't. Neil was just that one in a hundred."

"Neil's dead?"

"He is, Vann. Yes. He's dead."

"Uh . . ." I tried to think of something. Six days before, I carried a girl named Sheela on my shoulder out into the soft ravine in the dark. I committed her into the earth and said the prayer I had learned to say: God protect and cherish this Sheela. Bear her grief as only you can bear it. Sheela was number three. I imagined carrying Neil.

"Honey, I've got this plane to catch."

"I'm sorry."

"We all are, Vanny. We're all very sorry."

After I hung up the phone I sat on the floor with the covers around me, thinking poison—putting Naomi and poison together in my mind until they seemed a perfect fit and there was no getting around the fact that this was how she had accomplished something necessary. I recalled a Naomi from the Bible who I believe committed a poisoning. The truth of it struck me. I smoked a cigarette and listened to the wind progress downward from the tops of the birch and fir trees to the level of the cabin, like a shiver. I heard the rivers wake and stir and begin to vie and bicker amongst themselves, and begin, together, to focus in on me. I pictured Neil getting into bed, almost for the final time, holding a rum-and-Coke in his hand and wearing his colorful boxer shorts. He offered Naomi a sip, but she pretended to be sleeping. Then he touched the bottom of the cold glass against her nearest breast and she shuddered and started crying.

According to Tim, if you want to poison the person bit by bit over time, the best thing to do is to dip the toothbrush in the mixture every night. So then I imagined that this Naomi—short and pretty, with green eyes and a waist too small to contain all the usual organs—told my brother Neil to hurry up and finish his drink and go brush his teeth, and come back and turn out the lights so they could fall asleep. And he did. Like me, Neil did exactly what anyone told him to do. He was perfect and good-natured.

"You do it with the toothbrush," Tim had said. But then he smiled and raised his eyebrows and said that's not quite what he'd done with Evan Tyrer. "No, ma'am," he said. "I just put the stuff in the jar where he soaks his combs."

If there had been anyone with me in the cabin, they would have come over and put their arms around me and been of comfort. They would have asked if they could make me some coffee. But I was alone and continued to sit there thinking. The rivers hid themselves in the terrible hiss of falling rain. I pictured Neil in the dark sleeping. I pictured small Naomi next to him, up on an elbow, staring in his ear, waiting for the end.

I decided to go to Philadelphia.

Jane Dean prepares to leave town. I brew my coffee on the hotplate. While the coffee perks I open my door and listen down into the house. I hear the packing and telephoning. I hear the name of daughter Dean said often—Karen—and I fix her as the cause of this, whatever it is. Doug asks Jane over and over, are you gonna need *this,* do you want to take *this,* do you want to take *this?* His voice is helpless, pained. He is frightened of something in Jane, and in return she is silent, dreadful. All I hear are the drawers sliding open, banging shut, the heavy hangers screeching sideways in the closet.

When I speculate what happened to daughter Karen in South Carolina, my first thought is she might have met up with someone like me. Secondly, I picture an auto accident with a drunken boy. Or a rape—the college campuses are full of boys who feel entitled to it. Or she married someone suddenly or joined a religious cult. A daughter can go away from home and fall into anything, meet anyone, floating along through life from danger to danger, never knowing what can hurt her and what will not.

I hear their feet on the carpeted stairs, descending heavily. I hear them deep in the house, the tread of ownership. The back door opens and shuts. I go to the window with my coffee mug. Doug unlocks the trunk of the Chevrolet and puts the suitcase inside. He slams down the lid. He and Jane are breathing vapor. She waits for him to open the passenger door for her. He goes in first through the driver's side and reaches across to the lock. She gets in. The visible stub of the tailpipe shudders; blue-white smoke shoots out. Doug guns the engine in high-revving bursts, then lets it settle. The backup lights go on. The Chevy eases slowly out the driveway, out of sight beyond the corner of the house.

Alone, I spend this pointless Sunday morning wandering through the house where I don't belong, looking in the drawers and closets, turning on and off the television with the remote from Doug's leather recliner. A table next to the chair holds a two-tiered pipe rack, fully loaded. I watch cartoons and fuss with the pipes until I hear the Chevy drive back in. Then I move quickly up the stairs to my rooms, hoping I've left nothing out of place.

I hear the back door open and then slam shut. Doug stamps his feet from habit.

From the airport in Philadelphia I called Naomi's number and got her friend, Placide, who was protective and strange and made me repeat three times what relationship I had to Neil.

"He was my brother," I said each time.

"Okay, okay," she said, seeming to accept it, but then asking all over again. Only later in the conversation did she apologize and tell me how the annoyance calls had been pouring in all day and the night before from people she said were probably the neighbors, although she didn't know exactly which ones.

"It's just a thing you do when someone dies," she said. "You call up and ask for them. You pretend you don't believe they're dead. It's cruel, it's sick. Kids do it, mostly."

"I'm taking a cab in from the airport."

"Tell him you'll do it off the meter for ten bucks," said Placide. "It'll be twenty minutes, half an hour at the most."

When I got to the address my mother was standing on the sidewalk with Naomi. Naomi looked like her child. The top of her head was by my mother's chin. They stood in front of the stoop.

My mother had a bag of groceries. She stared at the cab before she knew who was in it. When I got out she shook her head and gave the groceries to Naomi and ran to the curb.

"Let's go for a drink," she said, and we wandered off down the street in some direction, leaving Naomi there holding the groceries.

I hear Doug's feet on the stairs, and they do not stop at the usual place, but continue up an extra flight to my door. He knocks.

"Come in," I say.

The door swings open loudly in front of him. He stands in the threshold with a fuming pipe in one hand, a bottle of vodka in the other.

"Hi, Vann."

"Come in," I say again. He steps inside and closes the door behind him carefully.

"It's like another world up here," he says. "I never came up this high when Karen was here."

"Uh-huh," I say.

"She hung a Holiday Inn do-not-disturb sign on the door handle. I took her at her word. People say you've got to respect what children say they want. That's what anybody would tell you. I don't know. She would sit in the window and stare out. Hours on end. She was stoned. Often. You could see her from the yard. Her hip against the screen."

Doug goes to the comfortable chair and sinks into it as though he owns it. The cushion splays out around him, expanding, hissing. He sets the bottle on the floor by the chair. He guides the pipe to his mouth. He opens his palm completely and lets the slim silver pipe lighter drop out from behind and into the other palm. He thumbs the lighter to life and sends down a jet of flame into the bowl of the pipe.

"I'm . . . tired . . . of . . . this," he says, sucking the flame as deep as it will go. Smoke spills out around the stem along with the words. "She's . . . had a . . . goddamn abortion."

"Karen?" I say, not knowing if I am supposed to know her name or not.

"Karen. Yes," says Doug. "She calls this morning from the dormitory phone and tells her mother. When I was my daughter's age, there were things you never told your mother. Now there's nothing hidden. Everything comes out in the open. Can I tell you something?"

"Sure."

He lights the pipe again. Smoke rises and clings to the ceiling, spreading out slowly from the point of first touching it like the roots of a plant, spreading and seeking tenderly.

"I'd rather be alone."

At first I think that he wants me to leave him sitting by himself in my two rooms, but then the meaning sinks in. He reaches for the vodka without looking, and holds it out to me bottom first.

"No thanks," I say.

"I was actually glad when Karen left home," he says, unscrewing the cap on the vodka and drinking. "Really glad. It was like there was more air to breathe. It was cleaner, clearer air."

"But now you got me here instead," I say.

"That's different. I don't have to think about you the same way— hardly at all if I don't feel like it. You wouldn't expect it, and what would it matter if I did or didn't? No. But being a family is complicated."

"Sure it is," I say.

"Karen. She was an angry kid from the start. It actually surprised me that she didn't get any nicer growing up. I waited and watched for some kind of change. You always had to be careful what you said around her. It would be like living with a minority. You walked on eggshells. She gave you the feeling you'd always just done something new and unforgivable to her. In my own house I was on trial every day. It was such a big relief when she got to be sixteen or so and suddenly didn't want to spend any time with her parents. That was how I noticed the first small changes in myself—that I didn't really miss her company. She was here and not here. Who cared? Sometimes dinner, sometimes not. Or you could hear the music coming down through the floor. But never loud enough that I had to go and yell at her. She knew exactly how far she could go and still keep herself alone. I appreciated her distance. Now there's just Jane."

"One down, one to go," I say. Doug nods and drinks carelessly from the bottle.

"Jane's gone to visit Karen," he says. "A mother is a comfort." He holds the bottle out to me like a friend. I shake my head.

"No thanks," I say again.

"Believe me . . . ," he says. He pulls hard at the pipe; the smoke builds and billows. ". . . I'd rather be by myself. Genuinely. I think I could relax." He smiles through the cloud. He offers the bottle again. I finally take it.

Naomi confided in me that my brother was an unhappy man. She didn't quite say that's what he died of—unhappiness—but you could see the direction she was headed in.

"He cried in his sleep," she said, which sounded so much like "He died in his sleep," which he did, that it nearly sailed right past me. We were standing in the kitchen of their large apartment, and I was pretending to be helpful, which it was not in my nature to be. In actuality I was waiting only for the chance to search for the poison, which I was certain she would not have disposed of. I washed the few dishes slowly and shut off the water after each one, wiping it carefully and fanning the damp dish towel in the air like a flag to dry it out and refresh it for the next dish.

"He always did," I said. "He did that when we were kids. We shared a room. It used to wake me up."

"He did?" Naomi was at my shoulder, so close I could smell the sweetness of her hair. Then Placide came in with a large, pale green ceramic bowl of something a neighbor had donated. She said it was called a "sealed salad," meaning that it had over it a lid of creamy dressing that was to be punctured and stirred in only when the salad was about to be served. Until then it stayed intact like a hymen and kept fresh the salad ingredients underneath.

"The Souzas brought this up," said Placide.

"The refrigerator, I guess," said Naomi. I was circling the rim of a plate with a soft, round white brush at the end of a stick. The warm water bubbled through the bristles, spreading and twisting. My circles got smaller as I entered the middle of the plate. Behind me I heard the refrigerator open and close.

"Not much room," said Placide. "What if I take it down to my place?"

"Okay," said Naomi. "That'd be good."

I heard Placide's footsteps go away. Naomi whispered up to me, "She'll eat it all herself. She's so overweight, you can't ever trust her with food. For her, it's like a disease. She can't help herself." Naomi laughed lightly.

"Here, let me dry," she said. She tried to take the towel, but I landed my wet hand on a corner of it and took it back.

"I *want* to do it," I said. "You go rest."

"You're the one who ought to be resting," she said, "coming all that way."

"I hardly ever need to rest," I said, which was true. I'm like an Indian. I can go for days without it. I shut the water off and began to dry.

"Did you cry, too, in your sleep?"

"No."

"But how would you know?"

"Because nobody ever told me I did," I said.

"Maybe they didn't want to hurt your feelings."

"People know better than that," I said, and she moved away slightly. I had put in my voice something hard of the kind she had surely never heard from Neil.

"I used to think I was a nice guy," Doug says.

"You are," I tell him. I take a small sip of the bitter vodka.

"No." He shakes his head. "That's just more or less of a mask." He clenches the pipe in his teeth, and it jitters like a just-used diving board. "It isn't possible to be a nice guy," he says. "Not really. I used to think it was. But I'm not, you're not. Nobody is."

"You could have fooled me," I say.

"I did," he says. "Fool you, I mean. I do. I always have. I fooled Jane and Karen. I fool everyone at work. Sometimes I fool myself. I go in the bathroom in the morning and look in the mirror and see my nice face, needing a shave, and my eyes all puffy and harmless looking. Soft and old—an old pleasant guy—not too far away from still being asleep. A nice guy."

"I know what you mean," I say, believing that I can probably make him feel better if I tell him about how the facial reality forms itself slowly upon the morning blankness of slept-in flesh; that nothing at all is there in the early moments of the day except emptiness. Then the eyes open and catch the edges of blur that float like fog just above the surface of the skin. It isn't easy to hold the framework of the self together. You need strength and patience; you need to give the process time to correct itself and find its level.

"And then I start to wake up," says Doug, "and the muscles begin to take hold, and the brain. I see that kind of semi-hardness arrive upon me. So I cover it up by shaving. And in the nearly total silence I'm putting the shaving cream on my face when I hear Jane turn on the radio—the soft click of her fingers on the switch, and then the stupid contest types of voices suddenly blaring out. And this is the first thing I think about Jane each day: her stupid radio thing."

Doug lifts the vodka to the light and stares deep inside it, shaking the bottle gently so the liquor careens against the sides and splashes up toward his thumb, which stoppers the opening.

"No kidding," he says. He looks at me like a brother unloading a deadly secret.

"That really isn't so bad," I tell him. "Everybody has bad thoughts."

Then he starts to talk about delivering the mail day in and day out.

I searched Naomi and Neil's apartment quickly, in five minutes or maybe seven or eight, after my mother and I got back from a place called The Rabbit's Foot. Naomi helped my sotted mother to bed and excused herself backwards from the dark bedroom, saying she had to go out and buy a pillow.

"We only had the two," she said. "And now there's three people staying here."

"I can do without," I said, but she shook her head.

"No, I'm going to get one." It was an errand I couldn't imagine stopping.

I waited until I heard the door close and her feet on the stairs going down hard, and then I started at one end, one room, and thought I would just go through the whole place looking in all of the clever niches in which a person like me would have hidden something. I looked up in the milky globes of lamps and behind the rows of books on built-in shelves. I unscrewed the brush of a broom from its handle and stuck my finger in the dark, threaded cavity. I unscrewed both pieces of the telephone handset because I thought I smelled something strange through the tiny holes. I overturned two wastebaskets to see if something was taped to the recessed bottoms. I took the valves off radiators and the vitreous lid from the toilet, looking for a plastic bag or a plastic bottle floating a secret inside.

When I looked at my watch and saw that the time was passing so quickly, I realized how many were the possibilities. I could have brought in ten people—twenty people—just like me, and we could have searched cleverly for hours, exciting ourselves with deeper and deeper unpeelings of the settled appearance of Neil and Naomi's layout. When you set out to discover a hidden thing by first imagining hiding it yourself, you open the world completely, as though by surgery. I was nearly breathless in thought when I heard Naomi on the stairs. Who would have believed that a pillow could be found so fast?

"Hello," I called as the handle clicked and turned. I stood in the center of the living room and watched.

But it was only the overweight Placide.

"Hi," she said. She had a magazine in one hand and the remote-control unit of a television in the other. "My set's on the blink," she said, falling backwards onto Naomi's couch—Naomi and Neil's couch. While falling she pressed a button that brought the television to life with a crackling bloom.

"You don't mind, do you?" she said. I shook my head and stared at the television news face, talking and smiling. From the bedroom down the hall I heard my mother cry out.

"Did you hear something?" I asked Placide.

She shook her head. With the remote-control she turned the volume up.

Doug laces and unlaces his hands around the neck of the vodka bottle. "I think that actually delivering the mail is the hardest job.

People are always talking about how boring it is to work on the big automated sorting machines at the regional depots, but nobody ever thinks about how you go to the front doors of these same houses day after day, for years, without ever setting foot inside. All you know about the houses stops at the front door. You put the articles through the slot or into the mailbox, and then you turn right around and go on to the next place. This adds up. The repetition gets on your nerves. The repetition and the frustration, too. No one ever thinks, probably, that you might be curious about these houses or the people who live there. Sometimes I'll just get a craving in the worst way to go into a house—it could be any one of them on my route—and start living there, and read the mail that I've brought as though it was my own. But there's no completing the circle. I don't get anything back. The trays are heavy in the morning when I leave the office and light in the afternoon when I come back. Now, maybe if part of the job involved going inside the houses . . . There wouldn't be so much hidden from you that, over time, begins to weigh on your mind. For me, it's this fact of so much being hidden from view. The insides of the houses and the contents of the mail. Everything is sealed. And you are just the letter carrier. You are nothing. Sometimes I wish I could open up the letters and read them. And then my job would be to repeat the contents in person to the addressees. That way there's a larger part to play. You're personally involved. In the morning, when I organize my route, I look at some of the letters and the return addresses, and I picture the houses in my mind's eye and imagine the contents of the places.

"But it's changed so much since I started out. Almost no one gets any real mail anymore. Whatever isn't a bill is just all this crap from magazines and causes and charities and time-share vacation resorts. And they're all getting so slick—they make it look like the kind of real mail people might remember getting twenty years ago. Pale blue envelopes with handwriting. When was the last time you wrote an actual letter?"

"I don't know," I say. "Years. Maybe five years. I don't remember."

"Did you know every house has its own smell? Each one is

different? Like a person?" Doug hands me the vodka and watches me sip. He tilts back his head and sips with me, his mouth slightly parted, metering what I am taking in and wanting me to take more. I let it flow in and fill my mouth. He nods and smiles. I swish my tongue through the liquor and let it burn thoroughly around the top, bottom, sides. The last letter I wrote was to my brother Neil. It came back to me in a box from Naomi.

*"Dear Neil: Thanks for your card. I've had pneumonia or I would have replied much sooner. The weather is gray and quiet, and the outer walls of the cabin look soft and mossy the way they ought to in the fall of the year. As though the place is alive. The inside's exactly the same as the outside, this being the only season for things attaining an equal comfort both outdoors and in. One of Mother's cats has learned to turn on and off the television with a string contraption. She admits she spends all of her time teaching it these stupid things. She telephones when she has a nose full. The other night she put the phone by the television and let me hear it come on and go off. By now you've probably also heard the same thing, over and over.*

*"I'm sorry you're worried about Naomi possibly screwing some-one else. But you admit you don't have any actual proof, and you were always the one to say to me not to go off half-cocked with some lame suspicion. And now I could say the same thing to you. What if you're wrong? You could blow yourself out of the water, and then what? Have you mentioned this to Mother? Until I know one way or the other, I won't say anything. She calls often now. I'm thinking of having the phone undone. If you call and you don't get an answer, that's probably what it is."*

I picture Doug arriving at Neil and Naomi's apartment and being let in to read the letter to them in person.

"I never noticed this," I say.

"I mean it," says Doug. "There's really a smell. You don't notice it right away, but after a while you do. You begin to recognize the smell. It surrounds a house by five feet or so. And the first time it hits you, you think you've never smelled it before, but you've probably been smelling it all along—it's just that you haven't no-ticed it yet. The smell is stronger in the summertime because of the windows being open. You can still smell it in the winter too, but then it's more like a shadow of the actual smell." He nods slowly. His eyes go dreamy, and I think that maybe he's recalling the shadows of certain houses' smells.

"You begin to think you're learning things about people by the smell that escapes from their house," he says. "That it's a clue to the life inside. For instance . . . When Mrs. Rose Keller got sick, the smell of her house became sharp like cheese. Then after she died it changed again. She took something away from it."

"I never noticed this," I say.

"It's the truth. Every one is different."

Placide sat and watched the news and scratched the insides of her thighs—it was really more of a gentle tickling. Then she scratched her stomach, lifting up the T-shirt so her belly was bared. She dragged the tips of her fingers back and forth softly across the broad patch of pale flesh. She was careful not to snag the navel.

"I was struck by lightning once," she said. She turned around on the couch and looked at me, who was still standing in the middle of the room not knowing exactly where to be or what to do.

"I was at a picnic with my boyfriend, sitting on a bench underneath a tree. The lightning hit the tree and flowed around it like a snake. It went down into the ground and up my legs and deep into me. Deep in. Blew me right off the bench. Ever since then, I needed to scratch myself, which is mostly like erasing the feeling of it. Don't pay any attention."

She lifted the T-shirt off her breasts and stuck her fingers beneath the bra. The shiny white fabric of the bra writhed with knuckles.

"I apologize," she said.

Then I heard Naomi on the stairs. When she put the key in the lock and came through the door she was fully vigilant. She saw us right away and put the smile in place.

"Hello," she said.

"Hey," said Placide.

The new pillow stuck out the top of a big yellow plastic bag. She threw the bag at me and I caught it.

In the bedroom my mother cried out.

"Coffee?" Naomi said.

"Okay," said Placide.

The crying out of my mother is something only Neil and I could hear. I thought I might take the new pillow in to her and jam it on her face.

Doug begins to cough and weep.

"I'll leave if you want," I tell him. He shakes his head. He lets the bottle slip to the floor. It lands sideways and spins slowly, spilling nothing. He bends forward and holds his head in his hands. I imagine that soon he will vomit. I stare at his thinning hair. Sweat darkens the strands and makes them stand out more.

"I appreciate this, Vann," he says.

I clear my throat. "This is nothing," I tell him. "You think this is bad, this is nothing." And I am prepared to go on soothing Doug with what sounds like comfort. I'm prepared to put my hands on his shoulders like a brother and squeeze around the collarbone until the tears stop flowing out of him and he is grateful and weak and sorry. And I move just a step closer to him to be in place to deliver this consolation, but he suddenly straightens up and looks good.

We went the next morning to the funeral home—my mother, Naomi, Placide and I. My mother developed a disliking of Placide and began to say things about her body.

"Dear girl, you should wear a fuller dress. The cut of that is not forgiving."

Placide was in something tight—deep blue with small gold flecks—that stretched wide at the hips and sucked inward at all the adjacent creases. It was just the three of us standing on the street in front of the apartment building, waiting. Naomi had gone to get the car, Neil's car, which was parked around the block.

"I guess I should," said Placide. "But I haven't always been this big." Placide sighed. She turned to me and made a pitiful face.

We stood quiet again. Not once in the time I had been there had anyone said a word about Neil himself. Soon Naomi turned the corner in the car and pulled up in front of us at the curb.

My mother grabbed my arm. "Vann, wait," she said. "Let Placide have the front seat where there's more room."

This business with Placide I took as Mother's way of not looking closely at what was happening by looking closely at something else. She could always ignore the completely obvious. When Neil broke his leg at thirteen, she increased his household chores for the period of time he was in his cast. And he actually went around trying to do them. One afternoon I sat by my mother on the back steps and watched Neil mow the grass on crutches. When my father came out and saw this going on, he made me take over from Neil.

"What's wrong with you two?" he said to my mother and me.

"It's good therapy for him," she said. Then she went in and made iced tea for everyone. Placide was like the iced tea.

We drove in silence. I stared out the window. Naomi asked if anyone wanted the radio. No one answered, so she left it off. I was surprised that the trip was so short—a dozen blocks, then a left, then suddenly a right and into a driveway beside a broad, sloping lawn. The funeral home was low and white with drawn white curtains, lights showing behind them like moons. I imagined that the structure was an iceberg, descending deep into the earth with many hidden levels, like death itself.

Inside, Naomi went forward first. She shuddered in front of the half-open casket, beginning to weep in spasms.

"I wanted to have his babies," she cried. "His babies!" Her face was red. She was breathing in rapid gusts. Placide wrapped her arms around Naomi from behind and tried to pull her away. My mother looked at me and rolled her eyes. I was pleased that Naomi had not thrown herself upon Neil. I imagined the features collapsing, like the skin of a pudding, under the weight of the living.

"Oh, Neil . . . ," Naomi moaned. "Oh, Neil . . ." Placide was drawing Naomi away. Naomi finally turned and let herself be taken, and the two of them left the room—small and large.

I stood with my mother while quiet returned to the room. Neil was a feature of landscape, lighted in pink from above. His long, narrow nose poked up. I stared at the still point of it. The silence stretched deeper, and I felt my mother and me locked together, unable either to move closer to Neil or to go away. I waited for his face to change, to undo itself in some revealing movement of decay. But nothing at all happened until my mother grabbed my wrist and shook it angrily, spinning on her heel and moving quickly out of the room.

The funeral director met us at the door and extended his hand to my mother. "I'm sorry to have to meet you this way," he said.

"How else?" she said. "How else would you meet me?"

Outside, the engine was running. Placide was behind the wheel, and Naomi was in the backseat, curled in a corner like a dead spider, small and compressed. My mother took the front seat, and I got in with Naomi. I put my back to the door and watched her, watched the shuddering of her shoulders, the coil of her ankles, knees, hips and stomach. I felt the tight heat of her tension. But I also saw her cheek was dry.

"Placide," my mother said, but then she didn't finish the statement, whatever it was.

Doug gets up out of the chair and goes down on his knees and asks if I will pray with him. He pats the floor beside him as the spot where I should land.

"I don't mind praying," I say, and quickly join him. My knees feel good on the bare pine next to Doug's. He puts his arm across my shoulders. I smell the warm liquor and the grief on his breath.

"Dear God," he says. I bow my head and shut my eyes. "Help cleanse the hearts and souls of your servants Douglas and Vann. They are full of restlessness and complaints, which harden them toward their loved ones. Help them find contentment in the lives they lead and the relations You have given them. Help them resist temptation, which leads them astray, and bring them peace and understanding, which only You can bring. In Jesus' name they ask it. Amen."

"Amen," I say. Doug's arm slides off my shoulders.

"I'm sorry if you minded that I brought you into it so much," he says. "I know some of what I prayed doesn't really apply to you."

"It's all right," I say.

"It just makes me feel a little bit better, not doing this alone," he says.

"I don't mind," I tell him.

"I appreciate that," he says. He sips from the vodka bottle and sinks back into the chair and begins to weep again. He lets the bottle slip to the floor. It lands upright, teeters and settles.

"I think I can tell you this," he says.

"You can," I say, but he looks at me carefully, like someone waiting for someone else to blink.

"I don't know," he says.

"Well, whatever you want," I tell him.

"No. I think I can."

"Okay," I say. I watch his hands wrestle with each other. Then he looks me in the eye.

"I sometimes feel like I'd like . . . to . . . kill Jane," he says.

I wait for a decent length of silence to pass before replying. "You mean actually kill her?" I say. "Or just that she suddenly wasn't there anymore?" Again, he looks at me carefully.

"Well, I've thought about both," he says. "But I guess the best thing would be to wake up in the morning and she's gone. And the closet's empty, and the dresser drawers. And I never hear from her again. But that's not, it won't happen. So, what does that leave?"

I shrug.

"I never thought about an actual method of killing . . . No, that's not true. I have. Of course I have. At least a little bit. I know I couldn't stab."

"Me neither," I say.

"It's too personal."

"It makes a mess," I say. "It creates a lot of evidence, too. And from what I've read, you can stab a person thirty times and still not kill them. A hundred times."

"That's happened."

"Sure," I say. "You need to be accurate. Just being pissed off at somebody isn't enough." I take a sip from the vodka bottle.

"I couldn't do it," says Doug.

"No." I put the bottle back beside him.

"But I think I could use a gun."

"Do you have a gun?"

"No," he says.

He reaches for the neck of the bottle. His index finger plugs the mouth. He leaves it there.

"Then that's a problem," I say.

"Yeah. But what I meant was just, you know, in principle. Using a gun. It happens fast. It isn't brutal like a knife. It has its benefits."

"It's loud, though."

"Yeah."

"The neighbors come running."

"They do?" he says.

"No. Probably not. They probably think it was a car backfiring. Or a cherry bomb. Unless they know you've got guns in the house."

Doug grunts.

"My brother was poisoned," I say.

"To death?"

"He died. Yes. Five years ago. He was murdered."

"Did they catch the person?"

"No."

"Did they know who did it?"

"No. Yes. I knew. But nobody had any proof. There wasn't any evidence. It looked like a natural death. A sudden death by heart attack. He died in his sleep."

"Five years ago."

"That's right."

"Do you miss him?"

I see Doug wanting to be the new brother to me. I also see him wanting something back. He waits for an answer, and I weigh the right and wrong possibilities. I think back to Neil sleeping in the bed beside me for seven years, sitting up in his sleep like a ramrod and flapping his lips like a horse. I hear him getting ready to cry. I wait for him to cry. Then I hear the door to our parents' bedroom open, and I hear my father walking in the hallway, his feet swishing on the thin red carpet, getting closer to the stairs. Neil begins to cry.

"No," I say. "I don't even remember him."

Doug extends the bottle to me, and I take it off the end of his finger with a dull pop.

--

I smelled Naomi's breath before I felt how near to me she was. Geraniums. Then the heat of her. A big heat like a radiator. At first the living room was pitch-black. I slept on the sofa cushions arranged like a train in the middle of the floor. I pushed my hand out and touched her leg above the knee; the nylon nightgown slid against her skin before grabbing and sticking.

"Vann," she said.

"Naomi?"

Then the light increased, and I thought it might be dawn.

"Uh-huh."

I sat up, and in a whisper she told me she was lonely. The whisper swirled in the dark. Her hand reached out of the gloom and touched my arm. I tried to see if she was smiling at me, but her face was just a dim gas floating in and out.

"You should have thought of that before," I said.

"What do you mean?" she said. "Before what?"

"You know what I mean."

"No I don't," she said. "What *do* you mean?" She took her hand away.

"Don't pretend with me," I said. "I know what you did. Don't kid a kidder."

"This is . . . Vann, what are we talking about here?"

"About Neil," I said. "About what you did to Neil."

"I didn't do *anything* to Neil. Are you holding me responsible?"

"What do you think?"

"I don't know. Let me think . . . You think I'm responsible for his death in some way?"

"That's right."

"Well, how? What did I do?"

She reached her hand out again and wrapped her fingers around my wrist. Her fingers were warm. She leaned closer and started whispering again. "I know Neil wrote and told you about something I did that was very wrong, very stupid. But that was over. We put that behind us. Things were really, really good for us. I mean it. Vann?"

I felt the doors closing inside me. Blood was slamming against unmovable barriers and retreating. I welcomed the cold that crept over me. My thoughts were affected, too. A thought would originate in my mind and perish like a blown bubble, suddenly, without even reaching its full shape—it would simply quiver and vanish.

"Vann?"

She started weeping quietly, ashamed of her old unfaithfulness. Her shoulders shook. She waited for me to reach out and hold her, and give her the comfort that she craved, but I wouldn't. I was who I was—empty and dead and motionless. I lay back on the cushions and stared at the ceiling and watched it lighten tenderly with the dawn. Time crawled.

The next thing I knew, Naomi was gone. She might just as well have been a dream. From the bedroom down the hall I heard my mother cry out.

Later that morning we went to the funeral home and picked up the urn containing Neil's ashes. My mother spread a newspaper on Naomi's kitchen table, emptied the urn and divided the ashes into thirds.

"I'll keep the urn for myself," she said, spooning her own one-third back in.

Naomi provided jelly jars for the other two thirds—hers and mine. I knelt on the floor and packed my portion of Neil in the leather suitcase my father had given me that Neil had coveted. Somehow, on the flight back home, the jar broke, spilling Neil's remains and spreading them everywhere inside the bag. I recovered and saved the rougher parts—the irreducible gravel of bone—but some of the rest is probably in there still, deep in the pattern of the herringbone lining.

Doug falls asleep in my chair. I sit by the window and watch him sleep. The sun goes down beyond the Deans' back fence. I feel its winter redness warm and color the side of my face.

Through the floor I hear the Deans' phone ringing. It rings twenty-seven times. I count them while watching Doug's face, which slowly seems to lose its pleasant features and become an empty mask, like the faces of the dead. Each of the long, harsh rings hides secret words that are part of the air of the house, part of the history of its long-contained life. If you made a tape and slowed it down and carefully filtered out certain frequencies, you would hear the words distinctly. But watching Doug, I believe that he is hearing them now, that they are swimming through him, building upon all the secret words he has heard in his sleep already, for years on end.

When the room is dark I go to my bed and lie on it. I feel the cold creep over me. I lose track of time. I disappear completely.

When I wake up in the morning Doug is gone.

# SEVEN

‑‑

INSIDE ME THE URGE GROWS AGAIN, BECOM-
ing large like a fast-inflating raft, unfolding suddenly from nothing,
taking the familiar shape and crowding out the other organs. It
feels as if it will never stop growing. I go to a movie to take my
mind off. To get there I drive through Bledsoe and look at certain
people walking, leaning into the cold. I slow the truck. Their scarves
blow back; the wind is terrible. It whistles and mourns in the thin
struts of my windshield wipers. I look at the cold faces, half
sheathed—only the tops of noses and the eyes are visible, darting,
squinting.

But I do not stop. I struggle past and make it to the theater. The
ticket man pushes a button, and the ticket surfaces instantly
through a slot like a paper blade.

"It already started," he says without looking at me. I stand for
a moment and wait for his eyes.

"Next," he says, never looking up.

The urge keeps growing. In the dark I find a lonely seat at the
back, far from others, silent. Men are moving on the screen, crawling on their stomachs through a jungle at night, faces blacked and
glistening, cradling weapons across their forearms. All I hear is the
undergrowth rustling, the men trying almost not to breathe, the
weapons rocking with a soft chatter on top of tense muscles. Fear
shines bright in the wide, ready eyes. In the theater the dozen or
so heads are motionless, upturned to the screen. The screen ex-

plodes loudly in yellow, drifting to white as the sound of the explosion slowly fades. Then the screen becomes a sky. Geese fly across it. A single gunshot sounds, and one of the geese is hit and falls. A dog runs across a stubbled field to fetch the bird. A man with a shotgun runs after the dog. The goose lies in a heap.

"Trevor!" calls the man. "Trevor! Left!" The dog changes direction. "Left!" The dog can't see the goose. "Trevor! Left!" The dog is confused. It turns in a circle. The man is red-faced, angry. The dog breaks off to the right toward a grove of trees.

"Trevor!" The man chases after the dog. While running, he drops the shotgun. He follows the dog to the grove of trees. "Trevor, you piece of shit!" The dog disappears into the trees.

The man is seen approaching the grove of trees from the shadows just inside it. He nears the opening and quickly enters its darkness, angry and determined. Then suddenly he stops, looks shocked and surprised. Another man is waiting there with a shotgun, one of the men from the previous jungle scenes. He fires the shotgun and blows the first man backward, out of the grove and onto the bright corn stubble. The dog runs from the trees and sniffs at his owner, whimpering.

The scene changes to a city.

When I exit the theater snow is falling.

Heavy snow drifts down from a windless sky, big flakes that fall straight out of the soft gray clouds and strike my hair and face with a confident weight, so I feel each one as a cold pat or a melting kiss. My penis stirs and grows in my jeans as I walk to the truck; it heats like a radiator. My head buzzes in the thick snowfall. Already the ground is whitened by an inch or more of covering. My feet tread down upon the snow with a squeaking sound. I marvel at how everything—the air, the snow, the fog of my breath, the heat that tingles in my legs—is working upon me, boiling me like the coiled waves of California, where I happily watched my blue-suited father, standing far back from the surf with his cuffs rolled, observe me disappear beneath the rolling surface, my small feet flashing under and over, under and over. Caught in the wave, I was helpless and thrilled. My spine twisted against itself. My elbows twirled and snapped. I squeezed my lips shut to keep the water out until, slowly, I let the screaming build inside me to the point that it could push the water back. I opened my mouth and screamed. In the grip of tons of disorderly water it was only a quiet scream. The water pressed in around my head and surged back along my neck, confused. It wagged and twisted my lips, touched and chilled my front teeth, until the scream was gone and I shut my mouth again. The water, I told myself, was wondering who I was and why I was in it so softly, letting it do whatever it wanted to do to me. Deep in the boil, with all of the breath gone out of me, I smiled. I swear I did. The wave finally threw me up at my father's feet. He grabbed an underarm and a foot and pulled me up the beach. I was coughing and laughing. My ears were clogged, but I heard him yelling into me. I lay on my belly on the hard sand, panting. My father pounded my back. Other people ran up to see what was the matter. I felt my semi-stiff penis press warm against my thigh and bind. I was ten.

"Jesus, Vann . . . Jesus, Vann," my father cried.

Now that I know desire by its proper name, I am not surprised when it comes upon me. In later boyhood I tried it out in many ways and places. With baby-oiled palms behind the locked bathroom door. Sitting on shoes in the closet of my parents' bedroom, shooting carefully into a slipper. In the corner of the dark garage with the door down, accompanied by the smell of the cold engine and the damp, slow-growing circle of dripped oil. In Spokane, a girl named Amy Spinney walked me home from school by a different route. She said wait, and ran up to a certain house that she said she knew was empty. She disappeared behind it and soon came out the front door and called to me.

"My aunt says you can stay for dinner," she hollered.

I followed her inside and up the stairs. The house smelled of lemon and cedar. The dark furniture shined as though there was light inside of it slowly leaking out. In the bathroom the girl undressed and ran herself a bath. She made me sit fully clothed on the toilet and watch her wash herself.

"Come here," she finally said. I knelt by the tub. She put the wet soap in my hands and pulled them down under the water to touch her parts. "Wash it," she said. She threw her head back and moaned before I even made a move. I took the slippery oval of soap and squeezed it into her slowly from my hand. She jerked. The muscles in her legs tightened.

"Hold still," I said. "Don't move."

"That hurts," she said. "Cut it out."

The soap was gone. I waited for the soap to squeeze itself back into my hands.

"Don't do that again," she said.

"Be quiet," I told her.

I squeezed it in again. And again and again. I liked having something to do. I was busy. I stared at the graying water. My hands disappeared in the murk. I had no idea what her face was showing. I heard her crying. I didn't know whether she liked it or not.

The steam stopped rising from the water. Gradually, the soap got smaller and smaller until it stayed inside her and wouldn't come out. I waited for a while. I looked at her face. With her eyes closed she shook her head. I pulled my hands from the water. She brought her legs together and apart, together and apart. Lazily the water slapped the sides of the tub. She took my hands in hers and flung them up into the air. I felt them fly. Then she plunged her own hands in the water and dug out the soap. She held it in the palm of her hand and stared at it. Then she looked at me.

"What do you want to do?" she said.

"I don't know," I said.

She stood up out of the water. She was pink.

"Now you," she said. She pulled the plug. The water drained with a windy suck. When the tub was empty she ran more hot. She undid my belt.

"Go on," she said. "Hurry up." I finished undressing and got in the tub.

"Go ahead," she said. "Do yourself."

The sweat rolled down my forehead; steam drifted up from the new water. I was lost in the wave. I reached down under the water and found myself, holding on with my eyes closed. I felt her fast, shallow breathing on my wet shoulder.

When I was finished we heard a noise downstairs. We froze. It sounded like something, a cat scampering across a puddle. She crept out naked on all fours into the hall. Hardly breathing, I watched the water calm itself in the tub. She came back smiling. It seemed like forever.

"It was just the mail falling in through the slot."

She dried me and led me into a bedroom.

"We can do anything we want," she said. "There isn't anyone to say no."

At the idea of doing anything I wanted, my heart beat crazily. I walked toward her slowly. She had no idea what I wanted. Freedom is the absence of someone saying no. I felt myself slipping deep into the coiled and churning wave. I tried to think what it was I wanted. She smiled and held out her arms.

I start the truck. I start the wipers; they sweep in sudden arcs across the windshield, throwing snow to the side. I turn the radio on. There is a weather advisory affecting southern Massachusetts, Rhode Island, parts of Connecticut. I pull the truck out of the parking lot and turn left toward the interstate. On the interstate I drive no faster than forty, often much slower. Snow thickens on the road. A wind picks up; snow begins to blow from all directions at once, obliterating distance, tricking vision, darkening the afternoon to a swallowing smallness. The tires sing in a high-pitched tone. The snow intensifies until the picture of life shrinks to nothing but me and the truck, wrapped and muffled, flowing upon the immediate road. The small sky—farther above me than I can imagine—darkens to night. The distant movie disappears from my mind as though somebody rubs it out. The radio reaches into the sky for a signal, but finds nothing and only hisses and breathes. The yellow dial glows. I turn the headlights on, and the snow seems to flinch and jitter, sweeping straight into me, past me.

Slowly I deplete Rhode Island and begin Connecticut, still full of the urge to do anything I want.

East of Groton I take an exit. The truck slides mysteriously near the end of the ramp, but stops where it should. I wait there, at the edge of a rural road, wondering which way to turn. Minutes pass. Finally a car drives by, left to right. My headlights catch the silhouette of a woman at the wheel, the orange glow of a cigarette in her mouth. I turn right and follow, staying back. The road is treacherous. Ahead, she fishtails on a curve. I take the hint and slow the truck without braking. The road dips and rises, turning frequently in snakelike S's. The woman's car is in and out of sight around these curves. I see her headlights sweep high across the trees; my headlights follow, going where hers have gone, exciting me. She slowly climbs a hill that rises steeply between thick stands of snowy pines. I drop farther back, believing that she will not make the top. I turn my lights off. Her small car slows and stops, sliding backwards, wheels spinning. Her brakes go on—dim, snow-blotted red. She sits at an angle, resting short of the crest of the hill. She waits. I roll my window down and listen; her engine is inaudible, distant. I can't hear beyond what's occurring close to me: the sound of the filtered wind, squeezed through the trees, and the sandy pattering of snow—falling on the roof of the cab, drifting sideways against the passenger window, whispering. After a while she backs and straightens the car; she lets it roll slowly down the grade, retreating past the deepest part of the hill, toward me—fifty yards from me. Her brakes go off. I hear the engine revving. The wheels spin, and she moves ahead slowly, fishtailing, slowly gaining speed, but obviously not speed enough.

I wait where I am and watch her, whoever she is. Her car reaches not quite as high on the hill as the first time, the back wheels swinging in sorry arcs at the end of the climb. The brakes go on. She sits. The headlights sweat through the falling snow. She revs again, and the headlights brighten—the wheels spin and whine against the slick. She stops her revving, and the headlights dim. I wait. She gets out of the car and stands upon the roadway, in the shelter of the open door, looking up the hill and down, then directly into the darkened sky. I reckon her feet are two inches deep in the fresh powder, with more falling all around her. I close my eyes and feel the largeness of circumstance, in which nothing can be made by me to happen but can only be gone through patiently. In the depths of the wave I let the water work in whatever direction it will.

When I open my eyes I see bright headlight beams come crazing up over the crest of the hill, from the opposite direction. She is saved. I wait. Two stunning lights appear like suns; a car comes whispering behind them and glides surely down the hill, past the place where the woman stands in the road—first illuminated in a shock of brilliance, then plunged in a wake of darkness, invisible, alone. I duck down in the cab and hear the car approach and pass my observation post, a whoosh followed by a deeper silence.

"Shit!"

I hear the shouted word sweep down the hill, chasing the car, passing me angrily and dying against the endless trees.

"Shit!"

Snow stifles the would-be echo. I stay where I am, slumped down by the open window. The minutes creep by. Then I hear an unmistakable sound: the compacting squeak of footsteps trudging steadily through snow. The sound gets louder. Louder.

"Hello?"

I hear the anxious voice, rising at the end of the word, the hard breathing. I crack an eye and see the puffs of her breath come billowing toward me.

"Hello?" she says again. "You alive in there?"

I pretend to awaken. I groan. I stretch.

"Huh? What?" I say to the woman.

"Can you help me? My car is stuck on the hill . . . Up ahead? See?" She points. I follow the point. Her headlights skew off into the trees. She turns her attention back to me and tries to explore my shadowed face.

"Sure thing," I say, adjusting myself in the cab to be ready to drive. "Hop in." I turn the key and the truck shudders to life. She trudges around the front. I turn the headlights on as she passes. She throws a hand up to her eyes and squints. I open the door. She climbs in.

"I ought to have snows," she says, slamming the door shut. "I ought to have weights in the trunk. You live near here?"

"Uh-huh. Couple miles," I say. I push the button on the gearshift for four-wheel drive. I hear the klunk. I pull ahead slowly, building speed. The truck does its part. We climb toward her car.

"Think you can get me over?" she asks.

"We'll manage," I tell her.

" 'Cuz if you can't, you could help me just push it off to the side and give me a lift to the gas station."

"Okay."

The truck eats the hill. My headlights freeze her car, a flimsy red Japanese sedan. I stop and put my flashers on.

"Okay," I tell her. "Go get in it."

She jumps out of mine and runs to hers. Once she's in, I creep up behind her gently until the bumpers kiss. Then I take mine out of four-wheel drive—in this case, the plan that fails is the plan that works.

"Okay, hit it!" I shout out the window. When she does, her car sags back against the truck. I hear the wheels whine and spin, throwing slush. I punch the gas too hard to accomplish anything. The truck fishtails. Together we slide a few feet back.

"Again!" I shout. More spinning, whining. The same thing happens—we slip lower on the hill.

"Once more!" This time the bumpers grind unwholesomely.

"Stop!" she yells. She gets out.

"It's no good," she says. She heads back to my window. I watch her come. She has a small body, light blue down jacket, jeans and rubber boots that shine.

"The road's too slick," she says. Reluctantly I nod.

"I'm sorry," I say. "I thought we could do it." Her breaths puff in through the open window and disappear beneath my nose.

"Thanks anyway," she says.

"Well, at least I can give you a lift."

"Yeah, okay," she says. She glances at her car. "Can we just get it off the road?"

"Sure," I say. I let the truck roll back from her bumper. Then I get out and stand in the road. And I see how she watches me, wondering the things that all of us are taught to wonder about strangers. I look at her car and pull on my chin in a thoughtful gesture that I believe conveys harmlessness and good intentions. She walks up ahead of me, toward the car. Snow blows flat the helmetlike back of her dark curly hair. She looks up the hill to the top, wishing she were beyond it and on her way. Snow swirls there in funnels and plumes, dancing, tempting—cold life. The girl is young and tiny, college age. She reminds me of Naomi.

"Well," I say. She turns to me and waits. I look all up and down the hill. The shoulder is narrow and slopes off sharply into a ditch. "Best thing is just back it down and park it off there, where I was parked before." I point through the still-falling snow to the dark roadside of the recent past. But I'm busy thinking into the future.

"Okay," she says, and I notice for the first time that she has a cold.

"If you want to wait in my truck where it's warm," I tell her, "I'll back it down myself." She looks at me for half a second and nods.

"Thanks," she says, and heads for the cab.

The options are these. I can offer her the flask right now and in a few minutes climb up the hill from parking her car to find her cooling gently like her distant Japanese engine. Or I can wait until parking the car is done and be there with her when she drinks, and for all of the moments after. I find that I could think these choices through for hours, weighing two pleasures against one disappointment or one plus against two minuses. In my mind I could count my steps through the darkness and feel the wind and snow on my face and hair as I climb toward either the certainty of what I will find in the cab, or toward the warm prospect of what I will do and witness, which hasn't yet been set in its last delicate spiral. As she brushes past the right headlight and it heats the bright blue of her nylon jacket, I am running the two movies side by side in my thoughts. But a choice must be made. It almost doesn't matter. You can never completely eliminate regret; there will always be something important left to the imagination. On every occasion I have done this, after the cold stillness settled in beside me, I have thought of a question I should have asked.

She opens the door and gets into the truck. She slams the door. I look at her through the windshield. She blows in her cupped hands. The steam billows up warm around her cheeks. I go to the still-open driver's side window.

"There's a flask in the glove compartment," I tell her. "It'll help you warm up."

"Okay," she says.

"Help yourself," I say. "Might even cure your cold."

"Okay, I will," she says. She smiles. I watch her hand begin to move forward. I turn my back and march up toward her car. I get into the car and shut the door and slowly breathe in the atmosphere that she has gradually scented, which even in the cold comes through as cigarettes and something mint, and a flurry of perfumes and deep bodily warmths that are hers entirely and give her away to me. This is a new piece of the puzzle—having access to the now-empty personal environment of one of my chance encounters. If there were no hurry I would close my eyes and let the tinny engine idle on the hillside; I would let the heater whir and blend the girl's private atmosphere in a small tempest of warmth around my head.

But there is no time. I depress the clutch and disengage the gears. I turn halfway in the seat to look behind, and ease my foot off the brake, steering carefully around my truck and past it, thinking I've seen the gleam of the raised flask in the lights cast back from her car. Through the cab's rear window I believe I see her head begin to tilt in a drinking posture, but the snow thickens in the brightness of her headlights, blotting the deeper background as I roll slowly down the hill.

I try sometimes to think what makes me do this. In my mind I prepare for the end, explaining myself to people I don't yet know but expect someday to meet. I envision my detectives sitting across from me at a dark-gray-linoleum-topped table in a room with fluorescent lights—the kind of lights that add weariness to the air and flatten the shadows on expectant faces, making them appear to be only bored or tired. But I can feel the magnetism in the solemn detectives raising the heat of the room, drawing the history up from inside me in a scene over which I have total control: I can tell them everything, and they will have to listen to me. Two tape recorders—one a backup—quietly rolling. Maybe three.

I would begin with my mother tying me to a chair in the basement in Tacoma. One of the detectives would break in and ask me how old I was at the time, which is what I was about to tell them. But I would give them a look that clearly said "shut up," and possibly also held the threat of my choosing not to continue. And another detective would help me out by saying it straight out: "Shut up. Let him tell it his own way."

My mother tied me to the bone-white wooden chair in the basement. I was four. Neil was at school. From the window I would watch him walk down the street carrying his lunch in an oiled canvas bag, swinging it by the army-colored drawstrings. Then I would sneak out and follow Neil, never catching him, and my mother would suddenly notice the door was open and have to run after me.

"If you don't stop following your brother," she warned me, pulling me home by the stretched arm, "I'll have to do something about it."

She used the bright white clothesline cord and looped it around my ankles, drawing them tight against the bottom rung and weaving the cord up through and around everything—my waist and wrists, chest and shoulders—turning me and the chair into a single object, dedicating all of her morning's energy to teaching the perfect lesson. She sweated from her forehead and nose, and her breath came in generous gusts of exertion that stank of coffee and of burnt, jellied toast. Nearing the end of the clothesline, she wrapped her arms behind me, tucking in the cord somewhere. Her dark hair brushed my cheeks.

"There," she said. "Lost liberty, Vanny. Freedom means responsibility."

She stood back and looked at me with her arms folded across her chest. Then she turned and stepped quickly toward the stairs up.

"Not a peep," she said, climbing.

With the door shut and the lights out, the rest of the day was a nothing. For most of it, she wasn't even up there—I would have heard her soft feet sliding above me on the wooden floors. Instead, soon after she left the cellar, the back door was firmly shut. Its double tongues and strikers met and clicked in their absolute way, and I was alone in the house. I listened to my breath. The chair and I floated through the darkness like a ghost. I played games with time, counting my steps on the stairs, counting the people whose names I knew. I closed my eyes and squeezed until there were sparks and pinwheels. Far above me it began to rain. I counted the times the shutters banged. Much later I heard my father's worried voice whisper in my ear from deep in California, from behind the wheel of his black Oldsmobile, telling me not to worry.

"I'm coming home," he said. "I'm coming home."

But my mother came home first and had me untied and upstairs sitting quietly beside her on the couch, reading a book about a timid worm named Norm, before Neil was back from school.

"Hi, Mom," said Neil. "Hi, Vanny." She called him over and mussed his hair and laughed. I sat with the worm book on my aching knees and closed my eyes, emptying darkness into the room.

I trudge up the hill through the snow. The car is registered to a Sarah Colven of New Tarryton, Connecticut. If this is Sarah sitting up ahead in my truck, I'm prepared to discover her motionless, eyes shut, the darkness emptying quickly, suddenly, into her life, sparking and pinwheeling. She will not be able to speak to me or turn her head to look at who I am. I have never done a death this way before, setting the event in motion through remote control. As I near the truck I think how future encounters might be carried out entirely through the mail. I think of Doug Dean's well-used, burnished leather mailbag holding a small parcel addressed to the randomly chosen "Occupant" of a certain house on a certain street in Bledsoe, Massachusetts. And yet it remains to be learned whether the pleasures of remote control compare at all with the pleasures of personal witness.

I am halfway to her. The engine of my truck still idles, the sound of it softened in the storm. I record all observable details. I am not different. Only the circumstances are altered. If the thing is to be felt from the outside, it must be felt in much the same way as I would feel it from the inside, with the same degree of attention. My climb flows by me like a movie, both slower than life and faster—it all depends. The rear red lights of the truck have a cherry beauty, gauzed by the snow. Their glow seems to tremble. I observe the head of the girl through the back window, the hair a wide dark blot. My ears buzz hot in the clamping cold of the storm. A dark bird glides across the road, from a tree on one side to a tree on the other, landing heavily in a way that shakes snow from the branch. A car approaches suddenly from behind me; the bright lights throw my shadow far ahead to where I would already like to be. The car slows, scaring me.

"Need help?" a man shouts from inside the car, the windows still rolled. I can't make out the face of the man, and I feel sure that he cannot make out mine. I shake my head and hold up my hand in the "okay" sign. The car drives on, its back end at first swinging slowly like a rung church bell, then straightening out and gripping, the good tires pitching back tread-shaped bites of compacted snow. Ahead, the car slows but does not stop going past my truck. The lights disappear over the crest of the hill. Snow hangs red in the air behind them, like a sunset. I quicken my pace. I think about time.

Tim assured me that death was never instantaneous. "It's like a piece of symphony music," he said. "Split up in different stages that stand for different moods and rhythms." He named four specific stages: Shock, Confusion, Understanding and Ending. "Once you learn what to look for you can see the changes. Everyone goes through them."

But he also said that death was like a good perfume, combining in each individual to create a unique effect, no two events being quite the same. I have tried to observe and learn the differences. For example, some endings seem to be only just a deepening of understanding. Others are a final struggle in which the muscles try to do something they can't at all manage anymore, because the lines are down. I remember also two cases where shock and confusion monopolized, and where there was no sign of any understanding before an ending that was no more than a sudden halt to the confusion. But Tim would say that the understanding was hidden someplace, possibly bundled in with the quick ending. (And what could be finer than having the two together? The peace would be lasting, uncontradicted. There would be no second thoughts.)

So while I am convinced that there is a sure and irreversible progress from drinking out of my flask to dying a death that passes through some mixture of Tim's four stages, I also know that time itself is a major variable.

Some people have died in three minutes; others have died in ten.

Eleven is the very outer limit, a fisherman named Lawson with a tweed hat. Younger people have seemed to die more quickly. This might be a metabolic factor—they say the metabolism slows down in the course of the aging process. And I once suspected that weight was a factor, with the heavier lingering longer, but my largest death turned out to be one of the quickest. There may be something, however, in how large of a sip is taken, which there is of course no way to measure (or in this case even to guess).

The science is not exact. Climbing the last of the hill that lies between me and my truck, I can't with any accuracy guess where Sarah Colven will fall on the scale of completeness. She could be a short death—in which case she is already gone—or a long one. She could be staring through the windshield sliding the focus in and out: the far treetops, the nearby bits of snow, the thick smudge on the glass to the left of the blue inspection sticker. She could be waiting stiffly, thinking "Where have I ended up?" Nothing can be completely controlled or predicted. And that is why it is important for me to clutch at all the surrounding circumstances, none too trivial, because they are all a part of the full event, which floods out into the night, over the whitening hill, across Connecticut.

With a gloved hand I pat the left side rail of the pickup bed and slide the hand along, piling up snow that spills over and down. Inside the truck I see the head and hair. The nose is sharp and still. The flask shines dully in her lap, held sideways in her enfolding hands. I sniff for the scent of something having happened. I open the door and she turns and stares at me.

"Hi," she says.

Once the detectives have heard about my day in the cellar in the white wooden chair, I will share with them my thoughts about freedom. Freedom is what you do with the leftover pie in the breadbox: You take it and eat it. It sits inside the breadbox in the dark and dares you. You open the breadbox and the light pours in on the pie, and the pent-up smell of the filling flows out. The light and the smell. You take it. I have been dared to be free too many times. Something has always dared me. Think of the words "taking liberties." The number of times I have heard these words. What does a person mean by using a phrase like this?

"Vanny, as usual you're taking liberties," my mother would say like a broken record.

We spent a year by ourselves in the house without Neil. And always when Neil came home from school we were quietly there on the couch, my mother working the puzzle and looking up and putting aside the pencil when Neil walked in and threw his empty lunch bag on the chair that no one ever sat in. I was running my hands across the pages of the various books, feeling the letters tremble under my fingertips as though they were insects being crushed.

"Neil, what's a four-letter word for little?"

"Tiny," I said, fast as lightning.

"That's right!" said Neil. "Ma, Vanny's right."

"I asked your brother, Vanny. You're taking liberties." She quickly snapped the pencil across my fingers. I felt Neil flinch.

When I look across the table at the faces of the bored, exhausted detectives, all I can truly see is how disgusted they are at the insignificant little troubles of my younger life. I imagine them thinking "So what?" They just about dare me to tell them something more troubling. One of them lights a cigarette and taps the pack over to me. I reach out my hand and stop it.

There is the time my father sat in the crawl space above the second floor and held the gun in his lap and said he would do it.

"Don't," I said.

"Don't," he said, imitating my voice, small and weird and accurate in a way that made me want him to do it.

I stood on the flimsy, pull-down ladder. My mother and Neil were at the circus that I had refused to go to. "What is a circus," I said, "except for elephant shit and people falling."

"I don't know what," my mother said, "but you don't ever have to see one again in your life. Neil and I will go. When your father gets home, fix a sandwich for him."

In this period of our life my father was like the ghost in the house. He was there and he was not there. My mother never spoke to him. He moved in and out of the rooms like someone who was not meant to be seen by the living. He picked up a magazine and was careful to put it down exactly the same way he found it, leaving no sign that he had touched it at all. For whole weeks he would be on the road, calling collect at night and making us promise that we missed him. Then, after we'd hung up the phone, my mother would say, "Boys, that was your father." As if we didn't know.

He came home from Idaho a half hour after my mother and Neil left for the circus. I heard the big engine of the Oldsmobile hiss loud like a rapids running between our house and the neighbors', the car gliding back to the garage. I decided I didn't want to be home alone to greet him, so I hid from him, first in the hall closet. He entered the house with a tread so light that he might have been on tiptoe. I listened from a crouch in the dark, the cuffs of his galoshes bending beneath me. He cleared his throat and cracked his neck. I heard him put the suitcase down and heard the suitcase fall sideways, as it always seemed to do.

"Hello?" he called once. I waited through the stillness. Then I heard him in the kitchen staring into the icebox, muttering, "What's this?" "What's this?" "Mmmmm, maybe," then closing the door of the icebox. I heard him at the counter. I heard him take a knife from the drawer. I heard the knife in a jar of something, probably mayonnaise, scraping the sides. Then I fell asleep.

When I woke up I didn't hear anything at all. I crept out of the closet and up the stairs. I saw him in their bedroom on the edge of the bed, just sitting, facing away from me, slouching forward with terrible posture so that his large back was squashed and shortened.

"Hi there," he said, but I didn't answer. On all fours I crept backwards in the hallway. He continued not to move. I got to the hall table and crawled underneath it. I waited there for a long time, cramped and drawn up. Then he finally stood and stretched, and I heard him open and shut a dresser drawer.

He walked from the bedroom into the hall and pulled down the hidden ladder to the crawl space. I saw the long-barreled pistol hanging from his hand like something almost ready to drop and be forgotten. He was barefooted. Slowly he rose up into the ceiling. He retracted the ladder behind him, its lower legs folding up gently, the steel springs making their soft boinging sound. Soon the hall was silent again, and he was gone.

I expected to hear the shot fired right away, but the silence continued. I waited.

"Dad?" I finally said softly. "Dad?" Then gradually louder, because most sounds from the house below did not easily penetrate
the crawl space, which had full insulation and a thick plywood
floor. With the ladder drawn up you could be perfectly alone in
the dim light that leaked in from outside through the soffits and
made the rafters glow blond.

"Dad?"

I got out from under the table and reached for the wooden knob
tied to the end of the rope hanging down from the ladder.

"Dad?"

"Is that you, Vann?" he said, his voice muffled.

I pulled the ladder down and climbed it, thinking I might stick
my head up into the crawl space and see the barrel leveled at me.
But my father was sitting cross-legged, five feet from the opening,
with the gun in his lap, perfectly still.

"Hi, Vanny," he said.

"Why are you up here?" I said.

"I'm thinking things over," he said.

"About what?"

"About how I feel," he said. "I'm away so much, I don't feel
connected to anything."

"What's wrong with that?"

He shrugged. "I don't know," he said. "But I don't like it."

I stared at his face and wondered what he would do. I didn't
think he would do anything. The unmoving air in the crawl space
was hot and piney. The air below, where my legs were, was cool
and agreeable. Now and then my father would close his eyes for
a few long seconds, and each time he opened them again there was
the fresh look of surprise that I was still there with him.

"Vanny," he said.

His face was damp and shining. A car went by outside with a
whoosh. He looked in that direction as though he could see the
car through the solid wood. He had his hands folded over the
pistol, hiding it from me. I tried to pay full attention to everything,
but my interest began to waver. Sweat formed on my upper lip,
and I was uncomfortable being half up and half down. I wanted
something to happen soon.

"Don't," I said, in a voice that seemed unconvinced.

"*Don't*," he said, imitating me, angering me.

Slowly I went back down the ladder and pushed it up toward the ceiling. But I was too small to make it rise all the way and seal itself. For a moment it hung there between up and down, a sloppy, half-completed event. I stood beneath and watched it. Then my father snatched the ladder upward. It went quickly, as if sucked by a wind, the lower legs folding back with a smack and the ceiling becoming again a healed surface.

I went downstairs and turned the television on. Later my father came down and sat on the couch beside me.

"Would you like some milk?" he said.

"Yes," I said, but he didn't move. He sat and stared at the television until my mother and Neil came home from the circus. Then he stood without a word and went upstairs to bed. My mother and Neil and I stood in the hall at the foot of the stairs and listened upward to the sound of him running the cold water and brushing his teeth.

"He doesn't feel connected to anything," I told my mother.

"He's not," she said dreamily. "He's certainly not connected to me. Is he connected to you?"

Later, when we had gone to bed, Neil told me that our mother spent the entire time at the circus trying to make him confess to her all of his negative feelings about her. When he wouldn't admit that he had any, she began to ask him questions about her appearance.

"Are my lips too red?" Neil told me she asked him. "Is my figure still nice? What dress makes my figure look best? Be honest." Neil said that during the aerial act she took a flask from her purse and offered him a sip.

"Did you take it?" I asked him.

"Yes," he said. "Of course I did."

"What was it like?"

"Sweet. And the flask smelled like the mixed insides of her purse—but mostly like her perfume."

I imagined my mother making Neil crawl down and put his face between her pale shaved thighs and then clamping them hard around his ears until he heard the ocean roar. I fell asleep to the sound of my father beginning to sleepwalk in the hallway and down the stairs, sliding his hand against the wallpaper with a soft hiss.

I would end it there. The detectives would sit silent and still in their chairs, or lean back against the empty walls, staring down at their shoes as though something small and unrecognized was crawling on one of the toes. Slowly they would look at each other, waiting for someone to crack, wondering what else was on my mind that was possibly even stranger. This would be a moment to covet. The silence would stretch and stretch, sucking the air from the room, until someone—his dry voice sounding like thunder—would ask me if I wanted more coffee.

"Hi there," I say in return. I stare at Sarah Colven. She smiles. All of this is wrong. Snow flies over her soft blue shoulders; birds swoop through the dim cab of the truck; headlights shine from beneath her sweater; the silver flask dances on the palm of her wool-gloved hand like a happy pig.

"You didn't have any . . . ," I say at exactly the same instant she says, "If you could just . . ."

Her words have a swooning echo.

"Just what?" I say. I hand her the keys to her car.

"Take me down the road? Please? It's a mile, mile and a half or so? There's the gas station there. You know the one I mean. Easy Ed's or something. Yellow sign? Shell? Sunoco maybe. They have the convenience store."

"Sure," I say. "No problem."

I'm getting into the truck. I notice the cold in my feet that makes the workshoes feel like spongy rotted wood. I roll the window and slam the door. Snow explodes off it into the dark. I put the truck in gear and ease it slowly up over the hill and down. Already I am forgetting everything. The details are flying backward in time until they can't be seen. In the corner of my eye the flask glints, still held warmly in her lap. We pass beneath street lamps that throw the vapor down upon the truck and in through the window, winking on the bright chrome finish.

"Here it is," she says. I slow the truck. The wipers slap. I pull in at Easy Al's, not Ed's, and it is a Shell sign after all that turns on top of a giant pole.

"Thanks," she says. "I don't know what I'd have done."

I nod. She opens the door. She reaches out and hands me the flask. I take it. It almost burns me through my glove.

"Did you get to have any?" I ask her, holding the thing up.

"Of that? Oh, yeah. I did. Yeah, thanks," she says. She smiles. She is just a liar, this girl.

"One for the road?" I ask, unscrewing the cap.

"No thanks," she says, and I know that this is how it goes. The moment is cold and uninspired. I hear the defeat in my voice and know that she is gone for good, saved by something I don't know the name of or understand that reached down out of the snow and kept her from doing what anyone else would have done.

"Okay," I say. "Good luck."

"So long," she says. "Thanks again." And I watch her turn her tiny back and walk off in the amber direction of Easy Al's warm doors, inside of which I can see the television, high on the shelf above the boxes of wiper blades and spark plugs, showing little colorful changes that might be the news or the sports or anything at all, too far away to know. Her hair blows sideways in the snow and a car pulls in and blocks my view of her. I consider the encounter ended.

I drive another mile down the road and turn around and head back the way I came. It's always faster going over new territory a second time. Long before I expect to have returned to the scene, my lights swing over the crest of the hill and down onto the girl's parked car, a shapeless heap beneath new snow. I have the flask between my legs and feel the liquor tremble inside it the way the urge still trembles inside of me—confined and wanting out. I reach my hand down and touch the knurled cap, thumb and forefinger sliding, rubbing. I think about taking the sip myself.

I would tell the detectives of the many times I sat with the flask in my hands and almost drank. It isn't possible to possess such a poison without sometimes coming to see it as a solution to a long-standing problem. I will always return to the theme of my freedom.

"You can try anything once," I would say, waiting until they— or at least one of them—nodded. "And some things only once."

I have sometimes closed my eyes and remembered a dozen deaths in as many seconds, the jelling faces flashing by like photos. After the images faded, with my eyes again open, I have wondered why I have not done this same thing to myself. If my actions amount to anything more than the quenching of a large, unbearable urge, I see that they bring me right to the edge of this final reluctance. I watch the others go over the edge the way I used to watch Neil ride a dented silver flying saucer down the icy hill near our house in winter. I stood perfectly still at the top of the hill and watched him get smaller, flying off the saucer on the bumps and landing on it again, speeding faster toward the sweep turn that finally took him out of sight behind some trees. When he was gone the held breath swept out of me in a plume of vapor. I was always scared to follow him down, until I finally did it.

I have unscrewed the cap and smelled the liquor. I have put my eye right close to the hole and seen the room light or sunlight leak downward into the darkness and wink back up. I have set my tongue against the threads of the neck and waited for something to happen, believing it wouldn't. I have come so close . . .

"You should have," one of the cops would be obliged by duty to say, breaking the spell.

I drive defensively on the interstate, out of Connecticut into Rhode Island. I slow and let the yellow sanders and snowplows pass me, then follow along in their cleaner, drier, safer wakes.

There is still the unsolved problem of the urge, which was brought so close to being satisfied and conquered, and now sits in the pit of my bowels and secretes some whining chemical, the juice of its weary, unappeased hunger. Today I think I have confused the urge. On other occasions when an encounter failed, it failed before things had gone very far—before the flask was introduced, before any large expectation of success had taken hold and raced the urge along. In those cases the solution was just to retreat and try someone else. (I have never had to try more than twice.) But now . . . I find myself passing the signs for towns whose lights might otherwise have caught my eye and caused my hands to bend the truck down the exit ramps to see what I could find. But the urge doesn't quite know where it's been left. It floats somewhere between need and satisfaction, not knowing whether to go forward to the end or backward to the beginning. And I feel that I am stuck along with it: The physical sensation doesn't grow inside me and doesn't shrink. I am only where I am, and there is no progress. If I were a machine, I would have a red reset button, and then the truck would take the exits and cruise the streets, and I would not have to try more than twice.

But nothing changes or is resolved before I arrive back in Bledsoe. The time simply passes on the snow-covered roads, and the weary urge grows older, and perhaps begins to shrivel up. I pull the truck into the driveway at the Deans', roll past the house and into my accustomed space, and sit in the dark while the engine cools.

"Home again, home again," I say in the same kind of singsong voice my father used to affect coming in the door from a trip in his happier years. I put the flask in the glove compartment and lock it. I reach in beneath my jacket and place a hand on my stomach and feel the heat coming through. I think back to Sarah Colven and imagine that this heat is hers, the heat of her lost-and-found life, which I had wrongly thought would be breathed out into the cab of my truck forever. I try to picture her face, but all I can get is the hair and a sharpish nose and dark eyebrows.

I get out of the truck and head toward the house, treading quietly on the snowy back steps, hoping to get inside without having to see any Deans. But just as I reach for the door the porch light goes on and Doug comes out to greet me and ask me in.

"There's someone I want you to meet," he says loudly, grinning. He takes my elbow and guides me through the back hall and into the kitchen, where a pale, slender, unhappy-looking girl is standing, leaning against a counter with a beer in her hand.

"This is my daughter Karen," says Doug, his voice full of pleasure. "Karen, this is Vann Siegert, who lives upstairs in your old room."

"Hi," she says. Jane Dean turns around from drying dishes and watches me reach my hand across to Karen, who obliges me with a handshake, her fingers cold from holding the beer.

"Nice to meet you," I say.

She nods. She lets go.

I'm about to make my exit when Jane asks Doug if he isn't going to "tell Vann the good news?"

"I was just about to."

"Good news?" I say.

"Well, not good for Joe LaMoine," says Doug. "He just had open-heart surgery this afternoon. Three bypasses. Stable condition. But good for you . . . They want you to come back and fill in until Joe's recovered. We're talking at least two months, more likely three."

"Geez," I say.

"Yeah. Big surprise. The guy's watching a Celtics game last night, and feels a little indigestion. And then, b-bing!—today he's on an operating table up in Boston. Anyhow, I said I'd tell you. They want you to start back right away. Is that okay?"

"I guess so," I say. "Thanks, Doug."

I look at the girl. She stares down at the hole in the lid of the beer can. Then she looks up at me and smiles.

"Okay," says Doug. "I'll see you in the morning."

"Sure thing," I say.

"Good for you," Jane says to me, shaking a plate in the air as though it means victory.

"I guess I better get some sleep," I say. The girl stares at me hard and then shifts her eyes suddenly to the ceiling. There is something about her that I do not like.

"Good night," I say, moving backwards out of the kitchen and into the hallway.

"Good night," say the three Deans all at the same time—none of them smiling, none of them looking either at each other or at me. As I close the door I hear Doug clear his throat in a way that indicates that some conversation that had been interrupted is about to begin again.

In the dark back hallway I wait to hear what will follow; but nothing does. On both sides of the closed door there is silence.

# EIGHT

---

IN THE FIRST WEEK IN WHICH I WEAR THE OLD leather mailbag of Joe LaMoine, I poison two people. The bag hangs from my shoulder and rides on my hip, a comfortable but heavy hump that moves against me like a new joint when I walk. The bag and I are together in this way, and I feel what Joe LaMoine has felt for many years, and it hardly feels strange at all. The leather of the bag is soft and ancient, warm to touch even in the winter air. Its creases catch the sunlight and shine like rivers crossing and joining.

Some of the streets of Joe LaMoine's route are like no other streets in town. Many of the houses are built into the side of a hill, and each front door is a climb of many steps from the street. Halfway down the first block of the first day of my replacing him, I think of Joe LaMoine's damaged heart and hear the thump of my own as I lean and catch my breath against the fence in front of a house whose steps turn twice and seem like a mountain trail, at the summit of which I see a curtain part and fall.

The first day I don't finish the route until six o'clock. Some of the people make a point to meet me at the door and snatch their mail from my hands before I can put it through the slot or into the box outside, and they look at me hard and strangely, as though I am defective, inexplicable. To some of these people I say I am sorry, and that seems to make a difference—they soften themselves or instead just look down at the mail in a happy, scrutinizing way, as though it has all been worth the wait.

When I get home that night, I'm too tired to eat. I stare at my shelf in the Deans' refrigerator and see that there are hot dogs and cottage cheese and a half gallon of Coke. But I can't make a decision. So I slowly close the door and turn around and leave. Going out to the back hallway I see Karen Dean coming down the stairs from my rooms.

"I didn't know you were home," she says.

"Well, I am," I say. I put my eyes right through her, trying to scare.

"I'm sorry," she says. "I didn't mean . . . I just wanted to see what it felt like without me living up there."

"Okay," I say. "Just this once. 'Cuz to me it's home." And I go up past her, not looking at her but feeling her eyes follow me from behind. I go through the two rooms and examine them for signs of her having disturbed me in some way. But she has been careful.

I lock the door and turn out the lights and undress. Naked I walk through the rooms and take them back. I sniff the air for her but find nothing left. Once I'm satisfied that mine is still mine, I go to the bed and sleep. The cold creeps up from my toes to my knees and beyond. I hear nothing but the soft fussing sounds of people kept waiting.

The second day goes better. Although I am sore from the walking and climbing of the first day, I keep a better pace and finish with the route by five. That night I have two hot dogs and some cottage cheese and a glass of the Coke. I take my supper up the cold back stairs. The steaming hot dogs roll from edge to edge, almost going over. I eat with the plate on my lap and watch the news from Providence on my little TV. The mayor's niece was kidnapped and held at gunpoint for two hours by her ex-husband before he released her unharmed and gave himself up. The mayor is shown slowly shaking his head and saying nothing. Then the ex-husband is shown being put in a cruiser, his hands cuffed behind him, a detective gently pushing down the back of his head so it won't bang getting in.

After dinner I feel rested enough to go out. I drive to the Keenan-town Mall and walk up and down the various indoor avenues. The piped music makes the place feel empty even though there are plenty of people doing just what I am doing—walking and looking.

For a time I sit in a booth at a fast-food place and drink a shake and read the paper that someone else has left behind. When I finish the shake I go up and buy a medium Pepsi. The place is busy and the lines are long. I take the Pepsi back to my seat and reach to the deep inside breast pocket of my leather jacket and pull out the flask. Taking the plastic lid off the Pepsi, I carefully pour in a generous sip of my liquor. I put the lid back on the Pepsi and sit with it in front of me, trying to think what to do next. I continue reading the paper.

The next time I look up, there's a man setting down his tray of food at the table nearest to me. He takes his coat off and drapes it over the empty seat across from him. Then he leaves his food and goes to the napkin and straw and condiment station to get other things he needs before beginning to eat. When he has his back to me, I take my doctored Pepsi and set it down on his tray, switching it with the drink that he has bought. I go back to reading the paper.

He returns and eats his meal quickly. At times I look up and see the frenzied eagerness with which he feeds french fries into his mouth, a half dozen at a time, as though the flavor gets better the more he can eat at one time. He chews with great energy.

Finally he takes a sip of his drink. He smacks his mouth thought-fully, noticing something odd in the taste. But he must decide that he likes the oddness of it, because he drinks more and more. I stand up and crease the paper and slap it down on the table and go to the other side of the room, watching the man from a distance as he reaches up and rubs his temples and lets his arm sink ponder-ously to his lap. He tries twice to stand up and falls back into the seat, both times landing heavily so that the plastic back makes a wrenching sound that is just on the verge of breaking. His head shudders. He clumsily pushes the tray forward and lowers his head to the table. Very soon he stops moving. I go to the counter and order coffee. I leave the restaurant and wander the indoor avenues some more. In ten minutes I hear the sirens. I walk outside and find my truck and drive home.

Sometimes it can go so easily.

The third day is harder than I expected. I naturally thought that the route would be easier on the third day than it had been on the second, but I am wrong. A delayed fatigue sets in and slows my step, and I take almost as long finishing as I did on the first day. The people who had met me at the door on the first day, but not the second, meet me at the door on the third and are plainly less pleased to hear my apology. The cold is sharper and the air more still. By the end of the day my lungs actually hurt beneath the ribs as though I have injured them from too much breathing.

In the Deans' kitchen that night, Karen sits doing a crossword. She asks me for a cigarette when I come in. Saying nothing, I put the pack on the table. The book of matches is nestled in the cellophane. I open the refrigerator door and stare at the hot dogs and cottage cheese and Coke. I hear her light the cigarette.

"Thanks," she says. "What's an eight-letter word for tyrant?"

"I don't know," I say. I take out the jug of Coke and drink straight from the bottle.

"Martinet," she says. I put the bottle back and take out the tub of cottage cheese. I close the refrigerator and leave the kitchen by the back-hall door. I can't get away from her fast enough. I even leave the cigarettes right where they are on the table in front of her.

I eat the cottage cheese and watch the news. I don't know if my man from the night before will be there or not. He isn't. People simply disappear. They are there, and then they're gone. I enjoyed watching him from a distance. It felt important. I felt the pity in my eyes.

Karen knocks at the door to return my cigarettes.

"Mr. Siegert," she says. I know immediately. But I don't open the door. I speak to her through it.

"What?"

"I've got your cigarettes."

"It's okay," I say. "You can keep them."

"Really?"

"Yeah. It's okay. I've got more."

"Okay. Great," she says. "Thanks."

Some kind of breathing on the other side. The wood tingles. I wait with my ear near the door for the sound of her feet on the stairs. Doug and Jane are out somewhere, dinner, a movie. It's just me and daughter Dean in the house. Finally she is moving. I feel relieved. I hear the steps. I imagine the breath and heat of her lingering afterward, trapped in the high spaces of the small landing outside my door. I go back and sit down and watch the sports and figure it out: She wants to get in. She hates me being here. She wants her room back.

On the fourth day I am not scheduled to work. I sleep until almost ten. I drive to the Canada Falls Diner and order blueberry pancakes with a thin blue syrup that stains the cakes and sinks in quickly and disappears. I keep pouring on more syrup until the steel container is empty. Then I eat them, going around the edges and progressing slowly in toward the thicker center where the pats of butter lie buried between the cakes, melting outward. I play some songs on the little wall-mounted jukebox in the booth. I look out the window. I see a duck standing on the hood of someone's car. Then the window fogs with my breath. I imagine the duck will be gone if I wipe the breath away, but it isn't.

I go to the library and sit in the stove-heated reading room and read the newspapers mounted on bamboo sticks. The varnished floor creaks companionably without anyone even walking on it. After I've read the paper I go to the desk where the two ladies sit.

"Do you have the Bible?" I say.

"I'm sure we must," one of the ladies whispers. "There's the catalogue." She points at the dark oak furniture with the many tiny morguelike drawers.

"Look under 'B,'" she says.

In the drawer I find cards for six versions and follow around the corner behind the ladies to the aisles with the correct numbers. The Bibles sit on the shelf side by side, separated from anything else. I pick the one that looks newest and take it back to the reading room. I open to any page and let my eyes fall upon it haphazardly, and slowly whisper the words to myself. "Set a guard over my mouth, O Lord. Keep watch over the door of my lips." Psalm 141, verse 3. Then I open to another page and set my finger upon it. "Behold, I am doing a new thing. Now it springs forth. Do you not perceive it? I will make a way in the wilderness and rivers in the desert." Isaiah, Chapter 44, verse 3.

Then a shadow falls upon me, and I look up to see what causes it. A tall man in a stained brown cardigan is standing in front of me, over me, staring down. I stare back at him coldly.

"Huuuhh," he says. "Huuh." There is obviously something wrong about him. I shake my head.

"Take a hike," I say. "Go on."

Then I feel a hand on my shoulder and quickly turn my head to see one of the library ladies. She bends down next to my ear.

"This is Mr. Gray," she whispers. "He's all right. He only wants to shake your hand, I'm sure. He always wants to meet anyone he's never seen before. He's harmless and very nice. You'll see." Then she stands up and goes back to her desk. Behind her the floor creaks.

"Hello," I say. I reach out my hand to Mr. Gray. He takes it with great eagerness and shakes it up and down. Others in the room pause in their reading and watch this encounter taking place. Maybe they, too, have had this same experience.

"Nice to meet you," I say.

"Huuuhh," says Mr. Gray. He smiles. I wait for him to go away. I nod and smile in return.

"Yes," I say. "Nice to meet you."

He turns and goes to the corner where the papers are hanging from a rack like drying hides. He returns with the local Bledsoe weekly, the *Transcript,* and offers it to me.

"Thank you," I say, and hand him the Bible in exchange. He takes it off to an empty seat and sits with it in front of him, softly rubbing the black cover.

I stare down at the paper he has given me. On the lower half of the front page is the dense headline, "FOUL PLAY IN MALL DEATH?" I read the story beneath it.

*"Police and paramedics responded to a sudden death Tuesday night at a Burger Boy restaurant in the Keenantown Mall. Pronounced dead at the scene was James K. Edge of Logan Court, Harding. Mr. Edge was found slumped over at his table by restaurant personnel, who summoned an ambulance. Attempts by paramedics to revive Mr. Edge were unsuccessful.*

*"The initial cause of death was given as cardiac arrest, pending an autopsy. But sources in the Bristol County coroner's office indicated late yesterday that forensic pathology tests are under way to determine whether foul play might have been involved.*

*"William H. Deven, a spokesman for the Bristol County district attorney's office, would say only that 'some evidence was collected by police at the scene that we are subjecting to lab analysis, and while we have no firm basis yet for concluding Mr. Edge was murdered, we are not at this point ruling out that possibility.' Mr. Deven declined to state the nature of the evidence, but said that police interviewed several restaurant patrons and employees and are 'pursuing some leads gathered in that fashion.'*

*"According to Mr. Edge's sister, Janice Fournier, of Daigle Road, Bledsoe, Mr. Edge, who was divorced, often stopped at the Keenantown Mall on his way home from his job as a state building inspector. 'He didn't like to cook,' said Mrs. Fournier, 'so it was easiest just to grab a sandwich someplace.'*

*"Besides his sister, Mr. Edge leaves a son, Roy, of New Bedford, and a daughter, Myra O'Rourke, of Taunton."*

When I look up from the paper I see Mr. Gray smiling at me and holding the Bible aloft, like a preacher, for me to see. I get up and put the paper back in the rack and leave the library and sit outside in my truck with the engine and the heater running, listening to the radio and waiting for something, I am not sure what.

I always try to be careful not to be seen. The murder of the man in the mall was a careless thing. I might have been noticed sitting there. I might have been spotted in the act of doctoring the Pepsi or switching the drinks. I might have been seen paying semi-close attention to the man after he drank the drink. But the restaurant was crowded and loud that night, and these are the kinds of places where people don't look at each other much, where many come in alone and eat alone, as I was doing and the man was doing, and where eating is a necessary chore done quickly. People don't linger and watch each other. They buy and pay and eat and leave, making little eye contact. No one could describe anyone they ever saw in such a place who was not crazy and babbling.

Another thing about the man in the mall is that he was the first of my victims who truly had no choice in the matter. He had no awareness of me. In that way, he died completely alone, drinking the drink he thought was his own. This was one of the reasons I had to move away from him, across the room, placing all of those others between me and the man who was dying. This was one of the odd dimensions of the murder, that it was shared with so many others. My pleasure in it was small, subdivided, short-lived. There was no relationship. All of the other victims had known that they were taking something from me; they had known that I was offering it, and they could think about me and decide one way or the other. But the man in the mall didn't know. He had no awareness of me, and was not in even the smallest way free to choose. So, of everyone I've done, I felt sorriest for him. He was only minding his own business, stopping on the way home from work because he didn't like to cook.

Later, in my bed, I vowed that I would never do such a thing again. Everyone must know me and not be alone. There has to be a relationship. My only excuse for the man in the mall was the recent frustration of the girl in Connecticut. This was a time, like no other time before, when I needed a sure deliverance. And so I eliminated choice from the process. Choice is the only element that threatens success, but it is also the thing that makes the encounter unfold in the proper way and deliver the deepest rewards. I need to know that they have taken it from me; when they take it from me, I am never ashamed. My life expands beside them. For an instant, we are together.

I look up and see Mr. Gray crossing the street from the library. He is dressed for a warmer season but shows no sign of being cold. He carries under his arm a stack of several books that makes him look like an aging high school student. The urge soon makes itself known inside of me and addresses itself eagerly to Mr. Gray.

"Him," the urge seems to whisper in the voice of Tim, spilling like a flood from my stomach down into my bowels. I pull the truck out and turn the corner onto Holden Street, which forms one boundary of the town square across which Mr. Gray is walking briskly.

Why did the urge say nothing when I first saw Mr. Gray inside the library? I don't know. I cannot answer for what is felt or not felt by the urge, or why it comes and goes, awakening when it does and sleeping otherwise. This is something the detectives will ask me: Why then and not the other time? Why would this suddenly opinionated urge say, "Kill *him*, but don't kill *him*." As a man immersed in the hot bath of honesty, I would stare the detectives straight in their eyes and tell them I just don't know. And one detective, the far one—the one who never sits at the table but always stands and paces or stops for long spells and leans against the wall—will say in a voice that reminds me of Tim's, "Look, pal, isn't all this stuff about the so-called urge just a lying-sack-of-shit way to get out of saying it straight out?—You wanted to fucking waste these useless bozos. Right? You. Vann whatever-it-is . . . Siegert. Not the fucking Green Hornet. Right?"

I can reveal to them exactly what it feels like to take the two slow lefts around the Bledsoe town square, following Mr. Gray: It feels slow, and yet exactly fast enough. I'm thinking: No matter how fast he walks I'll still get all the way to the other side of the square before he does, and park the truck and get out of the truck and get myself seated down on one of the old green benches that lies at the end of the path he's walking along so rapidly. And I do. I am sitting there waiting for Mr. Gray, watching the permanent eager look on the permanently eager face and feeling a deep love of the sodden disability that makes him so dear to the library ladies that they are moved, interchangeably, to go explain the odd rituals of his helplessness to a stranger—part of the small-town job description, this loving the everything of everyone.

He doesn't see me, and then he does. His face lights up with an extra eagerness that shames the customary eagerness. He moves forward to me like a thing that will not be able to stop in time. He smacks his free palm against the back of the bench. The iron front legs budge a little in the cold ground. He drops his books on the bench.

"Hi, Mr. Gray," I say.

He shoves the books aside and sits beside me and stares back along the path in the direction he has come from.

"Huhh," he says, pointing at the distant library.

"That's a long walk," I say. He appears to be thinking nothing about anything, and I have no idea if he understands what people say to him or not.

"Where do you live?" I ask him.

He reaches up and pushes the hair back off his forehead, long reddish-brown strands that twine through his fingers and settle and hold in the crook of the ear.

"Do you live near here?"

He shakes his head and points straight up. I follow the line of his arm and see the undifferentiated clouds, low and pewter, a simple ceiling. Mr. Gray is one of the homeless.

We sit together on the bench until he seems to find himself angry at something. He stands and rushes toward a tree and stamps his foot at the knuckle of one of its roots, stamping repeatedly. The ground thuds hollowly as his heel strikes the root. After a dozen of these blows he stops and gently probes the empty air with the toe of his boot, as though turning over the body of a ghost.

"Huh-uh-uhhh," he says, the sound of a car that won't start. He is out of breath and his face is flushed. He comes back to the bench and gathers his books and hurries away. I watch from where I sit until he reaches the corner and waits for the light to cross. I go to the tree and stare down at the root. The bark is worn raw. When I look back I see him crossing. I set out to follow him.

I haven't often followed someone. There's an art to remaining unnoticed. You invent a business for yourself to be doing that the person in front of you is an incidental part of, but not the main thing. You convince yourself of this. You appear to be going about this business. If the person in front of you stops to tie his shoe, you go right past him and don't even look down. You pass him close enough to make him feel the wind of your passing, so that he might envy your continuing movement but never think that you have some interest in him.

Mr. Gray doesn't stop and doesn't look over his shoulder and see me loitering along behind him. He keeps a steady pace, as though he himself is going about some invented business. Following him is easy. Someone observing me behind Mr. Gray would think nothing of it. And yet, we belong together like this. I think back to the moment when he came to me in the library with his curiosity, with his soft hand ready to be taken. If there has ever been a summoning, that was it. He had me. The urge must have stirred inside me without my knowing it, yawned and stretched and found itself waiting for the next sighting of Mr. Gray, all eagerness, ready to spread the chemicals of need through my lower parts.

He turns down Church Street, past the camera store that has no light inside, past the cleaners, the florist, the St. Stephen's rectory and the church itself. Then up the steep hill—Waban Hill—where we come to the midst of one of the neighborhoods that are included in the postal delivery route of Joe LaMoine, and now me.

Then Mr. Gray stops in his tracks and turns around and looks at me as though he has known all along I was there. I stop, too. From the house I am standing in front of a woman emerges with a snowsuited baby in her arms. This gives me the strangest feeling, as though the woman and the baby are entering something instead of leaving something; the interior of their house is the outside, and the neighborhood is the inside. This was the way I felt as a child: Outside was in, inside was out. I am swept back to Spokane, where I wandered the streets as though they were mine alone. The woman looks at me for an instant. The baby is rigid in the shape of the snowsuit. Believing that my stillness holds an element of risk, I look away from them and begin to walk toward Mr. Gray, who also turns back and resumes his march up the hill. Behind me I hear a car door open. I hear a short cry from the baby. A house and a half later I hear the car door slam. I survey the neighborhood. I do not gaze at Mr. Gray's brown sweater, at the back of his bobbing head. But he is there, rising higher on the hill, rising toward the tiny, pine-treed park at the top where the newspapers say young boys and girls buy and use their drugs and have sex in the cinderblock comfort stations, leaving a litter of stained underwear and condoms and tiny nibs of tin foil in the defaced, dented stalls.

I hear the woman's car start and drive off toward the center of town. Mr. Gray quickens his step and surprises me with the speed he attains. His legs are long, and he must be fit. My breath comes shallower as I try to keep up. The hill wears away, and finally he enters the park through a wooden gate. I see no cars in the dozen or so spaces.

Mr. Gray takes a path through the pines, which are snowy in their lower, sun-deprived branches. I hear him whistling tunelessly—a note held briefly that disappears, then another, and another. The sound of it surprises me after knowing him only to grunt. Soon he leaves the path and enters the thickness of the pines. I stop on the path and watch him twenty yards in, carefully placing his feet in footprints he has left before, broken through the crust of snow. Like a chimpanzee he reaches for branches and lets them bear his weight as he swings through the narrow route that is made more difficult by the need to set his feet just so.

When he is safely ahead of me, beyond veils of snow shaken from the branches, I too step off the path and follow in his footsteps exactly—we are much the same shoe size. Soon I see where he has gone. In a small clearing there is a shelter large enough for a man to crouch in, and perhaps, in places, to stand in. It is made of scavenged materials thrown together into a kind of lean-to slanting up against several trees and camouflaged with pine boughs. Beside it is a rusting shopping cart filled with leaves and snow. Mr. Gray sits inside the shelter's opening with his legs crossed and a poker expression on his face, watching me approach.

"Hello, Mr. Gray," I say. "Is this where you live? Can I see?"

I crouch down in front of the opening. The inside is dark but dry. Covering the ground are two oval blue shag bathroom mats and a large, thinly grooved black rubber mat that might have come from between the inner and outer doors of a supermarket. I see a sleeping bag. I see three plastic milk crates full of books and cans and candles.

I waste no time.

"This is nice," I say, nodding slowly, savoring. "This isn't so bad." Still crouching, I unzip my jacket and reach inside to my inner pocket and bring out the flask. I unscrew the cap, flip it off and let it hang by its chain. I begin to raise the flask to my lips. But suddenly I stop, remembering my manners, and offer the flask to Mr. Gray.

My hand trembles slightly. Mr. Gray would never notice. He reaches out fast and takes what is offered, drinking immediately and deeply, upending the flask and letting the amber liquor pour down his throat by gravity. I am almost ready to snatch back the flask, thinking he will empty it, when he stops abruptly and swallows.

He pats the pleasant burn as it makes its way deep down the esophagus. He smiles and stares at me. With one hand he gives me back the flask. With the other he takes my free hand and holds it softly, tugging me gently, relaxing his wet mouth into a whisper: "Haaahh."

He pulls me forward, into the shelter, bringing me off my balance. My knees hit the threshold, the edge of the black rubber mat. I accidentally drop the uncapped flask in the snow behind me. He has me by one hand and the opposite underarm. He possesses considerable strength. He pulls me into the dark. I land on top of him. He groans. His breath comes out with the sweet orangey taint of the liquor.

"Huunh," he says. Then I hear a long breath come slow from his nose. It mourns and drifts like the whistle of a distant train. He shifts beneath me. He raises his hand to one temple and rubs. I roll off to the other side and watch. The hand stays at the temple, the fingers stilled. The head rolls toward me. The hand falls away. The eyes are steady and unfocused. I touch his forehead and find it damp. I let my fingers drift slow across the flesh, thinking maybe he feels the tickle somewhere deep inside. This is the closest I have ever been.

"Mr. Gray," I whisper.

I put my palm on his chest, the place on the brown cardigan that would be just over the heart. The beats are slow, thick and ponderous. I count the lengthening seconds that elapse between them. Finally comes the time when I am sure that the counting will never end. Fourteen, fifteen, sixteen . . . My pants are tight with the pleasure of this closeness. I lie beside Mr. Gray in the dark until I begin to fall asleep. I fight against it. I get to my knees and roll my neck around, letting the bones crack. I reach down and pick up one of Mr. Gray's recently borrowed library books and open it roughly in the middle. I place the opened book face down on his chest. My own heart slows and I feel the silence. For the first time I notice the invading cold.

Outside of the lean-to I find the flask. The snow beyond its mouth is stained in a circle the size of a silver dollar. Carefully I enclose the stain in a larger snowball. I roll up the stain until it becomes the size of a human head. Using two hands I launch the head between two trees, as far as it will go. It falls to earth twenty yards away and disappears to my satisfaction. I screw the cap on the flask and shake it—there is still some liquor left. I take a handful of snow and wash the flask; the snow melts beneath my hand as I rub, and the cold and slippery friction feels good.

I leave the shelter the way I came, placing my feet exactly in the footsteps already made. But then I decide not to walk down Waban Hill. Instead, I go toward the oceanview prospect for which the park was created, a bluff that drops to a marshy wetland that stretches out to Coffin Creek, which in turn runs into one of the several bays that Massachusetts and Rhode Island share.

I descend the wide wooden steps of the nature walkway that switches back three times from the top to the base of the bluff. There are instructive legends, mounted on pedestals at each turning, that describe the geologic and wildlife characteristics of the views. Under weathered Plexiglas, typical coastal birds stand in postures that are cooperative and revealing. At the bottom of the bluff the walkway narrows, offering the choice of a trail that winds out through the marsh in a deceptive loop that seems not to be returning at all, but eventually does. I take this trail and feel myself disappear. Spindly cattails rise to my shoulders as I walk, and the path jogs and twists after every ten yards or so.

I look out across the marsh to see if other heads are floating above the reeds; I don't see any. The olive-stained two-by-fours ring sharply under my heels. I stop and listen for the sounds of others' footsteps beyond the cattails, but there are none to hear. The path is mine alone.

I try to smell what's left of the sweet, muddy decay of the marsh, but the winter cold has deadened it. In the spots where rivulets cut beneath the walkway, a skin of blue-gray ice winks up. I stop once and kneel on the walkway and peer down into the ice, trying to see through to something moving underneath; but there is only a stillness.

Before I have completely circled back to the edge of the bluff, I step down off the walkway into the midst of the brittle reeds. The mud is crusty and firm; but I hear countless crystals of ice breaking softly under my tread. I walk in the vague direction of the parts of town beyond Waban Hill. The cattails break aside as I pass through them. In my wake I leave a short stubble at ankle height. Soon the bluff is gone and the cattails thin to nothing, and I am on the browned and bleached grass plain of gentle hummocks that leads to the blocked-off dead ends of residential streets that are also part of the postal delivery route of Joe LaMoine and me. As though I have only come for the view, I sit on the edge of a ten-foot section of guardrail sealing the end of Bethany Street and smoke a cigarette, blowing rings through rings and seeming to be lost in admiration of the distant marsh.

When I finish the cigarette I stub it out against the cloudy gray steel and walk back along Bethany Street, then right on Union Street and left on Bellow Avenue, which feeds back into the center of town at the corner where Church Street leaves the town square.

I walk to my truck and get in and start it up. A song ends and the news comes on the radio.

*"The Bristol County coroner has identified traces of a rare poison in the body of a man found dead Tuesday night in a Burger Boy restaurant in the Keenantown Mall. The ruling of coroner Dr. Roland Mayo contradicts a preliminary finding that James K. Edge, of Harding, died from cardiac arrest. Police are said to be treating the case as a homicide, but Mayo refused to speculate . . ."* Then comes the voice of the coroner: *" 'The only thing the autopsy showed was that the poison was present in lethal quantities in the victim's body, but not how it came to be there. A death of this*

*type could just as easily be suicide as murder. From the evidence available to me at this point, I can't make a ruling one way or the other.' A State Police spokesman said that the uneaten remnants of Edge's meal are undergoing toxicology tests in the state lab to determine the source of the poison. An inquest is scheduled for next week."*

I grip the wheel stiffly. The truck goes slowly along the route to home. I remember back to Mr. Gray, wishing to be able to say to myself that he was a perfect wonder and by far the best. But I can't. The truth is, they do not stay with me. No sooner is the full encounter ended than it begins to be forgotten. The urge erases carefully the path it has traveled, drifting across the memory like snow. The people are all a blur of equal stillnesses: set jaws, fixed pupils, hands half closed, half opened, the skin becoming stiff and strange, hardening like wax.

The detectives are suddenly busy now. I see their squints of concentration. They read, again and again, the coroner's report, missing nothing but finding something new each time. They pore over the interviews with the Burger Boy patrons, searching for someone who isn't short and isn't tall, and isn't yet anything at all. But they begin to feel my presence here. There begins to be a picture—shadows drifting on white, like fog. The truck takes shape in their minds' eyes, its color shifting through the spectrum—red, blue, yellow, green, violet, white. The truck turns gently into the driveway at the Deans'. The front shocks creak and sigh. I am becoming a fact. They know I am here.

Inside the back door to the house I find Karen. She opens it for me. My hand is on the handle on the outside, hers on the inside. Between us the door moves as though the spirits controlled it.

"I've been waiting for you," she says.

"Why?"

"I don't know," she says. "I wanted to talk to someone. Not my parents."

I pass her by and turn to climb the back stairs to my rooms.

"I'm sorry," I say. "I'm tired." I let the exhaustion pour out of me and show itself in the slow pace and soft shuffle of my feet on the steps. She can't fail to notice. "And even when I'm not tired," I tell her, "I hate to talk."

"You look like you'd understand," she says, her brittle voice aimed up at my back.

"I wouldn't." I turn the first landing and go out of sight. "I'm sorry."

But by the time I get all the way up to my door and unlock it, I hear her two floors below beginning to climb. And there is only the one destination.

I close the door quickly and throw the bolt. But the feet of Karen keep coming, getting louder. I wait, and soon she knocks.

"Mr. Siegert?" Behind the door she sounds like her mother. There is a hint of echo from the dim stairwell where all the surfaces are hard and cold in the winter.

"Yes," I say.

"Can I come in?"

"Not now."

She tries the door. The bolt rattles.

"I like my privacy," I say.

"I don't," she says. "Please. I'll just come up by the inside stairs. Please."

I glance over my shoulder at the other door, unlockable and frail.

"I mean it," I say.

"Please," she says again.

"I'm just a tenant here."

"So what. Come on. Please . . . Let me in."

I listen to the sound of her breathing. If I wait long enough she will go away. I put my palm flat against the door and try to direct my banishing feelings through the wood and into her small head, with the dull brown hair pulled tight against the scalp and coiled at the back in a knob.

"Come on," she says again, this time so softly I can almost not hear it. "Please?"

Then her body slumps against the door, her back or shoulder sliding down. The slow sound of it draws my eyes lower on the wood. She begins to cry. I stare at the bottom of the door.

There is no sound like a woman crying. My own mother has sat in front of me hundreds of times and begun so silently that only a

dog could have heard it at first. From there it would quickly grow.
Her eyes would show the sudden heat and moisture of the deep
alteration within her, and she would fix those eyes upon me and
let me see how they asked for something. Always I knew it was
something I could not give her, although she acted as if she believed
I could. Any tiny event might be the trigger. If something fell and
startled her, she would shiver hard and sit herself down in the
nearest chair and begin. Once, with the tears still drying on her
flushed cheeks, she knelt in front of me and took me by the shoulders and clamped down hard. "Life is a mystery, Vanny," she said.
"It holds no pleasure for most of us. It's best not to want a thing
from it." Then she took me by the hand and led me into the
bedroom she shared with my father, and she took her blouse and
brassiere off slowly, not caring that her breasts were mine to see,
and lay on her stomach on the bed and made me sit across her
narrow hips and lean far forward to rub her shoulders. She bur-
rowed her face in the bedspread and reached back to pull the hair
off her neck, groaning as though I was paining her.

"Vanny," she said, beginning to cry again. Something like this
happened almost every day during the year when Neil began school
and left me home alone with her. In the summertime, when Neil
was also home, she would make us compete to see whose turn it
would be. We would have to hold a heavy book at arm's length
for as long as we could. To keep us each from trying not to win,
she sometimes chose the loser. And sometimes the two of us got
to do it together, she stretched out in the middle of the bed with
a son to either side. When we had made her feel better she sat up
slowly and thanked us both with a kiss.

"You are both so eager to please me," she said. "That's the way
it should always be." Then she went to the pale blue vanity, where
her combs and brushes lay on the covering glass in a perfectly
parallel arrangement, and slid open the middle drawer and took
out her flask, which is now my flask, and unscrewed it and drank
what she called her pick-me-up. It made her close her eyes for a
moment and sway left and right like a tree in a breeze.

"Go out and play," she said, and we left her alone.

I unlock the door and open it. Karen sits outside hunched over
on the landing, her shoulders curled around like folded wings. The

cold air of the stairwell stirs and surges in upon me. Karen stands, sniffing, and says, "Thank you." She comes into my rooms with her hot eyes lowered.

"I just felt like talking," she says. Like her father, she goes straight to my chair.

"That's *my* chair," I tell her. She gets up quickly like something launched and says nothing. She goes to the window and sits sideways on the wide sill, staring out into the gray afternoon that looks as though it could snow again. I sit in the chair and wait. The cushion hisses as I settle. Karen continues looking out the window. I wait for her to talk. I can sit all afternoon like a statue. It is my day off—Thursday.

"I had an abortion," she says.

"Okay," I say. I imagine that she is paying me to sit here and listen to her.

"It still hurts." She turns around and places the palm of one hand flat on her abdomen, inches beneath the waist of her jeans. "Here." She rubs the hand slowly from side to side. "Somewhere in the middle. It aches."

I nod my head. My temples buzz. I feel summoned into the midst of Karen to touch the ache. She wants me to know. But I only want to turn away and not look. Her hand remains on the front of her jeans, still rubbing from side to side. "In here . . . ," she says again, and I am almost ready to stand and go over to her and still the motion of the hand, pull it away and place it firmly beside her, as though she is improperly using the positioning of her limbs to create an effect in me that is unpleasant, bothersome. If I had a child of my own, I would see to it that the child understood exactly what the effects of all of its possible actions were upon me. Then the child could make its decisions with the fullest information. My own mother instructed me in these sorts of things. I grew up knowing how to chew my food in a way that she would not be set on edge by. My father also knew this, but ignored her instructions. And soon I, too, learned to be set on edge by the sounds my father made eating. My eyes would meet my mother's, and there would be the flash of understanding. We grew closer.

Karen takes her hand away and stands and begins to walk around the room.

"Do you have a cigarette?" she says.

I fish the pack from my pocket and light two, keeping one for myself. I hold out the other and she comes and takes it.

"Thanks." She stands above me and draws deeply from the cigarette. She closes her eyes and holds in the smoke like marijuana. Then she steps backward and turns and heads over to the window, resuming her sideways position and the earlier silence.

I wait again, hoping that she will do nothing more than finish smoking the cigarette and leave. I urge the silence along by closing my own eyes and cherishing the stillness. In the dark I hear the smoke rise, the oiled white paper burning itself to ash in tender circles, whispering. She smokes and sighs.

"So, what do *you* do about pain?" she says.

The sound of her voice is sudden, jolting, and I realize I've begun to fall asleep. Maybe I was asleep already, passing down through the upper depths, on my way to a place unreachable, until the question sharply tugged me back. I feel the flaring heat between my knuckles and look down to see the long ash teetering and the orange coal creeping closer to the flesh. I quickly stub the cigarette out in the amber ashtray on the table by the chair.

"I do that," I say, pointing down at the broken filter and the black smudge.

She stares at me.

"Do you have anything to drink?"

I shake my head. She stares at me. I wonder if she has been in my closet and dresser drawers and boxes, or looked beneath my bed or up in the cupboards and the medicine cabinet. Her old rooms littered meanly with a new life, a stranger. I saw her coming down from here. She must have searched. Maybe she found the half-empty fifth of Southern Comfort on the floor of the closet, standing amid my three pairs of shoes. Possessing knowledge of where everything is is a kind of power.

"Oh, wait a minute," I say, having now seen her in my thoughts finding the bottle. I go to the closet. I get down on my hands and knees and reach back in the corner. My hand closes around the cold neck. I draw it out into the light and hold it up—the uncontaminated raw material.

Karen smiles. I deliver the bottle to her. I let her unscrew the cap herself and swig from it straight. As she drinks with her head thrown back, I half expect the urge to wake from its slumber and address me on the subject of what to do with her. But all that occurs inside me is the fathomless silence.

"Here," she says. "I love this stuff."

I take it from her and drink a small sip myself. The burn goes around my mouth and down my throat, slowly heating outward through the thick bone in the middle of my chest, dying and flaring at the same time. She reaches up and places her palm against the burn, the size of a quarter, as though she knew it was there. I lower the bottle.

"Hey," she says, breathing the orangey smell of it up into my face. She moves the palm against me. Rubbing from side to side, the edges of her hand compress my nipples, which are hard and still sting from the cold. For a girl in the first year of college, she has an old face, narrow and worn. I see nothing in her features that resembles Doug and Jane Dean. She could be no relation to them. Her lips are thin, bluish, experimental. I think of the ache inside her, not so much a wound as the absence of something that had begun to settle its weight in the tight, cul-de-sac organs and make a place for itself, mapping out new paths for the circulation and digestion. Something created, wanted by the body, then expelled. What remain are the first adjustments, slowly undoing themselves.

I take her wrist in a solid grip and deliver it back to her body. "If you want to talk, okay. I'll sit and listen. But anything else, I'm not in the mood."

"It was just an idea," she says. "I'm sorry. Sometimes I just think it's what I need, like breakfast or a beer."

She watches me go back to the good chair. Outside the window the sky is darkening. I fix my eyes on a smudged location in the clouds beyond her shoulder. And suddenly we are settled in like an old, familiar pair. She stares at me, then turns and looks out the window in the direction of my spot in the clouds. You can take an isolated instant in time and freeze it, making anything out of it you want. The room is quiet and warm, and I feel we are two people perfectly in tune and without the need to ever speak. The

electric clock groans unevenly on the wall; the sweep hand strug-
gles, climbing up the bright red numbers. I could stand and go over
to her and put my hands on her narrow shoulders, and she might
reach up with one hand or two and cover mine. This can proceed
in any direction. We could stay together like this for a minute or
an hour, and then break apart. Or she could turn to me and say
something foolish or cruel in her flat, dull voice, and it would be
as though she never walked up those stairs at all—five minutes
after she leaves the room the memory is erased, and I am sleeping.

The window rattles from the wind. "My father likes you," she
says. "He really does. He looks for people to admire, the way they
live their life. He collects examples. There's always someone on
the top of his list, and right now you're it."

"He says so?"

"Yeah."

She stares at me, and I imagine her thinking about her father the
way I sometimes thought about mine: that he was out there in the
world like a good-sized rock hidden in the grass that I was mowing.
For most of the time he wouldn't be a factor, but then suddenly
the rock would get in between the blades and stop me cold, and I
would pitch forward, my chest bone ramming the smooth wooden
handle and my elbows wrenching back, chickenlike. And this would
be over in a second. I would bend down and take care of it and
go on and feel no lingering trouble from it. My father would go
back to being not much of a factor. I think of this because he was
exactly the kind of a man who always had someone he admired,
and talked about that person at length and what that person might
do in a certain situation. Neil hated this aspect of my father more
than I did. It made him ashamed. But slowly, as Neil got older, he
began to do the same thing himself, giving allegiance easily to
others.

"He says you know how to take care of yourself."

"I guess I do," I say. "He's right about that."

She nods and gets up from the window sill. "Okay," she says.
"Thanks for the audience."

She goes out the way she came, down the cold back stairs. I
listen to her entering the house again. The sound of her movements

shifts to the interior, and I hear her below me, now through the inside door, the one she could enter at any time, unimpeded.

I turn on the television and watch a line of women in chairs telling of how they kept up secret lives for years before they were discovered, or else confessed. One was a lesbian with a normal marriage, one was a prostitute with a normal marriage, one was a nun with a normal marriage, one was a woman married to two men in different cities, and one had pretended to be a man for the year and a half she was married to another woman, who never found out.

The audience, mostly women, are shown staring at these guests as though they don't believe such things are possible, but when the host goes up the aisles and lets the audience ask questions, it's obvious they would all like the chance to lead secret lives. When the questions come pouring down, the women on the stage listen courteously and smile. They look so happy to be there, as though their experiences with secrets were all completely satisfying and untroubled, and have led to this easy pleasure they show. Their answers are all to questions that sound like requests for the recipe— how did they do it, exactly? The five women go into great detail, the details sounding much the same from one to another, until finally the host asks one of them, the prostitute, "But isn't the *real* secret that you have to have a spouse who's about as dumb as a cinderblock?" And the camera comes in close on the prostitute as she pouts for a second, apparently considering that possibility. But then she says something that keeps everything from falling apart and the rest of the show from being completely pointless: "It's not so much that they're dumb. It's that they're really all just sweet enough to want to believe what we tell them. What they really are is *nice*."

And the audience bursts into loud applause. The camera goes from face to face on the stage, the women nodding and smiling, and then into the audience, where the women are also nodding. And then to the host, who nods and looks humbly put in his place, and seems just about sweet enough, nice enough, himself to believe anything he's told. The thought of there being a supply somewhere of truly nice husbands—husbands so trusting they could fail to detect a hard-to-manage double life—sweeps the applause along, and quickly the barriers break down between the audience and the guests, the way they often do at some point in all of these shows, and there is only love flowing everywhere, unrestricted, and it doesn't have to be explained. For the moment, there is nothing more to say.

"We'll be back after this," the host yells into the camera, nodding. The applause continues, mixing with music, then fading, and the commercials begin.

I get up from the chair and turn off the television. Then I go into the bedroom and lie down on the bed to take a nap.

I draw the thin, white knit blanket up over my knees and chest. A gust of wind hits the back of the house and rattles my window. The coldness leaks into the room and settles softly around my head and shoulders, searching for a welcome home.

On the fourth day of subbing for Joe LaMoine, I finish the route almost on time. The ache and fatigue are gone from my legs, and my heart and lungs are suddenly in synch—I'm not out of breath. No one comes to greet me at the door and remind me that I am late, and I imagine the mail falls through the slots at some of these houses with an unexpected shock, startling women on their sofas in the midst of groggy naps.

When I am parking my Jeep high on Church Street, near the top of Waban Hill, a police car races past me, heading up into the park, followed by a second cruiser and an ambulance. Mr. Gray has been discovered.

I continue delivering the mail, beginning with the house at the very edge of the park and descending Church Street for twenty houses or so, then crossing the street and working my way back up to where the Jeep is parked. A half-dozen houses from completing this loop, I see the paramedics come out of the trees with a dark green body bag sagging between them. They strap the bag on a long-legged stretcher which they slide into the back of the ambulance; the legs collapse so the stretcher can roll in easily on the ambulance floor.

By the time I am back at the Jeep, the ambulance has left and the police are threading a yellow crime-scene ribbon around and through the trees.

This is the first time I have ever been present to see the removal of one of my people. How strange it is to have one life come close to and mingle with the other. There is the fear that if the edges were somehow to intersect, a kind of conflagration could occur. I remember that Neil went through a time when he couldn't bear to have his whole meal put together on a single plate. It had to be meat on one plate, potatoes on another, vegetables on a third. He was almost thirteen. My mother catered to this and brought the smaller plates in one at a time. He wasn't ever ready for the second thing until he had finished with the first. During the period of this ritual my father would stare at Neil like a murderer.

"What is your problem?" he sometimes said.

"Never mind," my mother said.

One night Neil told me that he feared the mingling of things that were not alike. "If I see you go to put catsup on something," he said, "I want to stop you. I hate the sight of it. Catsup is not like anything else."

Until he recovered from this, for his benefit I ate my food plain. It was not such a terrible sacrifice. The length of the spell was only three months or so, after which Neil slowly began to allow the foods to be brought back together on his plate—first two things, then three or more. My mother believed it was a chemical imbalance that Neil either would or wouldn't get over.

"It has to do with his puberty," she said.

I see the yellow police ribbon cordoning off my secret life. The tape appears friendly and pleasant. The police are sometimes visible, sometimes hidden by the trees. They go in deeper. The ribbon weaves in and out of sight, its continuing deployment stretching and shifting the visible portions. I stand by the Jeep with Joe LaMoine's bag on my shoulder. I hear the policemen shout to each other. I watch the lights flashing on top of the cruisers.

Slowly the question comes to me: Why do they think this was a crime?

# NINE

÷

ON A WARM DAY EARLY IN MARCH, A DAY WHEN
the wind is out of the south and the temperature rises suddenly
into the middle fifties, the frozen seaweed thaws on a Rhode Island
beach and a college girl is out walking her year-old German shep-
herd dog off the leash. The dog runs up over the rim of a dune
and disappears. The girl doesn't see where he's gone and keeps on
walking along the sand, nearer the water, until she notices that the
dog is no longer with her. Then she turns around and retraces her
steps, whistling and calling. The dog is named Duke. When the
warm wind dies for a moment, the girl hears a strange commotion
and trudges up the slope of the dune. Inside it, in the middle of
the bowl of the dune, she sees Duke digging furiously. Behind him
is a growing pile of damp, darker sand. There is a shoe near the
top of the pile, new sand beginning to cover it. The girl goes over
the edge and down toward the dog.

"Duke?"

The dog keeps digging. He is positioned between the girl and
any revealing view of the object of his digging. The girl circles out
to the dog's flank to get a better look.

"Duke, what is it?"

She sees a ragged edge of pant, a sock in tatters around a tattered,
indistinguishable ankle. She goes closer with the halting tread of
someone who thinks she begins to know what she is finding—what
the dog has found for her.

"Duke?"

This was how it unfolded that the dog Duke, belonging to a girl named Libby Strobell, discovered Gene Fowler buried in the sand. I sit in front of the television. My teeth are slowly chewing on my lips, bottom then top, bottom then top. Already, in the late evening of the day on which this discovery takes place, the wind has swung around to the northwest and brought back the frigid wintertime Montreal express. Libby Strobell stands out in front of her dormitory and shivers in the bleaching light of a TV crew, worrying out loud to the reporter that dogs aren't really permitted in the dorms, and this is probably going to develop into a problem for her, "*even though Duke is a kind of a hero.*"

Earlier in the report they showed the body coming over the edge of the dune in a zipped-up bag that sagged between two paramedics exactly the way the bag that held Mr. Gray had done. Then they showed the fully excavated hole, pulling back to show the reporter talking about the as-yet-unknown identity of the victim, a white male thought to be still in his teens, and saying that the dental records of missing persons would be sought and compared with the teeth of the victim.

Now the camera pans away from Libby Strobell and pulls in tight on the reporter. "*An autopsy is in progress at this hour,*" he says, "*and Rhode Island State Police detectives say they are confident pathologists will be able to determine an exact cause of death.*" The face of a State Police spokesman, taped earlier, comes on the screen. "*Because of the cold winter months and the relatively preserving effects of it being buried in sand, say, as opposed to soil, this has slowed up the decomposition process on the body a lot. The body is in not too bad of a shape, even though we think it has probably been in there for a while. But we are definitely optimistic, yes.*"

Then the report cuts back to the live shot outside of the dormitory. The reporter exhales a dense cloud of cold-air vapor onto the microphone. "*So there you have it, Jack and Liz. For Libby Strobell and her dog Duke, a walk on the beach on a springlike day turned into a grisly encounter with murder. Back to you.*"

The anchorman thanks the reporter and turns to the weatherman, who sits beside him at the anchor desk, and says that "*it may have been springlike earlier in the day, but it sure isn't springlike now.*" And this is the point where I stand and begin to pace around the room.

I believe that someday I will hear from Tim. He will discover me. I have no doubt that he could close his eyes at any moment and picture me well enough to capture in his thoughts the location of the picture and go directly to it, like a psychic. He would find me in the pose he pictured me in, maybe sitting exactly as I am now, in my truck out in front of the post office, waiting for a song to end on the radio and staring through the windshield at Ferrin, who is walking toward the truck and waving at me.

"Hi," I say soundlessly, my mouth aimed out at Ferrin and forming the *H* and the *I*. The song continues. The hinge of my jaw creaks so that I can feel it deep in my right ear. Ferrin comes up beside and opens the door and gets in.

"You're gonna be late," she says.

"I'm waiting for this song."

"I like that one, too," she says. She taps her foot in the dark underneath the dash.

If Tim closed his eyes and pictured me now, he would see only me in the truck, not Ferrin. She would be invisible to him, like a vampire in the mirror. Likewise, I believe that if Tim were to come to find me he would be unseen by others and be visible only to me. On those occasions when I become afraid of what I've done, I often think of Tim rescuing me, coming in at some important last minute and taking me out with a stroke so surprising that no one could rise up and prevent it. He would be invisible and undetectable. The rescue operation would be carried out in absolute silence by Tim, who would not allow me to talk to him until we had achieved some level of safety that only he could determine. Then, as suddenly as he had appeared, he would be gone again.

The song ends. At the corner of the block snow swirls up in the shape of a man about to cross the street. I think of Tim taking form before my eyes as Ferrin tells me the song is over.

"Shouldn't we go in?" she says.

"Okay," I say, still staring at the coiling snow that suddenly blows apart and becomes nothing. She reaches across and lifts my nearby hand from the wheel. I feel my fingers go limp. "Okay," I say again. She scratches a nail across my palm.

I do Joe LaMoine's route as though it is mine. I believe I am bringing a new sense of style to the same streets that Joe LaMoine has served for many years. I go along the sidewalks deliberately choosing a left or right tangent based on what I suppose Joe LaMoine must have done, and doing exactly the opposite. If the steps to a certain porch have a single railing, I climb the side that has no railing. If the steps have two railings, I climb up the middle, touching nothing.

The route is mine.

I begin to hope that someone will come to the door to greet me. The more this happens, the more I will be able to say something of my own and be the different face that they slowly grow used to seeing. I wait for the first smile that comes from someone who recognizes me for myself and shows that she was expecting no one else. I hear the gruff dogs barking on the other sides of many doors—sometimes deep in their houses, beyond vestibules that are empty and cold and full of light. These dogs are getting to know my tread, a weight and pace that are different from Joe LaMoine's. I expect the barking will slowly disappear, except for the few hard cases. Most of the dogs will only lift their heads and not get up at all.

I inhabit the route. It becomes like a trance in which I am transformed into someone with only the sweetest intentions and can forget that there is anything else to my being. When I say that I make the route my own, I more likely mean that I make myself the route. I seem to absorb the streets and the houses and the slanting steps and the dull clacking sound of the brass mail-slot doors that fall back shut as the mail drops through. These things that are pure sensations bring the trance upon me. I walk up Church Street feeling good—opened up and included in life—exactly the opposite of the bitter frustration that Doug says comes to him from never being allowed inside the houses. To me, that barrier between myself and the houses is the beauty. I stop at the front door and slip something through and inside that disappears. And you would think that would be the end of it. But something still comes back to me in a kind of unexpected exchange that opens a picture in my mind of the people moving inside, or of the stillness of an empty house just waiting for something to suddenly occur. I can feel the throbbing of the television, like a heartbeat, which awakens in me the urge. And I am pleased then to turn away from the house, not to go in, to be able to turn down the urge the way I might turn down the television so that I could hear the voices of the Deans bickering below me in the house.

I wish that a person could come out into one of these air-lock vestibules and see me bent over, pushing through the mail, posing no threat of any kind, even smiling to myself the smile of being in this trance in which the urge behaves like one of those dogs that have finally grown used to my tread—lifting its head just briefly and then putting it down again.

For the detectives, things begin to fall into place. Autopsies of Mr. Gray and Gene Fowler turn up traces of the same rare poison found in the tissues of James K. Edge. The death of Mr. Gray is ruled a homicide. It's always said that police from different states and agencies don't cooperate easily, but they begin to show signs of at least talking to one another. The television news from Providence reports a press conference in Washington County, Rhode Island, where the district attorney mentions having been in contact with the Massachusetts State Police and the district attorney of Bristol County. I get the clear impression that these three deaths are soon to be linked. In the same press conference, the Washington County district attorney reveals that a match of dental records will soon be announced. "*I can't say anything more specific,*" he says, "*except that we are beginning to believe the crime may not actually have been committed in Rhode Island. We may have just been the dumping ground—the burying ground, I should say.*" Then he walks away from the microphones as people yell at him to answer more questions. And for a second there are just those empty, waiting microphones, the air above and beyond them. I imagine my own face being led up to these microphones, eyes half shut, people shouting, a police at both elbows, each with a firm hand wrapped like the blood-pressure cuff around each bicep.

A Boston station mentions that the State Police are following up on reports from Maine that a cross-country skier discovered a body in the woods, and that an autopsy showed the victim had been poisoned. *"We've sent an officer up to the town up there, yes,"* says a State Police spokesman whose face is beginning to seem familiar to me, who is in fact becoming one of the foreseen detectives who comes in and out of the small, smoky room in which they do not empty the two ashtrays, letting them both turn mountainous with my stubbed, bent cigarettes to impress me with the length of time I have been kept there without once being asked if I needed to go to the bathroom or wanted a glass of water.

I am fascinated with all of the news. The reported information hardly seems to fit together properly, and I wonder how much they are getting wrong—or else what I have forgotten. Some detective mentions footprints in the snow in the park where Mr. Gray had his tent, and that these footprints *"don't match the running shoes found on the feet of the decedent."* I have no recollection of his running shoes. I distinctly remember hard-toed, round-toed work shoes, scuffed and worn to an ashy blondness. But another station also reports about these running shoes. It bothers me so much to think that I could have remembered this detail incorrectly that I hardly give a thought to the second set of footprints the police have collected as evidence of my—of someone's—being there.

The New Bedford station runs an entire report devoted to the poison. Tim called it sedgewort, but the reporter interviews a historian and author of books on poisoning who calls it by a Latin name that I do not recognize, translating it to mean *"soft cudgel— because of the way it paralyzes the victim suddenly, but gently, without undue pain, inducing a pleasant sleep before it brings death. It was used in medieval times by wives to kill their husbands and, less often, by husbands to kill their wives. It would only appear that the victim had died in his sleep."*

The reporter asks why the poison is considered rare if it's been around for such a long time.

*"Because it derives from a variety of fungus that is itself quite*

rare," says the poison expert. *"Even experienced mushroom hunters can go a lifetime without ever seeing this fungus. It grows between the bark and the wood of decaying trees, once the bark has begun to separate. Under only the right conditions of climate— fifty to fifty-five degrees and a relative humidity higher than eighty percent—the fungus appears virtually overnight and lasts only two to three days before degrading into a custardy soil. It has a reddish, mottled crust and a white tissue. The crust must be scraped from the tissue, which then must be minced, dried, baked and powdered to yield the poison. In its powdered form it is extremely dangerous to handle because it can be absorbed through the skin."*

A Boston station sends a reporter to Maine and embarrasses the Massachusetts State Police by getting a local police chief there to identify the rare poison by its proper Latin name, verify that it was what killed the man found propped against the tree by the cross-country skier, and shake his head vigorously when asked if he'd yet been contacted by any Massachusetts officials. *"Nope,"* he says. *"Not a one."*

On the evening of the day Gene Fowler is positively identified as the Rhode Island victim, I am standing in front of the television, moving around it at various angles, when Doug knocks at the inside door. I can hardly sit still for a second now in the presence of the television when it's on. The beady bright screen is an agitation that drives me into movement. As I move in an arc, the light changes. A reflection glides across the screen and off the edge. I expect the ruddy faces at any minute to start to use my name in their reports, to say that I am the same Vann Dothan Siegert who lives in the Dean residence in Bledsoe, and to flash my picture up in a little square box in the field of blue beyond the shoulder of the anchor. It doesn't even have to be the news—suddenly I will be there for all to see—just a figure standing quietly in front of the camera or moving restlessly through my rooms—and everyone will know my innermost self. All the truth about me will be telepathically conveyed in a glance, leaking out from my eyes and pores as an odor, a heat, a field of charged atoms, a stream of invisible information. People will just know. There is no concealing.

My mother said it best: "Anyone can see right into you." She meant herself, but she also meant me. "If you don't believe it, just look at your father." Which, as usual, was a joke, since he wasn't anywhere to be seen. She walked away from me, laughing. She would always seem to leave the bathroom door open whenever she went in there. First I heard the rustling sounds of clothing being undone and arranged; then I heard the urine spattering upon the water, the agitation of the water growing, growing, until the hiss was a roar and I heard words hiding within the sound. Pairs of words that seemed to belong together: flowers, couches; weather, waves; pails, showers.

"Vanny?" And the sound ended. "You can come in here if you want," she said. "I hate like hell to be alone." Her voice reached around the corner and into the hall, seeming to carry with it the sour, coffeelike smell of what she had just finished doing.

Doug knocks again.

"Just a second." I turn off the television. Suddenly the silence is like the end of life, and I am frozen here in one position, with the tip of my finger still touching the stubby button that pushes the television off and pulls it on.

"It's me," says Doug. I am struck by the fact that you can never be alone that someone can't suddenly reach out and get you.

I go to the door and open it. The light pours out onto the dark landing. Doug squints and smiles. The sharp, salty smell of the Dean dinner surges past Doug and in through the door.

"Did you hear about Gene?" he says.

"I did," I say. "Come in." I turn aside and leave just enough room for Doug to slide by me.

"I can't believe it," he says. "A guy like that."

"I know," I say.

"I mean, I knew he was dead. I *believed* he was dead, but . . ."

"Yeah," I say. I shake my head.

"It's got to be some sicko."

"Have a seat," I say.

Doug goes and takes the good chair, the comfortable chair. He stares at the silent television. I follow his eyes and expect the screen will suddenly awaken with my image on it, and Doug will sit forward and watch me, both of me—the TV image and the person standing nervously in front of him in the room.

"Jane is still on the phone with Lois," he says. "We haven't even eaten dinner yet." He takes out his pipe and passes it back and forth between his two hands, as though neither hand can decide which hand will finally hold it.

"It's good they had the funeral and didn't keep up any false hopes," I say. Doug nods.

"I guess," he says. "It's what they wanted, both of them, Paul and Lois. We've all heard about those other kinds of parents. The stories are unbelievable. All these kids, and the parents are waiting for years. In their heads, the kid gets older . . . Poor Gene."

"You said it," I say.

Jane calls up the stairs. Doug's name floats lightly into my rooms like a fragile bird that has flown too high. I barely hear it, but he stands like someone launched.

"I guess it's dinner," he says. He leaves quickly without saying anything. Halfway down the stairs to the second floor he turns and looks up at me. I look at him. Light from a hall lamp falls on the bottom part of his face, splitting him as though a crack has formed. I don't know what he's thinking.

The next morning I wake up with Karen standing over me, looking down. When I was a boy I slept in a forest for almost a week one summer. In my memory Spokane is surrounded by trees. From any point in the city you could walk to a dense forest, and the walk would take no more than fifteen minutes. The forests sprang up in the midst of a neighborhood and twisted through it, behind the backs of houses, into shallow ravines with dry brooks covered over in brittle leaves. I wandered away from home and stayed away for that whole week. My father was in town and sat still in his chair staring at the worn knees of his olive chinos. He was like half a moon waning to nothing. My mother would bring him a drink and set it down on the shiny oak table by the chair. He would turn his head and stare deeply into the drink, low and amber, with ice cubes floating lazily, still twisting slowly from the motion of the drink having been set down. In the silence we all heard the drink breathing, settling, the ice cracking. My mother stood by the table like a statue, waiting for something.

"You're welcome," she said.

Then his gaze returned to the knees of his trousers. I sat on the couch with Neil and waited for my father to say something. Neil believed that some important statement was building up inside him. And it was true that my father had the look of a man who was pondering difficult questions. I could see how Neil might think that something was about to issue forth. But it never did. He sat that way all day. What looked like tension in his forehead remained in place, slowly becoming frozen and permanent, no longer a sign of tension. My mother refused to allow the television to be turned on. When I cornered her in the pantry and asked, she whispered that what she wanted was for the total silence of herself and her sons and the house to punish him back for being this way.

"He is a failure," she said. "Your father can't sell anymore. And he knows it."

In the late afternoon, when Neil was reading a comic book and my mother was up in the bathroom showering, I walked to the back door and out to the garage. On a shelf in the back I found a dusty old cloth sleeping bag, rolled and tied. I took it with me. I went over the fence behind the garage and through the yard of the neighbors. I walked straight to the nearest forest and in. I stayed there for a week. I met three hoboes who kept me with them and gave me food. At night they tried to scare me by talking about the things they'd like to do to me. But they never tried, and I was never truly afraid of them. They drank and fought with each other and left me alone. Their names were Gabe, Dex and Saul. I had no idea that there were still hoboes.

During the days they went their separate ways into town. I stayed in the woods, going just to the edge of the trees and looking out at the traffic shooting past, or watching the backs of houses, hearing the radios playing inside and watching mothers in shorts and untucked shirts fill plastic wading pools with dark green hoses.

One afternoon Gabe brought back a newspaper with my picture on the front page. He threw it down and told me to get lost.

"You're a missing kid," he said. "There's people looking for you. I'm not gonna do no kidnap time." The other two stared at the picture and then at me, repeating this several times. Slowly they gathered their stuff together and rolled it up and drifted away. I sat in the dirt and watched them go.

That night I slept a perfect sleep, lying on my back and closing my eyes and conking out in less than a minute. The night seemed to pass instantly. I woke up in exactly the same position and saw a girl staring down at me. For a moment she appeared to be curious and disbelieving that I was actually there. Then she smiled and hugged herself.

"I found you," she said, almost in a whisper. "You're Vanny."

Then she turned and started screaming, in a shrill voice that frightened and annoyed me, "I found him! I found him! I found him!" And suddenly there were dozens of people swirling around my sleeping bag, leaning close to me, asking questions and beginning to touch me and pull me out, and deliver me. There were photographers. There were police. There were men with microphones. I was brought home on a wave of triumph, carried like a trophy. I was the human thrill of rescue that everyone who had helped search for Gene Fowler longed to know. I was all of the possibilities gone right. My mother and father and Neil blinked back their tears on the front steps and said all the things that people say: "We're glad he's back. We thank God. We thank all the people who looked for him. We're just glad he's all right." And then I was hugged by my mother and a cheer went up, and slowly the world emptied of all these happy strangers. Everyone went home. My mother called a doctor, who came and examined me from head to toe, touching and probing and asking questions in a soft voice, the voice of someone who pretends he doesn't care what the answers are. "I don't remember," I said. Or "I forget." Or else I didn't say anything. He left, shutting the door softly. Later my father came in and stood at the foot of my bed and just stared at me silently, with the same expression of permanent dismay with which he had stared at the knees of his pants.

I once knew the name of the girl who found me, but I forgot it. It began with an *S*, an *S* sound, possibly a soft *C*.

Karen smiles and lowers herself to the edge of the bed. It amazes and confuses me to find myself suddenly not alone when I have expected to be.

"What are you doing here?" I say.

"I'm leaving," she says. "I'm going back to school. Mom is driving me to the airport. I wanted to say good-bye."

"Good-bye," I say.

She stares at her hands. She looks nervous. "I wanted to thank you for kicking me out," she says. "I was going to let you fuck the sadness out of me. Afterwards I would have been sorry. I thought that if someone fucked it into me, then maybe . . . But it was definitely always there. I know it was. It would still be there even if we'd fucked. It still *is* there."

She looks around the room. I draw the covers to my throat. She stands up. The bed rises, shudders and settles. Outside, I hear the car engine start.

"Gotta go," she says. "Good luck." She reaches down and puts a hand on my leg and squeezes. "I'm sorry I woke you up."

"Good-bye," I say. She lifts the hand and leaves. Soon I hear the outside door open and close. I hear her feet on the stairs, sharp, echoing.

An amazing thing happens overnight. A story more horrible and baffling than the apparently connected poisonings suddenly drives them from the television and newspapers, almost without a trace. A white suburban man named Boyd Little who had claimed a black robber shot and killed his pregnant wife Sherry and unborn child in downtown Boston, while critically wounding him, now turns out to have done the shootings himself. He had a girlfriend; he needed money; he was cold and empty and evil. The city of Boston—the entire region—has gone completely crazy with a hunger for every fact about this story. The black community is enraged at the slander and racism that arose from the evil lie of the husband, the true killer.

I pace in front of the television and see faces that are not mine, that bear no resemblance to me. I have been given peace and continued anonymity by this other killer, who killed himself by jumping from a bridge over Boston Harbor when he learned that he was soon to be arrested and charged with the murders.

In my mind's eye I see my own detectives fleeing out of the room in which they are holding me, leaving me alone to feel the air stop moving, the door left unlocked, unclosed, behind them. They are gone. I get up and leave. I walk unnoticed down the hall, down the wide steel steps, my feet clanging loudly, and out the door at the bottom of the steps, onto a side street. Cars are rushing by with blue lights flashing. No one cares about me anymore.

I can almost stop pacing in front of the television. I put on my postal uniform and heat water for coffee on the hotplate. I settle back in my chair and drink the coffee and watch the breathless news. There is nothing about the three linked poisonings. Boats are shown with divers falling backwards into the harbor. Then the body of the husband and killer is shown being brought onto the boat from the water. He wears white sneakers and blue jeans. He killed his pregnant wife.

I get up to go to work. A leader from the black community is shouting into microphones: *"When a wife is killed, who's the one who most likely did it? The HUSBAND! That's the way it always is in America. Every forty-three minutes, someone pops his wife. So, why were the Boston police out rousting every African-American male in Roxbury? Why were they out invading apartments in the housing projects like soldiers in Panama looking for Noriega? I'll tell you why . . ."*

I turn off the television. I feel light-headed and suddenly safe again. Some wheel has turned somewhere and rolled me back into the darkness, where I need to be. I leave for work, smiling, relieved. I open the door to the back stairs, and there is Doug on the landing, his hand hanging high in the air, poised to knock.

"Hi, Vann," he says. His forehead is sweating, but the stairwell is cold.

"Doug," I say, surprised.

"Can I ask a favor?"

"Okay," I say.

"Can I borrow your truck?"

"My truck?"

"Yeah. Jane took the car to take Karen to the airport, and I need to go up to Taunton to the dentist."

"I guess," I say.

"I can take you to work."

"Okay. I guess. I'm not gonna need it."

"And I'll drop it off after."

"Okay."

"Great. Thanks." He turns, and I follow him down the steps.

I drive to the post office slowly, savoring the changed air of public interest. The radio news talks about nothing but the Little case. When the news ends the DJ announces a call-in for listeners to voice their opinions on the motive. The first caller appears instantly.

"*You're on the air, Worcester,*" says the DJ.

"Some case," says Doug.

"Unbelievable," I say.

"*He had to have a girlfriend,*" says the caller. "*The guy had to.*"

"*I'm with you, caller,*" says the DJ.

"*He's in some jeweler's last week buying necklaces,*" says the caller. "*So, who is he buying necklaces for? Some broad. I'm telling you, Dick, this is some cold bastard.*"

"*Okay, Worcester, thank you. Brockton, you're on the air.*" I hear the DJ push a button.

"Unbelievable," says Doug.

Brockton says the wife was carrying the baby of someone else, and Little found out about it.

"*Do you know this for a fact?*" says the DJ.

"*What do you mean?*" says Brockton.

"*Is this something you know? Do you have some way of knowing? Are you acquainted with someone in the case? Hello, Brockton?*"

"*I don't know what you're asking me, Dick. That's why I hesitate here. What I'm saying is this. A guy finds out the baby isn't his. So what does he do?*"

"*You tell me, caller . . .*"

"*Ba-boom,*" says Brockton.

"*Okay.*" Click. "*Scituate, you're next.*"

We pull up at the post office. I do not turn the engine off. The heat is finally warming the cab. I put my hands in front of the vents.

"Okay," I say. I look at Doug and think of him sitting in the chair at the dentist. I run my tongue over the soft spot near the point of one of my canines, behind. It's soft, but it doesn't hurt yet. "Good luck," I say.

He nods but doesn't look at me.

I get out and he slides across.

"See you later," he says. "Thanks a lot for the truck."

I slam the door, trying to think if the glove compartment is locked. It doesn't matter; he has the key anyway. If he wants to get in, he's in. I am trusting fate. I go around the back of the truck and pass my hand across the tailgate's cold, raised letters. The truck pulls away. Suddenly, everyone in the world knows everything about the Little case.

Inside the post office, there is no one talking about anything else. Little this, Little that. The animal. The creep. Yesterday, it was the poisonings. But the poisonings were a mystery, and the Little case is a mystery solved. Everyone knows enough to be an expert. Everyone knows all they need to know. I notice the difference from yesterday: When people talk about a true mystery, they talk softly; when they talk about a crime that's been solved, they talk loudly. The noise of it rings from the shiny green walls. The routes are being sorted into cardboard-and-plastic trays. A huge card is circulating for Joe LaMoine. I sign it down low in a corner: "I'm taking good care of your route. So take good care of yourself. V. Siegert." The writing is cramped and dark and looks like a fence is drawn invisibly around it.

"What did you write?" says Ferrin. She leans her shoulder against mine. She reads it out loud.

"That's nice," she says. "I'm next." She takes the pen from me and licks the tip and looks up at the lights. Her eyes are blue and gray with dark flecks of floating minerals. She bends down to the counter and forms swift letters that are low and wide, that seem to have been crushed beneath a falling sky: "If you don't hurry back, this girl's gonna die of a broken heart. No pun intended. Get well soon, Joe—Ferrin."

I am sorting mail into my trays. The route goes together quickly.

My hands pull the pieces into streets. Each number equals a kind of dim picture that grows more complete by the day. Tomorrow I will see not just the low fence, but the color of the fence, the shape of the spindly bush behind it. Next week I will know the jagged cracks in the corners of the large rectangular windows on the wraparound porch. I will know the patch of blistered paint on the blue garage and the dull, heavy rhythm of the exercise tape that plays and plays inside the house as I am climbing the endless flights of steps. I place the numbers in order. I walk the route in my head, rehearsing. Already, I have found some of the holes in the soffits that the squirrels go in and out of.

I imagine that I have seen hundreds of things that escaped the attention of Joe LaMoine.

Ferrin slowly closes the card for Joe and moves away from me. "Who hasn't signed this?" she hollers. No one answers.

On Church Street, halfway up Waban Hill, at a green-shingled house with white shutters and a low-sloping red-tile roof, I have a certified letter to deliver. Mrs. John H. Chenier. I ring the bell; the round button lights, and I hear a murky chiming. Then I hear the sound of someone moving closer to me. The inside door opens, sucking cold air in with a hiss under the rubber strip along the bottom edge of the storm door. There is a young woman standing inside with a baby on her shoulder. She looks at me without opening the door. Her eyes widen.

"Certified letter," I say through the glass. "Chenier." I hold up the fat white envelope with the pale green card attached. She opens the door. Her face is familiar, but I can't place it.

"I need a signature," I say. I detach the card along its perforations. I get the pen from my pocket, but I can see she will have great difficulty signing unless she does something with the baby.

"Never mind," I say. I hand her the letter. "Just tell me what your name is, and I'll sign the card myself."

"Kathryn Chenier," she says. She looks at the letter. "It's the goddamn car insurance," she says. "I hate these people."

I write "Kathryn" slowly along the tiny line and have hardly enough room left for the "Chenier," which goes past the boundary of the space provided.

"Thanks," she says. She looks at me again, and I remember her. She is the one who saw me following Mr. Gray up toward the park at the top of Waban Hill. She pulls the storm door shut and backs deeper into the house and closes the inside door. She never takes her eyes off me. I feel held tight by her. All the while the baby hasn't moved a muscle. I hold the green card in my hand. The weight of Joe LaMoine's leather bag shifts on my shoulder.

I find my truck parked outside the post office in exactly the spot where Doug had promised to leave it. A piece of an obvious note sticks out of the ashtray. I extract it and unfold it. "Keys under mat in front of passenger seat," it reads. "Thanks."

I lift up the mat and find the keys. I check the glove compartment; it's locked. I drive home in the dusk. The days are getting longer. I am arriving back at the Deans' without having to turn on the headlights. I pull the truck into the back and see that the Deans' Chevrolet is not there. When I go inside, I see that a light is on in the kitchen, but the kitchen is empty. I climb the stairs to my rooms.

I turn on the television and watch the news. At first I stand and pace. Then, slowly, I move backwards toward the chair and down into its softness, settling. On the news the Little case takes up all the time. The weather and sports are compressed into shortened segments that one of the sportscasters complains about. *"Because of the latest sensationalism, we won't have time tonight for our regular 'Student Body' feature. Maybe we'll get it in sometime when all this stuff dies down. Chet?"* I switch from channel to channel, but I see nothing on the poisonings. They have disappeared.

I fall asleep in the comfortable chair. I wake up when someone knocks at the door that leads down into the house.

"Vann?"

Doug. The television shows a college basketball game. The play-by-play announcers are silent, but the players' sneakers squeal against the varnish of the bright court.

"Vann?"

"Coming."

I go to the door and open it. Doug looks disheveled, strange.

"Jane's missing," he says. He comes in. "She never came back from taking Karen to the airport." Doug stares at the basketball game.

"Maybe she decided to go with Karen," I say. "Last minute kind of thing."

"No." He shakes his head slowly. "I called Karen. Jane waited with her inside the terminal until she got her ticket and went down to the gate. Karen looked back through the metal-detector thing and waved. And that's it."

"Would she be visiting someone up in Boston? Maybe staying over?"

"Maybe. But don't you think she'd call and let me know?"

"Yeah . . . But maybe she told you before, and you just forgot. Have you called around to some of her friends?"

"Nobody's seen her," says Doug. He paces in front of the television. "Nobody. I'm worried."

Time runs out in the half as one of the players sinks a miraculous shot from in back of the half-court line. But an official goes leaping down the floor flinging his hands out sideways above his head to wave off the shot because the clock had already expired. Several players, including the one who made the shot, rush the official and jump up and down, but the official just turns and walks away, keeps turning and walking, turning and walking, until the players give up and leave the court.

"I guess you should call the police," I say.

"I know. I'll do that next," says Doug.

And something in the way Doug says the word "next"—as though it indicates some items set down on a list and crossed off one by one—draws me to the haunted look in his face, a grayness that is hopeless and guilty and frail. He lingers in front of the television as the game gives way to an advertisement for cars. His shoulders are narrow and curved around to the front. Not once has he looked directly at me. And I think that, of course, he has murdered Jane. And I know that if I called his dentist in Taunton, I would learn that he had skipped his appointment or had never had an appointment or, if he had had one, that it was much later in the day than he led me to believe when he borrowed my truck.

He drove the truck to Boston and murdered Jane, and she is somewhere cold and folded up and waiting to be found. It is only a question of how long it will take. And this is the process that Doug will set in motion when he calls the police, which he is delaying doing.

"Have you tried the hospitals?" I say.

"Do you think I should?"

"I do," I say. "You can never tell. Maybe there was an accident."

"I'll do that. Thanks."

I put my hand on Doug's shoulder. "I'm sorry," I say. "I hope it works out."

He moves slowly away from my hand. Am I the contagion of what Doug has done today? If I had never come to this house would Jane Dean be alive downstairs on the couch, doing the puzzle while Doug watched the basketball and puffed a cloud of sweet smoke around himself? Does Doug think that I have held his hand through all of this and have silently helped him form the plot that he carried out?

Halftime brings the opportunity of a news update. Doug pauses at the door and turns back to watch. His face is pale and squeezed.

*"State Police report that the body of a woman presumed to have died of a drug overdose late last fall contains traces of a rare poison that was also found in the bodies of three other victims of a presumed serial killer operating in Bristol County. Cheryl Casper, the Dartmouth woman whose body was found in an outdoor toilet at a rest area off route 495 near Fall River, was last seen in a Fall River bar in the company of a man who, police say, would at this point be their logical suspect in the serial murders. Police are pursuing leads that they hope will result in a physical description of the killer, who poisons victims with a lethal paralytic drug.*

*"In a related development, Maine State Police confirmed this afternoon that they are treating the homicide of a York Beach resident as the work of the Bristol County killer, bringing the total of known victims to five. Guy Hudson will report live from Maine on the nightcast.*

*"And Veronica LaPierre will have the latest bizarre turn in the Little case. Join us after the game."*

Doug sways in the doorway like a drunken man, his eyes still stuck to the screen, his heart still pumping hard at the words: "*the body of a woman . . .*" I feel the cooler air flooding up from the house below, Doug's house, the currents bending around and past him, keeping no secrets. This is a changed air—differently thin. It has no smell but carries with it the total emptiness of all the rooms in the house—all the rooms except mine, which is full of chemistry and knowledge, swirling. The cool thin air mixes in.

Doug and I are alone together tonight, breathing shallow, both of us watching the television, both of us waiting in fear.

# TEN

⁎

IF EVER THERE WAS A BAD TIME AND PLACE TO kill your wife, Doug Dean picked the very worst. With the Little case in full swing and the city of Boston feeling duped and guilty, any wife found dead in the trunk of her car, in the shadow of a tree on a street in a neighborhood near the airport, was bound to bring her husband into the brightest light.

I sit with Doug in the dark living room. We are waiting. He calls it keeping him company, but all I am to him is another organism with a beating heart, sharing the air. We do not speak. It's a Sunday morning. He has the television on without the sound. Cartoons and ads for bright sugared cereals and dolls. The TV is the third organism, winking and struggling—pleading to have its sound turned up. Doug smokes his pipe and stares into space. The silence in the room is brooding and tense. He hasn't spoken in an hour. His last words to me persist in the air like a jet trail, waiting for a swift current to blow them apart: "I wonder where she is," he said, but without the force of genuine curiosity. The words seem to float from place to place—across the mantel, around the pipe rack and curling over to the television. They caress the screen like fog and drift down to the dark blue carpet, hovering and sniffing. Then they sweep up to the valance over the picture-window curtains. Later, they repeat the route.

This is a vigil. I listen to my own breathing. The only other sounds have been the pipe lighter hissing to life every five or ten minutes or so. Or the clink of him setting the pipe in the large, clear glass ashtray. With the pipe set aside, his hands founder and search, kneading his knees and rubbing his elbows, or gripping the arms of the heavy chair. He hasn't confessed to me; I haven't confronted him.

I stare at Tweety and Sylvester. Tweety climbs a ladder up to a tiny helicopter. Sylvester follows. Tweety flies the helicopter over the yard of Butch, the bulldog, who is asleep half in and half out of his doghouse. Before Sylvester can make it to the top of the ladder, Tweety pushes a button on the helicopter control panel labeled "Ladder Release." Sylvester falls from a tremendous height and lands on the head of Butch. Butch chases Sylvester. The fur flies. Tweety watches from the helicopter.

Outside, when a car drives slowly by or a door slams somewhere, Doug snaps to and becomes alert. But when the telephone rings he doesn't move a muscle, like a deaf man. I rise to go get it, and he tells me, "Never mind." The ringing of the telephone erases the words of an hour before, but the ringing itself now hangs in the room with us, repeating and repeating.

Time passes slowly. I get up and go to the window. A tiny bit of snow floats in the air. The flakes are small and far, far apart, and some of them seem to rise more than fall. Doug coughs. I turn and stare at the back of his head. He reaches for the pipe in the ashtray. I hear the lighter come out and click and hiss. The smoke begins to rise and spread, forming a familiar pattern—seeking the ceiling, which is yellowish and darkened just above his chair.

I hear a sound outside. A black sedan without hubcaps comes down the street. It slows in front of the house and stops. Two men get out and stretch. Cops.

"Doug," I say.

The two doors slam—*whump, whump.*

"Somebody's here."

I hear Doug get up. I hear him set the pipe down in the ashtray. The two men come up the walk slowly. One reaches out his hand and feels the snow and says something. The other looks up. But they don't stop walking. They are both white men. I turn and look at Doug. He stands in a spot deep in the room where he can see the front door without being seen from outside of it. When I am delivering the mail I imagine that sometimes people do exactly what Doug is now doing, wanting not to be seen by the mailman to be just waiting.

The bell rings. Doug stands still, hardly breathing.

"Doug."

"It's Jane," he says. "Something's happened."

The bell rings again. Too soon.

"Doug," I say. "Do you want me to get it?"

"No," he says, and I see him begin to come forward to receive the news that he looks so frightened to hear but already knows.

I stay out of sight.

Doug opens the door. I hear the bright, cold sound of the outside fill the dark hall.

"Mr. Dean?"

"Yes."

"Douglas Dean?"

"Yes."

"I'm Detective Sergeant Pate, Boston Police. This is Detective Creech."

There's a pause, but Doug doesn't say anything. Or maybe he only nods.

"Ah, there's sure no good way to say this, sir . . . The body of a woman that we have reason to believe is your wife has been found in the trunk of your car, a car registered to you. Up in East Boston, sir. On Falcon Street. We're sorry to have to be the one."

And there is only this continuing silence in which the cold air pours steadily into the house, around the corner to where I am standing perfectly still and listening, my hand on the top of a warm radiator.

"I'm sorry, sir," says the detective who hasn't yet spoken. Creech.

"Are you sure?" says Doug. "It's Jane?"

"We will need you to positively identify the body, sir," says Creech. "Until then . . . No, we can't be completely sure."

"Then maybe . . . ," says Doug.

"But we don't have any good reason to think it's not," says the first detective, Pate.

"Oh, Jesus," says Doug. And I think that he is about to perform his sudden grief, and will sink to the floor and huddle himself and shake. But the cops don't let him get started.

"We can drive you up right now and bring you back after," says Creech.

"That's right," says Pate. "That's really the best thing. You can just sit in the back and not have to think about driving."

"Okay," says Doug, in a voice that is meek and awestruck. I hear him beginning to like the two cops, and I know that I should warn him. But I do not move a muscle. These are *my* detectives; I recognize them. They have that false politeness and that way of seeming to mean no harm and of seeming to regret that they are intruding on and interrupting the straight-moving line of your life. But in fact that is what they enjoy. They like the sight of someone suddenly not knowing what to say or how to behave, and that they can powerfully offer this degree of unmeant kindness that will never be seen through as insincere by a certain kind of person that they are trained to recognize. Someone like Doug.

They are my detectives. They are only temporarily assigned to Doug, and I do not wish to meet them now and have them turn their thoughts to me. I stand like a statue. My eyes search the room for mirrors or other surfaces that might reflect me out into the hall where they are standing. I see that I am safe.

"Let me get my coat," says Doug.

"We'll be out in front," says Pate. "Just come out when you're ready, sir. Take your time."

"Thank you, officers," says Doug.

The cops go out the door and down the walk. Doug closes the door. Instantly, the warmth of the house recovers; all of the cold air that has drifted in is swiftly canceled out as if it meant nothing. Doug walks in slow motion through the front hall toward the back of the house where the closet is. He seems to float.

"Doug," I say. He stops and turns around. He resembles my father sleepwalking.

"Jane is dead," he says in a dreamy way.

"I'm sorry, Doug," I say.

He shakes his head. "I can't believe it," he says. "I can't believe it."

And for the first time I think that maybe he didn't do it. Then he turns and goes to the closet door and brings out a dull green parka.

"I've got to go identify her," he says, putting it on.

After zipping the coat, he stands in the hall and stares at me with a blank expression on his face, his eyes not blinking.

"I'm sorry, Doug."

"I'll have to call Karen," he says. "Jesus." Then he moves forward to the door and takes the handle and goes out. I stand by the radiator and watch Doug make his way down the walk to the black sedan. I take care not to move. I don't want to draw the eyes of the cops away from Doug and up to the house. Pate opens the door for Doug and holds it, shutting it once Doug is safely inside. Then Pate gets in, and the car does a three-point turn in the street and heads back the way it came, slowly. I watch it out of sight. I continue to stand very still while considering the fact that when Detective Pate closed the door on Doug he turned his gaze quickly back to the house—the clapboard front, the picture window, the unmoving shadow of my arm and shoulder within—and he looked at it steadily, deeply, carefully, as if to show me something about himself. I believe he knew, in some animal way, that I was here. He marked me.

Sunday, after Doug has gone, becomes a day of rest for me. I spend it enclosed in my rooms. Wind rattles the windows, a dry, wooden rhythm. The snow thickens and thins. The neighborhood whitens. I roam both rooms. The house below me is quiet; I am its only life, confined to the very top.

I leave the television on. Cartoons give way to religion, a tall man in a cobalt blue suit who knows the strength of his eyes and has the camera deliberately come in close and hold them tight as his mouth moves below unnoticed. Eyes are the human center of gravity. There are mostly two kinds of people: the ones whose eyes absorb light, and the ones whose eyes give it off. But there is a third kind, very rare, that can do both at the same time; the light pours in and out simultaneously, defying nature and making the eyes seem to glow. This preacher has that gift and takes advantage of it. I stare at the screen. The choir hums and sways behind him in a blur—bright blue collars, white gowns. I have no idea what he is saying. My chest tingles; I feel the will go out of me. Then the camera suddenly pulls away, sweeping back into the depths and heights of the enormous church, and he is just a patch of blue on the altar, swaying and losing his power over me. My heartbeat slows, and I begin to hear the words of the choir: "In my father's house there is no dark, there is no dark, there is no dark."

Inside me, the urge to go forth begins to stir, and I wonder immediately where it has been that I have not felt it in a while. I stare at the window; snow scratches the air, swirling and thick. The urge grows in my stomach, warm and strong, and I think that the blue-suited preacher in some way has brought it to life. But there is no way to know.

"What can I do?" I say. There is nothing I can do. Its power is absolute and irresistible. I could walk down the stairs like my sleeping father and go out into the world with a sleeper's readiness to show no resistance to biology as it works itself through—as I have always let it do. I stand up from the soft chair and go to the window. I look down at the snow in the bed of my truck and prepare in my mind to start the engine and brush the snow from the windows.

"What can I do?" I say again. And then the urge simply dies down to nothing, like a dog that decided it was going to get up but then thought better of it and put its head back down and closed its eyes.

I encountered my first urge at what age? Seventeen? When Tim discovered me, could he have suspected that I was experienced? Probably he gave it no thought at all. He stared down at my face and wiped the mist and sweat off my forehead and saw that my eyes, when they opened, absorbed all the light in the room.

"My name is Tim," he said. "I have your medicine."

One Saturday when I was seventeen I hitchhiked from Spokane to Vancouver. On the north side of Everett a man named Avery picked me up in his Oldsmobile. He was pleasant and talkative and said he was a salesman. He pointed over his shoulder to several sample cases in the backseat. He said they were filled with electronic parts that he repped for a dozen manufacturers, including the Japanese and Dutch.

"We Americans are the best whiz-bang inventive geniuses," Avery said. "But those Japanese really know how to make things. And the Dutch know how to design."

He described what the parts were for, that they were used in radios and tape recorders, electric shavers, televisions, toys.

"You'd be surprised how much I sell to toy makers. A lot of stuff for dolls. But if I opened those cases up, you wouldn't be able to tell what went into what. An untrained eye. Sometimes I can't even tell myself. The pieces are getting more and more the same. And smaller. Incredibly small. Something the size of your thumbnail is about as much smarts as needs to go into a walkie-talkie. A tenth of an ounce where it used to be a pound. A little yellow nugget of enameled crap with a tiny number on it."

Avery was a careful driver, not fast, not slow. In this way he reminded me of my father. Anyone who drives for his living finally reaches a level of comfort in being on the road. Nothing ever bothered my father when he drove. The car just floated beneath him. He touched the steering wheel lightly, with his fingertips, and looked out ahead—half squinting, half smiling, as though a joke was running through his mind. He could have been sitting at home on the couch with his feet up on the coffee table, watching *I Love Lucy*. Avery was like this, too—relaxed. His Oldsmobile was a place. I let him talk and hardly said anything in reply. If he looked over at me, I would shake my head in wonder and say "Jeez" or "That's really something." He didn't need much encouragement. He was someone who was used to doing most of the talking. His voice swam around the inside of the car. It was a damp, chilly fall, and the windows were rolled up. There was a sweet, slightly sharp smell in the car, and I thought that it must have come from the stuff in the sample cases. I was sure that it did.

Avery began to ask me questions. How old was I? Was I running away? What sports did I like? Was I hungry? Did I think the war was right or wrong?

All of a sudden, I had to both talk and listen to him. But I answered his questions politely and as briefly as I could, thinking that he would either be satisfied with short answers or would get the message that I didn't much feel like talking. Unfortunately, he had an inexhaustible supply of questions, many of them having no connection to the ones that had come before, and some of them being a lot like questions on a personality test.

"Are you comfortable being on your own?"

"I guess so," I said.

"When you close your eyes and think of home, what do you see?"

"A door."

"Just a door?"

"That's it." A silence.

"Do you follow baseball?"

"No."

"Do you follow any sport?"

"No."

We stopped for lunch in Bellingham. Avery insisted that he would treat and told me to order anything I liked. I got poached whitefish with a yellowish sauce and a side order of hot potato salad with the skins still on. I separated the fish into flakes, slowly, spreading the meal across the pale blue plate and hardly eating it. He ate his own lunch much too fast, greedily, as though there would never be another.

"Is the fish good?"

"Yes," I said, looking at his empty plate, streaks of catsup. "You can have some of mine, if you want."

"No thanks."

I never formed a plan to kill Avery. The moment just materialized, and I can look back on it and recognize many aspects of the incident as setting a pattern that I would grow familiar with the more the pattern repeated. But that day it was all so new to me. After lunch I sat in the car and felt the urge for the first time, mistaking it for unappeased hunger. I should have eaten more of the fish. I shifted in the seat uncomfortably. The feeling spread through my belly, then down and up at the same time—legs and chest. Avery belched and struck himself lightly on the breastbone with his fist and smiled out ahead to the road.

"Thanks for the lunch," I said.

"You hardly ate a thing," he said. "A growing boy."

I stared out the window and waited for the strange sensation to go away. But it stayed and grew. Just short of Blaine, where the border with Canada lies, Avery stopped the car at the side of the road.

"Gotta take a leak," he said. "That Coke."

"Me, too." Maybe I did. The urge was a weight on my bladder, a weight in my body that spread like fevered blood and touched a thousand nerves and made them buzz as they never had buzzed before—as they were not meant to.

Avery sighed and got out of the car and walked off the shoulder, down a gentle slope into trees and underbrush. I followed him. I had no idea what I was doing, but I believed I was on my way to empty my bladder, which swung inside my body like an angry bell. There was no plan. I stared at Avery's back. He wore a much-too-small blue suit, as though he had grown up big inside it and was ready to leave it behind like a husk. He looked back, beyond me, to see how far from the road we had come, to see whether it was far enough for privacy. He stopped in front of a tree and spread his feet. I heard the zipper go down. I stopped, too. Beginning slowly, he spattered the leaves; the leaves tipped and shuddered. The sound grew louder. I stood ten feet away. The urine flowed out of Avery endlessly. I reached down and picked up a rock that was suddenly there, and I ran the rock toward the floating brown hair at the back of Avery's head. His face drove forward, into the tree. The bone yielded front and back. He slid. I let go of the rock and jumped away, as though something was going to touch me. Avery was curled and still, in the shape of a C that wrapped around the tree. His penis was hanging out of his pants, still urinating. His hand was stuck underneath him somewhere. My heart was going like crazy. I heard myself screaming silent questions at myself, asking me what I was doing. I sat on the ground next to Avery and stared at him. I went through his pockets and found his wallet and took his cash. Doing this made me feel more like a thief, as though I had a reason that someone could understand. I counted the money and flung the wallet through the woods—it spun itself open and took a jagged, boomeranging path, glancing off the side of a tree and falling. I didn't hear it land. I picked up the rock and looked for blood. There wasn't any. I stared at the back of Avery's head. I could see the pit that the point of the rock had made. But, again, there wasn't any blood. I always thought that head wounds bled like crazy. Avery's eyes were shut. On his forehead and the bridge of his nose were abrasions from hitting the tree. His lips were barely parted. I liked him. Before, I hadn't liked him at all, but now the barrier had been removed. I reached out and slid the top lip up and saw that the front teeth were cracked. Then his eyes opened slowly by themselves, and they were staring at me.

"Aaahh," I said, jumping back. The breath rushed out of me. But that was all there was. The lip slid down. I crept back and put my finger on the vein in his neck and felt for a pulse. There was nothing. The eyes were just a helpless reflex carrying on. I bent down close and examined them, and it was as though a fog had filled them—like dolls' eyes. I looked back out toward the road.

I thought of taking the car. I thought of doing what a fool might do. I could go up north in the car, through the border, and absorb for myself the possessions of Avery—the mysterious sample cases. But I knew I was not a fool. I sat in the leaves and surprised myself with the knowledge that I would not be caught if I did not behave like a fool by doing the things a criminal does. I tried to think clearly and to make a careful plan. I walked south through the woods. I could hear the cars headed north, whooshing. When trucks passed, the leaves rustled and I felt the wind. But I stayed deep enough in the woods to remain unseen.

I was not a fool.

After a mile or so I came to a road that ran under the highway. I walked east along that road for twenty minutes, until I came to a school where boys were playing touch football. I went up and leaned on the fence beside the field and watched them play. When one of the boys quit and went home, the others asked me to take his place. I played with them for half an hour. Then the game broke up. I sat on a bench with one of the boys and smoked a cigarette. His name was Jimmy. I told him mine was Dennis. I told him I lived in Blaine. He asked what street, and I told him I didn't know the street names, but it was near the border crossing, a small red house where I lived alone with my mother.

We walked back to Jimmy's house and watched television. No one was home. Jimmy made us open-face toasted-cheese-with-bacon sandwiches. I had never had it done that way. He cooked them under the broiler until the cheese went from yellow to crusty brown. Then he laid the bacon strips across the cheese in X's. We ate them with knife and fork. We watched the U. of Washington play Stanford. Jimmy's father came home and sat on the couch beside me without even asking Jimmy who I was. He turned and asked me the score.

"I don't know," I said.

At five o'clock I said I'd better be getting home. Jimmy said he and his friends would be playing touch football again tomorrow and I should join them.

"What time?" I said.

"One o'clock."

"Okay," I said. "I'll be there."

I walked out of Jimmy's house and back toward the highway. Once there, it wasn't ten minutes of trying before I got a ride. A man and a woman in a pickup truck stopped and motioned me into the back with their dog, an Irish setter. They said they were going all the way to Vancouver. I rapped on the window to let them know I was settled, and off they drove. The sun was going down. We sailed past Avery's car. I looked off into the woods, but I couldn't see him. We were going too fast. The dog crept over and rested his head on my leg. The wind whipped around the sides of the cab and chilled me. I petted the head of the dog. Through the window I heard the woman yelling something at me. I turned and saw her pointing at the dog. "His name is Monkey," she said. I nodded. I petted Monkey's head and shoulders.

All the way to Vancouver I thought about the day. The sudden movement of the rock toward Avery's head played like the start of a movie. The scenes unfolded from that moment in all directions of chronology—a jumble. I recalled the sight of the suit stretched tight across Avery's back, and recalled the deep insistence of the unfamiliar gnawing in my bowels, which I suddenly noticed was gone by the time I was walking south in the woods, and before I had found the road that led to the school. Then Avery was alive again, belching and striking his breastbone gently, saying something empty and annoying. Then the rock shot forward again like a comet, landing furiously, hissing. And I was catching a pass and running out of bounds as Jimmy tagged my hips.

Unerringly, the dog would move his head to the spot on my leg that felt the coldest. I stared back at the lights of cars and trucks behind us, gaining and growing brighter. My white face floated in space like the moon. The lights caught and held me. I squinted through the dazzle and petted the dog. As the cars and trucks moved out to pass us, the movie of the day played on. The rock soared forward. I searched my heart for a signal of guilt, but felt clean and ready to carry on.

Doug knocks on the door. I am staring out the window at the dusk and have seen the unfamiliar beige sedan drive back and into the garage. A rental car. I have watched Doug walk to the house and seen the fatigue in his step, then heard him climbing up my private stairs, his feet sliding heavily on the bare wood.

"Vann?"

I go to the door and open it.

"It was her. It was Jane."

"Oh, Jesus, Doug. I'm sorry."

"They think I did it." He comes inside.

"Did they say so?" I say to the back of his head.

"No. Not in so many words." He goes to the comfortable chair and sinks down into it.

"It's this Little thing," he says. "They keep apologizing to me. They say they know how hard it is, but they gotta ask me these awful questions. They gotta take the hard look. The whole world is watching, they say."

"How did she die?" I say.

"A blow to the back of the head. Somebody beat her to death. Some bastard beats my wife to death and stuffs her in the trunk of the car, and the cops are talking to me."

"It's like they say," I tell him. "It's the Little case. You know . . . Fool me once, fool me twice . . ."

"That's right."

"Jesus, Doug. I'm sorry."

"They're gonna want to talk to you."

"They are?"

"They said so, yeah."

"Okay," I say. "Anything I can do to help. But what do I know?"

"Well, see, that's the thing."

"I don't know anything."

"Right. So, nothing to worry about."

"Okay."

"You might do this, though . . ."

"What?"

"Well, you might, you know, when I borrowed your truck?"

"Uh-huh."

"That day I borrowed your truck."

"Okay."

"That was the same day. Jane was taking Karen to the airport."

"Right."

"I think the police might think that was my opportunity."

"How?"

"Don't ask me how. I don't know how. It's just that they might think. They could get the idea."

"So, it might be better if you didn't borrow it?"

"Well, yeah. Maybe."

I stand in front of Doug and nod slowly, thinking it over.

"Okay. Sure," I say. "Why not. What difference does it make?"

"Probably not a bit," says Doug. "But maybe."

"Okay," I say.

"Just do what you feel comfortable doing."

"No problem," I say. I nod. "Anyhow, I'm sorry."

"Thanks a lot," says Doug. "I appreciate that. I mean it."

He pulls himself up from the chair and heads for the inside door. "I've got to call Karen," he says. "She doesn't know. She doesn't know about her mother."

"If I can do anything to help," I say.

"Okay," says Doug. He opens the door and steps down into the darkness of the stairs.

"Thanks," he says, and he disappears.

I am doing the hillside houses, up and down steps, when the police from Boston creep up along the curb, scraping the tires. I descend from the Stuart O'Learys' and see the window roll down and hear my name.

"Mr. Siegert?"

"Yes?" I go over to the black car. I recognize the same two cops.

"Boston Police, Homicide Division," says the senior one. "I'm Detective Sargeant Pate. This is Detective Creech. We'd like to ask some questions, if you don't mind."

"No," I say.

"Would you like to get in the back? We can do it right here. It won't take a minute. You can get right back to your route."

"Okay." I get in the car. I look around to see who might be seeing this. But nothing catches my eye.

"Okay," says Pate. "We're investigating the death of Mrs. Dean. Jane Dean."

I nod.

"I understand you are a tenant in the Dean household."

"Yes, that's correct."

"Your first name, Mr. Siegert . . . Is that one N or two?"

"Two."

"Middle initial?"

"D."

"D," he repeats, writing it down. "And you are on friendly terms with the Deans? You knew them both?"

"That's correct."

"Are you aware of any problems in their marriage? Was there any tension between them? Any friction?"

I slowly shake my head. "No," I say. "At least not that I noticed."

"Where your apartment is," says Creech, "is it the kind of thing where you would have overheard if there was an argument?"

"If it was loud, yes. Probably. If it was shouting."

"Did you hear anything like that?"

"No, I didn't," I say. Pate takes notes in a tall white notebook with narrow pages.

"Oh, come on," he says. "You mean to tell me there wasn't a single time when—how long have you lived there?"

"Since what . . . October," I say.

"You're telling me in nearly six months there hasn't been a single time when one of them lost their temper and was yelling at the other one? Have you ever been married, Mr. Siegert?"

"No."

"Well, let me tell you. Married couples fight. It's part of the freakin' deal."

"But, all the same," I say, "I didn't hear them fighting. That doesn't mean it never happened. I'm just saying I never heard it."

"Okay," says Pate. He flips back through the notebook, to pages of notes on other interviews. "When was the last time you saw Mrs. Dean?"

"I don't know. I guess Thursday. I'm not even sure I saw her then. I heard her. She called to Doug to come down for dinner. Calling up the stairs—he was at my place. Then on Friday she drove Karen to the airport. I didn't see her then either. I was still in bed. I heard the car start. I heard voices. It was her."

"You're sure?"

I shrug. "I guess."

"What were *you* doing Friday?" says Creech.

"I was at work."

"Doing this?" says Pate, pointing out at the street.

"Right."

"Talk to anyone?" says Creech.

"Sure. I'm sure I did. I always do."

"Out on the route?"

"Yeah. That's what I mean."

"Okay," says Pate. "We might want to talk to someone who saw you, who could place you there."

"Chenier," I say without thinking, remembering the woman and the baby. "Church Street. I had a certified letter for them." I watch Pate write the name and the street, and the words "certified letter."

"I think it's at one-ten. A Mr. and Mrs. John H."

"Thank you, Mr. Siegert," says Pate. "You're being real helpful here. Anybody else?"

I shake my head. "I'm sure there were, but I can't think of them off the bat."

"Not like Chenier."

"No," I say. "It's that certified letter."

"Right," says Pate. He pokes the page with his pen. "I think that's about gonna do it for now. We don't want to hold up the mail for too long. We appreciate you taking the time."

"Do you have any leads?" I say.

"We *think* we do," says Pate. "But then, we *always* think we do, and sometimes it turns out we don't have shit. You can see that in the papers this week. The Little case. The big fuckup."

"Vince," says Creech, laughing.

"Okay," says Pate. "Thank you for your time, Mr. Siegert. If we need to see you again . . ."

"Okay," I say. I reach for the door handle, but the inside handles have been removed. Pate gets out of the car and opens the door for me.

"Thank you," I say.

Stepping out, the air is cold and the sun is dazzling. The world feels new to me. I squint hard. Tears come to my eyes.

"Take it slow," says Pate, getting back in the car. The car pulls away. The tires sigh leaving the curb. I believe the police know everything.

Doug goes to the interment of the body of Eugene Fowler on the day before Jane is to be buried. He comes up to borrow shaving cream and asks me if I will go with him.

"No," I say.

He stares at me out of eyes that are wet and deep. I have lost some of my goodwill toward Doug. He waits for me to say something else that would take the sting out of the simple "no." But I only turn and go to the bathroom to get the can of shaving cream. I come back to find him still in the posture of waiting for my goodwill to return, as he seems to believe it must. This makes me think that perhaps he is right, and that it will. I, too, begin waiting for it. I hold out the can to him. He takes it.

"Thanks," he says. He continues standing in front of me, watching me reconsider what I have told him.

"You're sure?" he says.

He has spent his whole working life walking alone up and down the same streets in four or five towns in the Bledsoe environs. He has had the opportunity to know the pleasure and loneliness of his own uninterrupted thoughts. And yet he is not used to going out without Jane to anyplace that is not work. He wants me to be his substitute other. He is lonely and pathetic. He should have thought of this.

"Yes," I say. "I don't feel like a funeral two days in a row."

He looks down at his feet and nods. He sags back from me toward the door. The can of shaving cream seems to pull his shoulder impossibly low, like a great weight.

"Okay," he says. And he turns and leaves me alone, down stairs into darkness as deep as a nighttime fog. I decide to call in sick.

Later in the afternoon I look out the window and see a man in a shiny blue Red Sox jacket bending down behind my truck, looking underneath, writing the Oregon license number in a notebook. I think of the two investigations proceeding separately, without relationship or awareness of one another, but suddenly coming together at this address, the Boston detectives asking the State Police detectives, "What are *you* doing here?"

The man circles the truck closely, and then at a distance of ten feet—orbits offering different kinds of views. He isn't one of the two Boston cops, but I have no way of knowing which investigation he represents. He looks in the passenger and driver's side windows. At no time does he actually touch the truck; not even his jacket grazes the finish. He goes by the book as far as what is allowed without a warrant: observation from without, but not entry.

He stands and reaches behind himself and massages his lower back. He looks at the sky and turns in a circle. His eyes graze my window, and I wonder if he sees the pale oval floating inside, looking down at him. He sticks the thin notebook in his back pocket—the spiral coil rises to the middle of the knit waistband of the baseball jacket—and walks out of sight, toward the front of the house.

I am thinking it is time to move again. I am turning a circle in my room, observing my possessions spread across all of the surfaces, planning the packing.

Where will I go?

--

Doug rents a movie. He knocks on the door and tells me to come and watch it with him. He is drunk. I follow him downstairs. He slips on the last two steps and lands hard on his heels in his stocking feet. I look around. The house is a wreck. It is as though he has invited people in to help him disorder it methodically. Cabinets and drawers are open. Paper is everywhere. Shades are off the lamps, and lie on the carpet on their sides. Plates of half-eaten food have been left on tables, shelves, the floor—more meals than it seems Doug could have tried to eat in these last few days since I was here. The place is transformed. I expect to see big rats hunching over the plates, indifferent to us. But we are the only living things.

The television is on in the dark, white snow hissing. Doug bends and pushes a button. The screen fills with a bright blue silent warning from the FBI. Then the movie. I stand behind the couch and watch it—a comedy, called *I Now Pronounce,* about a wedding between two homosexual men. Doug moves here and there, quietly, restlessly. He comes over and puts a drink in my hand. I sniff it. Bourbon, straight, no ice.

"Thanks," I say.

He drifts away. Neither one of us sits. As the movie plays I stand in one place, but Doug tiptoes around picking up plates and glasses and carrying them out of the room, which the changing scenes of the movie illuminate in blues and pinks and whites. I don't like comedies, but I find myself laughing at something. After a while, I lean forward and rest my hands on the back of the couch. I look down and am surprised to see Karen Dean stretched out below me, on her back, asleep. If she opened her eyes I would be the first thing that she saw.

In the kitchen Doug turns on the garbage disposal. It grinds and whooshes. Karen stirs but does not wake up. The father of one of the men in the movie is chasing him through a shopping mall with a gun. Innocent bystanders scream and throw themselves on the ground. The father fires wildly, hitting nothing but a little girl's heart-shaped silver balloon. Doug, who is suddenly standing right behind me, laughs.

"I love this film," he says.

A minute later I hear his feet on the stairs and turn to see him carrying a broad-leafed potted plant up to the second floor. On the couch Karen moans and coughs. The cough changes, becoming deeper, more violent, and soon she is awake and sitting up, vomiting and choking. I stare at her T-shirted back as she heaves. I move silently out of the room. I climb the stairs past Doug, who is coming down again, without the plant.

"I'm tired," I say.

"Okay," he says.

"Karen's getting sick," I tell him.

"She drank too much," he says. "She passed out."

I hand him the glass with the bourbon.

"Good night," I say.

On the second floor the doors are open and the lights are blazing, and all of the rooms are in perfect order. It is another world.

I am sorting the mail for Joe LaMoine's route, picturing the houses, counting the steps in my head, when Ferrin places her hip next to mine and asks me if I will go with her to Jane Dean's funeral.

"Okay," I say.

"They talked to me," she whispers.

"Who?" I say.

"The cops."

I stand with a wad of chain-store fliers in my hand imagining Ferrin and cops. She would work hard for them and woo them with her honesty and amazement. She would help them through their questions; she would phrase the questions over again, more clearly, and wait until they nodded—yes, that's what we mean. Then she would answer perfectly, slowly, watching one of them write her answers in his notebook. There would be no need to ask the question again, or ask another question on that same topic— the answer she gave would be complete, it could stand and walk around the room unaided. Ferrin would smile at the cops, ask them if there was anything else and, in the meantime, think back to see if there was more she could remember. She would rub her eyes in concentration.

"They scared the shit out of me," she says.

"Why?" I say.

She stands on her tiptoes and puts her mouth to my ear and whispers, "Because I think they think Doug might have done it."

While Ferrin is whispering her hot breath into my ear the room grows quiet. And for an instant I think that Ferrin has drowned out the rest of it in the sound of her avid fretfulness. But when the mouth goes away and the cool air chills my ear again to normalcy, I understand that everything in the room has stopped completely—that no one is sorting his route or hollering or throwing an empty mail sack into one of the canvas hampers or stacking a tray on top of another tray. No one is moving. I am afraid to look at what is happening.

When I finally turn around I see Joe LaMoine standing in the doorway smiling, tears in his eyes, taking in the silent stillness as though he owns it and deserves it. Slowly he comes into the room, and people start to clap their hands for him. He looks pale and thin, like a man who will never climb a stair again. And yet it is only, what, three weeks, four weeks since surgery? He waves like the pope. I look next to me and see there are tears on Ferrin's cheeks, and she is smiling and clapping her hands. She waves at Joe with a terrible energy. Her body shakes. Behind Joe come his wife and his son. Someone is whistling shrilly.

I have never felt so alone.

The mass for Jane Dean begins promptly at noon. Most of the post office people are still in uniform—I am, Ferrin is. We are all supposed to be back at work by one after taking lunch hour at St. Stephen's. The organist plays high notes held for a long time, brittle and disappearing, then beginning someplace else. Doug and Karen sit by themselves in the front row with nearly the width of a person between them. Many people stare straight ahead at the stained light coming in through the rose-shaped, passionate window, the glowing colors slanting down. The casket gleams. I imagine Jane's small face inside, the made-up pinkness sunk in a generous, cream white cushion in the dark.

"This is so sad," says Ferrin.

I nod. But Doug's thoughts begin to infiltrate me, as though they have crept backward down the aisle and into this pew, past Ferrin's jittering legs. He is thinking about what he would like to be eating for lunch. He is thinking of going on a long trip by himself. He is worried that he has been constipated for more than three days. He is pleased at the sight of the casket. He feels the terrible heat of Karen's slowly forming anger accumulating between them.

While Doug's thoughts are floating through me, I cannot take my eyes off the casket, expecting that Jane too will notice his thoughts and unleash a lingering spasm of stored electricity that I might observe some sign of—I look for the casket to tremble slightly or for the falling light to arrange itself around the casket in a sudden, new, unusual way. So not to miss it, I don't even blink. The priest drones on exactly as he droned last year for poor Gene Fowler. Nothing has changed since then in this religion. Ferrin's small, strong hand closes tight around my forearm. I look away from the casket and see the face of Jesus standing among his followers. He is pale, and his white robe covers him completely and reveals no line of his figure, as though there is nothing underneath the robe, only air—he is only hands and a face, an invisibility canceled by the light. Birds hover close to his head. A white sun hangs above cedar trees. There is a peace about to be shattered. The sun above Bledsoe dims, and the shafts of colored light are rescinded, back to the window and out.

When the service ends I follow Ferrin down the aisle. The two Boston homicide detectives stand at the back by the tall oak doors. They nod at us. Ferrin says hello, an echoing whisper. The detectives nod again, looking beyond us. We go out past them through the doors. Ferrin turns and looks at their backs. I am so close to my interrupted route that I only have to walk up Waban Hill to my Jeep and begin where I left off.

"I want to cook you dinner," Ferrin says. We stand together on the sidewalk, waiting for something.

"Okay," I say.

"Tonight."

"Okay."

"Is there anything you don't eat?"

"No, nothing," I say, though there isn't very much that I like the taste of.

"Will you just come down there, to my house?"

"I will."

"What time?"

"I don't know. After work?"

"That's good. We can leave together. You can follow me."

Everyone from inside is now standing outside the church, waiting, looking back at the doors. Soon the casket comes out, a rounded prow of shining varnish. Doug is at the front of it, the right corner up on his left shoulder. Two men in dark suits are behind him. One of them is Paul Fowler. Three other men are hidden on the far side of the casket. The back of the hearse is open. The pallbearers move in a slow shuffle, carefully. The crowd of people watches silently. The pallbearers' feet scuff and slide. The casket tips and bobs above them. Jane.

"I'll see you later," I say to Ferrin. I move away from the crowd, up Church Street, up the rising slope of Waban Hill, not looking back.

Ferrin makes a pan of lasagna with green noodles and broccoli, a tossed salad on the side. She serves red Italian wine in a bottle wrapped in a sleeve of basket straw. I eat the food as though it pleases me, faster and faster. I ask for more. Steam rises out of the pan between us. Ferrin smiles to see my empty plate and cuts me more. I hold out the plate and feel the weight of the food settle upon it. Strings of elastic cheese stretch thin between my plate and the serving tool. Finally they break. Ferrin laughs. She puts the tool back in the pan and reaches for her wine. We clink our glasses together. She smiles.

"To Jane," she says.

"To Jane."

Later she puts music on and lights candles.

"Where is your dog?" I say, remembering all of its energy.

"In the bathroom, in its basket."

I go to the bathroom door and look in on the dog. It looks up at me from the basket and wags its tail.

"Hello," I say. But it stays where it is, as though it is sick or drugged.

When I come back from seeing the dog the room is lighted only by candles. They shimmer and throw soft shadows of themselves. Ferrin holds her wine in a way that catches the flickering light of a candle behind it, placing the flame in the depths of the glass. Her teeth shine. Her skin in the dark glow of the room is the color of weak tea. I am the sorrowing victim of wine and lasagna, and whatever Ferrin wants. She drifts through the space between us. I feel my weakness grow, and by the time she has reached me I am nothing. She throws her arms up around my neck and buckles me down to the ground. My knees hit the bare wood. My head is by her zipper. The zipper moves hard across my lips. My heart speeds. I hear the wineglass fall and shatter. She pounds my shoulders with her fists. My strength floods in. I wrap my hands around her thighs and lift, pulling her back over me and onto the floor behind. I hear her hit and slide. She shouts. I turn and crawl after her. She looks back at me. I grab the waist of her pants and pull. She slides to me on the smooth wood. Her one cheek squeaks against the varnish. She cries. I take an arm and twist it behind, pinning it to the small of her back. Then I reach around front and unzip the pants. I pull them off. She is pink and warm. Her legs kick. Her knees and toes bang the floor on either side of me.

"Let me go!" she says.

I obey her instantly. She crawls ahead and leaps to her feet.

"What are you doing?" she cries.

I am squatting on the floor with my hands on my knees and the empty space in front where she had been.

"I thought . . ."

"Jesus Christ!" she says. "I thought you were going to *kill* me."

"No. I thought."

"Jesus . . ." She stamps her foot.

"I got carried away," I say.

"No shit . . ."

"I thought you . . ."

"You thought I *what?* Is *this* what you do? You *need* to do this?"

The tightness aches inside of my jeans.

"I'm sorry," I say. I get up and go toward her. Her shirttails stick out beneath the waist of her sweater, covering her underpants. She starts to cry. I stop and reach out my arms in a way that would welcome her in. She continues crying. She stares at me and takes a step away.

"I'm sorry," I say again. "Why can't we start over?"

"Forget it," she says.

"I can't," I say.

And it is true. Something has happened here that it is important to return from and erase from memory. I am going to need her help, and she is going to need my help. It is as though we had walked through a door and gone a certain distance down a dark hallway, and had decided that we didn't like the feeling of this particular hallway and, so, we should be able to simply turn around and walk back. It's not such a hard thing to do. I go to the edge of the bed and sit there, folding my hands in my lap in a gesture of meaning no harm at all. I try to explain my thinking to Ferrin. She paces back and forth in an arc ten feet away from me, not taking her eyes from mine as though she could freeze me if I were to leap.

"I feel bad," I say. "I need to feel better about this."

"What about me?" she says.

"It goes both ways," I say.

She nods at the truth of this. She goes and gets another wineglass and pours herself more wine. She brings me my own half-full glass and hands it to me.

"I started it, didn't I?" she says. I remember her fists on my shoulders, and immediately I begin to feel better. I sip some wine, which is warm and tart.

"Yes," I say. "That's true."

"I'm sorry," she says.

"Thank you," I say. She comes closer. She stands right in front of me.

"And then you just got carried away."

"That's right," I say. "I'm sorry."

"It's all right," she says. She sits beside me on the edge of the bed. She takes the wineglass out of my hands and puts it gently on the floor. She leans over and kisses the rim of my ear, and I hear the breath that rises from deep inside her.

"Thank you," I say. And I feel her leaning against me, pushing me sideways. I let myself go. She pushes me out of the dark hallway and into the growing light, where I will be still and take no action. Where I will be perfect.

"Just pretend it's drugs," says the voice of Tim, surfacing as a whisper inside my head. He laughs warmly, and the laugh bends and flies. My head falls back. Ferrin crawls upon me, tongue and fingers. I twist my head from side to side, captured, speechless. Yellow-white candle flames hiss like comets across my eyes.

# ELEVEN

-:-

ON THE LOWER HALF OF THE FRONT PAGE OF
the *Boston Globe* (the Little case gets the top half) is a police artist's
composite sketch of the man authorities believe has been abducting
and poisoning people in Bristol County and, possibly, in Maine.
The man is gaunt with sunken eyes and dark hair, a long chin and
a wide expanse of flesh between the nose and the upper lip; the
lips are delicate and dark in the sketch, and the man's forehead is
lined with hard furrows that give the impression of permanent
worry. His eyebrows are heavy and very black, and a tender line
of hairs continues across the bridge of the nose, where there also
appears to be a slightly slanting scar.

I stare at the sketch and then into the mirror. I am in the toilet
at the post office. The door is locked and the water is running. I
hold the sketch up next to my face. I smile a smile the man in the
sketch could never manage. He looks like a million people, and
hardly anything like me. His face is too thin, his eyebrows too
heavy, his chin too long, his lips too fine; I have no scar on the
bridge of my nose, and my eyes are farther apart. This is my first
lesson in the encouraging truth about these flat depictions: They
are patches of dim, contradictory fancy stitched together with hope
and compromise. I smile the smile. I wish I had the handsome
cheekbones of the man staring out from the page.

I shut off the water, flush the toilet and leave the bathroom. I
place the newspaper, folded so the police sketch faces up, on the

counter where I begin to assemble Joe LaMoine's route. I feel Joe's presence hovering near me, approving each piece with a faint, pope-like, heart-preserving wave. The trays fill up.

Behind me someone is telling Boyd Little jokes. "What's the Boyd Little cocktail?" Restless silence. "Give up? Two shots, a twist and a splash." People are laughing, spinning, clapping. "What's the difference between Larry Bird and Boyd Little?" Pause. Someone coughs. "Larry jumps *before* he shoots."

Some days I get more addresses in a single tray than I do on other days. But there is surprising uniformity. More often than anyone would think I get the same number of addresses in one tray day after day. Frequently, it breaks at 56 Chandler Street, the next tray beginning at 58. It's like a card trick governed by complicated mathematical odds, beyond my power to understand them. The amount of mail received by each house varies from day to day, and yet it often evens out over the course of many addresses. There is a mystery here that someone might be tempted to explore. But there is another possibility: That I am doing something unconsciously in the process of loading the trays that affects the fullness of them in a way that predetermines 56 as the cutoff point. Maybe if I just packed them tighter I could fit in another four houses, possibly up to 64 or 66. Mail is not an uncompressible commodity. And maybe on some of those days when the tray "feels" full at 50 Chandler Street, I cram in the extra pieces that get it to work out perfectly. These are possible explanations. I can't exclude that something like this could be at work here. And yet, a tray that is loaded too full runs the risk of unspringing, launching mail up into the air from the center of the rows, disordering the route. You learn very quickly how full a tray can get before reaching this point. Otherwise, you are suddenly down on your hands and knees scooping up envelopes while everyone else is clapping and laughing.

Ferrin comes and stands beside me and gives me a gentle hip check. I see her staring down at the police sketch in the newspaper, looking at it hard. She looks up at me and then back at the paper, and then looks up and back again.

"Hi," I say.

"Hello."

She opens the paper and turns it over and looks at the headlines on the stories about the Little case.

"Boyd Little. What a scumbag," she says.

Then she looks again at the sketch.

"Guy looks like me," I say.

She holds the paper up in front of my face and stares.

"No way," she says. "Not a bit." She puts the paper back on the counter. In front of us, across the room's back wall, Doug drifts as though he has misplaced his purpose but will find it again if he just keeps moving steadily.

"Poor Doug," says Ferrin.

Anyone would understand if Doug said he wanted to take some time off. But he insists on being here, and so he's been temporarily taken off his route and put at the counter out front—selling stamps, weighing mail, fetching parcels and certified letters, and refilling postage meters.

"Doug," I say, but he doesn't answer. He goes around the perimeter of the enormous room, searching shelves and cabinets and drawers with an exaggerated thoroughness. He lifts up volumes of postal regs and looks beneath them, running his hand across bare table space to verify the nothing that he sees.

I notice that others are pausing to watch him, too, and the room goes quiet for half a minute during which Doug either doesn't register this deeper quiet or pretends that he doesn't. He finally stops searching for whatever it is he wants and turns around and rubs both hands down the length of his face, slowly opening his eyes to the room and all the people in it after his fingers have passed down to the tip of his chin. He smiles. Everyone goes back to what they were doing, and the level of usual noise is soon regained.

I stare at my route and say to myself that this is what I have to do today. I stack the trays three high and say good-bye to Ferrin.

She sighs. "See you later," she says. Then she smiles and forms a soundless sentence with her lips: "I had a good time last night," she says.

"What?" I say.

She mimes it out again. I put my ear down next to her mouth to get her to say it in a whisper, which she does. I'm about to tell her I did, too, when I see that everyone who has just finished staring at Doug is now staring at me and Ferrin.

"Okay," I say. "See you later."

When I am out on the route I see the police sketches stapled to telephone poles, head high. The face of the man who stares back at me has no depth; it is flat and empty and conveys an anxious sadness owing to the forehead furrows and a deep, unreal, angry blackness to the pupils of the eyes. No one outside of comic books has eyes like this. More than in the *Globe,* it is obvious from these handbills that the individual features—the eyes, nose, mouth, eyebrows, hair—must have been selected out of a catalogue of facial pieces and thrown together by trial and error: "Did it look like this? No? A little thicker here? Yes? Did it look like this? It did? You're not quite sure? Suppose we try this one . . . Did it look like this?"

I fall behind my normal pace for the route. At every telephone pole that has a handbill stapled to it, I stop and experience anew the gathering interest of the unseen detectives—whose faces are to me more vivid and true than the face of my distorted self as seen and assembled by others. I stop and consider again the tenuous link between the sketch and me—I test myself against it. At some of the telephone poles I think it looks a lot like me; at others I think it doesn't. When a police cruiser goes slowly by, I wave. Another test. The cops wave back. I pass the test.

At 101 Spruance Street I drop mail through the slot for 101 Stallings, a block away. As it falls, I realize my mistake. I think of ringing the bell and explaining, but already I'm forty-five minutes off schedule. So I leave the problem to sort itself out tomorrow. I go back down the steps, my feet feeling heavy and chilled. I visualize the wrong mail lying in the wrong place. The thought of it troubles me, and I feel the mistake go rippling through the world in an uncontrolled way, spreading, communicating, revealing something about me to others. I ask myself whether Joe LaMoine, on the cusp of his heart attack, might have done something just like this which could have served him as an early warning. If, for Joe, the warning would have been of his coming heart attack, what would it be for me? If I get a warning like this, how will I know how to use it? Have there been other warnings before that I have missed?

At the dead end of Spruance Street, which abuts the marsh, I experience dizziness that compels me to lean against a tree. I close my eyes, and the dizziness gets worse. I open them and see the lace curtains part in the picture window of 77. Mrs. Lentowski. Her glasses wink in the reflected sunlight. Then the curtain falls back again. Seconds later she opens her front door and calls out to me.

"Are you all right?"

"Yes," I answer. "Just resting."

"You're sure?"

"Yes. I'm sure. Yes, thanks."

"You could come in for tea . . ."

"It's all right," I say. "But thank you anyway."

"Well, all right then."

The door closes slowly. I stare at it, thinking how kind she must be, Mrs. Lentowski. The curtain parts again, and I push myself away from the tree and cross the street to the even-numbered addresses. Gradually, the dizziness wears away. By the time I get over to Stallings Street it is gone completely. On Stallings Street, for some reason, there are no handbills, and I begin to make up time.

No rational system governs the timing of the urge. It comes and goes without consulting me to see if I would find it convenient or useful, to see if I would welcome it. I am its host, it is my guest, and yet it follows none of the rules of that relationship. Instead, behaving like a ruthless bully, it makes me its hostage.

I would offer this analysis as a gift to my attorney, whose face and shape are beginning now to emerge in my thoughts from a kind of generative mist, the plume of steam hissing up from the radiator in the room where I am questioned. She hovers faintly over the shoulders of the imaginary detectives who sit and stand and pace around me, never smiling, never sliding the book of matches across the slick gray table to me as I extract a next cigarette from the dwindling pack—I have to lean and reach. My attorney is the owner of a beatific smile sharpened by a deep red lipstick that is clearer than any other aspect of her features. At times she appears to me only as lipstick, the lips compressing and relaxing as though it were perfect exercise for them to hover and listen to my detectives belching and farting, to the sound of matches being struck, smoke inhaled and blown away, to my gentle and honest answers to their sarcastic interrogation. I begin to understand that she wants me to ask for her, not to talk to them anymore without her first becoming more real and entering the scene. She mouths the words: "Ask for me."

The inconvenient urge appears when I am hanging Joe LaMoine's old leather bag on a peg among other pegs bearing the bags of the other letter carriers, which are already in place because I am late to finish. As I reach up to drape the strap over its usual peg, it is almost as if I have pulled a muscle deep in my abdomen. I lower my arms expecting the dim flame to subside, but instead it takes a familar dimension and churns outward from a single point, affecting the large diameter encompassing lower chest down to knees.

There is almost no one else in the post office. Most of the lights are out, and the place is quiet, peaceful. Dan Shames is in his office doing paperwork, and because he is so handy at exactly the point when the urge asserts itself, I think for a demented instant of running out to the truck and getting my flask to offer some to Dan. But lately I have been careless enough. If I can manage it, I will suppress the urge. If I believed it would work, I would pray to Jesus for its annihilation, extinction. I would gladly see it killed like a monster, pierced by a sharpened broom handle through its one vital spot.

I stop by Dan's office to say good night. He looks up and merely says good night, and nothing else, before looking back down to his work. The urge flutters within me and asks for Dan. I pull myself away from the door to his office and leave the building, going out into a dusk that is cold and still, prepared to deal with the urge.

I drive north from town up to 195 and head east to the Cape. There is plenty of traffic, people heading home from work, and at first I do not notice that a car is keeping my pace exactly, a few cars back. But then it makes itself known to me, a subtle sameness in the midst of change. I begin to vary my speed, creeping up and back between fifty-five and seventy, and this car remains just where it is—never right behind me, but always close enough. When I pull out to pass, it, too, pulls out to pass. I memorize the headlights: dual rectangular beams on top of amber dashes. We could be innocently alike, this other driver and me, ensnared in the same rhythms and objectives of travel. But he could also be a detective— one of mine or, possibly, one of Doug's. In fact, he could be anyone at all. He could be the angry brother or father or son of one of my victims, way out in front of the dull police, pursuing leads of his own, perhaps with the assistance of a reporter friend. I have heard of such things.

After crossing the Acushnet River I signal to take the Acushnet-Fairhaven exit. The car behind me takes it, too. I slow at the end of the ramp and signal left but instead turn right. The car remains behind me. I follow the signs for Fort Phoenix Beach. Suddenly the car is gone, and I cannot say where it went. One moment it's behind me, the next it isn't. I have missed its disappearing. I circle through residential streets hoping again to be found. But the car is nowhere, and I am unfollowed. I head back out of Fairhaven with nothing behind me. On 195 I merge with the easterly flow. My thoughts again are filled with what I hope to find, and the urge flares hotly, as though in anger at having briefly been set aside by the drama of the car that followed me.

In Wareham I find a coffee shop called Dick 'n' Dot's and sit in a booth with red Formica tables. I have the open-face hot turkey sandwich with all the trimmings. I drink my coffee slowly and let the waitress continue filling it. Her name is Julie W., chiseled out in white letters on a thin black badge.

"Thanks," I always say when she pours. She holds the pot at a frightening height, but the column of coffee falls perfectly, steam coiling off it sideways as it descends.

Julie brings me pie that I did not order. She sets it down in front of me with a smile. I ask for a fork. The pie is cherry with a crumb topping. She waits while I try it.

"Good," I say. "Very good."

I hear the voice of Tim Jackson whispering, "Good, very good"—

which I take to be a reference to Julie W., whom at first I do not believe I have a ghost of a chance of luring. Then she returns from somewhere and swings herself into the booth across from me, rubbing her forehead and licking the tip of her pen to add up my pale green check. I see the dense blue spot of accumulated ink a half inch back from the tip of her tongue.

"Six seventy-eight," she says and rips the check off the pad. "More coffee?"

"Sure," I say, and I smile the smile.

Once I lured a waitress out of her job in Yosemite Park. She came to the point of dearly wanting me after having begun with only a mild curiosity. But such a beginning can be nurtured and grown. Observing it, I can often turn the gentle electricity of someone's wanting in upon itself, so that it amplifies out of all proportion until nothing can stand in its way—all good sense flies out the window. Imagine creating a feedback loop that circles and hums unendurably. This is the resonance which the urge seeks: to bring itself outside of me and into someone else. To create the companion urge. To be a mirror. The Yosemite waitress was perfectly tuned. She virtually did herself. I smiled the smile and saw her breathing change; I saw the color of the skin of her palms deepen, becoming purplish and exposing pale mottles in the fleshy parts, the tips of the fingers. She sighed as though the breath would never cease leaving her. It was too easy.

This waitress here begins to show similar signs. She has a skin condition and crusty makeup, but her hair is so beautiful that it takes the eye away from the pained, spackled cheeks. The honey hair rolls down in waves like a troubled sea. She smiles at me in return. She reaches up and plays absently with the plastic badge that holds her name. The black surface catches the light and winks. I turn my head to the window and look out into the night as though it is calling to me and I must go to it. In truth, all I see is my own pale reflection, a face that a younger woman like Julie W. might observe is still helpful, still magnetic.

I turn back, rejoining the smile in the air where I left it, and tell her how nice her hair is.

"Thank you," she says.

"Can I give you a lift anywhere?"

"A lift?"

"A ride. Do you need a ride anyplace?"

"Not really," she says. "I have my car."

"I can bring you back."

"You mean just a ride? Just go for a ride?"

"Why not?"

"And you bring me back here?"

"Sure. Back to your car. Why not."

I don't know how a girl can be this careless. The world is a dangerous place, and the fact of its risk is publicized and well-known. And yet the secret mystery is that there still remain many people who will meet a total stranger of unknown capabilities and step straight off the ends of the earth with him, calm in the grip of ignorance, of negligence. You will find them anywhere. I have counted my own in double figures. I reach across the table and softly pat Julie's warm left hand, which is shut tight around the pad of blank dinner checks. I celebrate her willingness which rises like a song above her fear. At exactly the moment of thinking of her death, I think of her opening to me. I feel the hum of resonance. The barriers fall. I can have anything I want. Freedom is wanting and getting.

"Okay," she says. "Why not."

She goes to get her coat. I stare at her dark brown apron knot as she pulls out the hanging loops, untying. The knot disappears.

"Okay," says the voice of Tim.

When I come home, Doug and Karen sit watching television in the dark. I come in uninvited and stand between Doug's chair and Karen's couch. They don't say a word. The television flashes light through the room. Pipe smoke hangs in the air and catches the beamed-out colors of the movie that plays: a boy spying on a woman swimming nude at night in a turquoise pool with underwater lights.

I turn to leave.

"Sit down," commands Karen.

I sit beside her on the couch. Without my noticing that he's moved, Doug suddenly is crouching beside me and putting a glass of bourbon in my hand.

"Thanks," I say. He lays his hand on my shoulder and squeezes.

"You're welcome," he whispers. His breath is murky and sour. He goes back to his chair in a crouch, as though he fears blocking the view of someone behind him.

The boy makes a noise that the woman hears. She stops and treads water. She calls, *"Who's there?"* Then she smiles. *"I know it's you, Matt. I think you're hiding behind that trellis. Am I right? You can come out now."* She swims to the edge of the pool and pulls herself out of the pool. Playfully, she creeps toward the trellis, dripping water. The boy's eyes widen.

"That's Matt," says Karen.

He is hiding not behind the trellis at all, but in the bathhouse on the opposite side of the pool, peeking out through the louvered doors. The woman slowly disappears beneath the trellis archway. Soon the boy hears what might or might not be a muffled scream, then silence. His face is both curious and afraid. He doesn't know what to do. He wrestles with indecision. Finally, he leaves the bathhouse and circles the pool to the trellis archway. He peers around the corner. The nude woman lies on her stomach with a knife in her back. Matt sees the dark figure of a man hurrying away from the pool area and around the corner of the house.

"I think it's his father," says Karen.

"You're supposed to think that," says Doug. "But it's not."

Matt kneels beside the body. The dead woman's head is turned to the side; the camera zooms in on her blue-lipped, open-eyed face. A drop of water clings to the tip of the nose, grows larger and falls.

*"Damn,"* says Matt. *"Damn!"*

Then the scene fades, and there's a commercial break.

"I'm going to bed," says Karen, stretching.

"Me, too," says Doug. "Gotta work tomorrow."

He gets up slowly, stares at the television screen for a moment and leaves the room. I hear his feet on the stairs, trudging and heavy. Karen stays where she is.

"G'night," she calls over her shoulder. Doug doesn't reply. Karen throws her head back and looks at the ceiling. Her neck is long and slender, her chin sharp.

She sighs. Then she turns and looks at me.

"Do you think my father killed my mother?" she says. "I really think he did it."

"Why?" I say.

"I don't know. It's just a feeling. It's not like he's done anything or said anything, specifically. It's more like what he hasn't said. Or what he won't. He won't talk about her at all. He won't sleep in their bed." Upstairs a toilet flushes. "The police think he did it."

"They say that?"

"No. But you can tell. They are asking about insurance policies. They want to know about fights and all that. They seem positive about it. They don't say they're looking in any other direction."

"It's the Little case," I say. "It's got everyone thinking. It's got their attention. The police's."

"Right. I guess."

"So, here's something . . . All things considered, wouldn't your father be totally crazy to kill your mother, under the circumstances? With the Little case and all that publicity?"

Karen shakes her head. "People don't think like that. They just go ahead and do what they do. Do you think someone weighs the consequences?"

I close my eyes and rerun the movie of Julie W. drinking from my flask and sliding across the seat to put herself right beside me in the last smiling moments, coming right to me.

"Yes," I say. "I absolutely do."

Then she stares at me. She takes the drink from my hand and has some. She puts it back in my fingers, which are still in the curled holding shape.

"No," she says, swallowing, shaking her head. "No way."

She turns and stares at Matt, who quietly opens the door to his father's bedroom and stares in through the darkness to the humped form under light white covers.

"*Dad?*"

The father groans.

"*Dad?*"

Matt turns the light on. The father sits up fast and blinks, bare-chested.

"*Matt?*"

"*Dad, we've got to call the police . . .*"

"*The police?*"

"*Yeah, dad, the police.*"

The father stares at Matt. "*What's going on?*" he says.

"*Dad. Meg's been murdered . . .*"

Karen points at the full-screen face of the father. "That asshole definitely did it."

Before the movie ends, Karen falls asleep on the couch with her mouth open, her lips and teeth slowly drying, the breath faintly whistling in and out. I stay awake all night for no good reason I can put my finger on. I stay and keep Karen company, sometimes sitting in Doug's chair, beside the rack of pipes, sometimes walking through the downstairs in the dark. I am serving no purpose. Time passes with a peculiar easiness, possibly because the Deans' downstairs has so many places to move among and things to explore. I open the dining room hutch cupboards and examine some of the porcelain pieces—open-backed brown cows for cream and sugar, large gold-rimmed plates with scenes from famous old movies. I stand by the uncurtained bay windows and let the moonlight filter in upon the things I hold in my hands. An extraordinary amount of time can be quickly consumed in looking at objects you've never laid eyes on before. The second time you see them, it's different—faster.

After a while, the sky outside begins to lighten. I go and turn off the television, which is now only snow and a gentle hiss. Karen lies on her side, her hair having fallen down across her face like a veil. I sit in Doug's chair and listen to the antique wooden clock ticking slowly on the mantel. The dry sound is homelike, heartlike. When Jane was alive something kept me out of the bottom half of the house, but now I am here in comfort, feeling welcome to whatever I find. I open the zippered pouches of pipe tobacco and close my eyes to the smells, which are deep and complicated, seeming to have been soaked for hundreds of years in sweet, intoxicating liquids. I assemble in my lap a half-dozen pouches and float my nose above them. The odors mingle and harmonize. An aromatic moisture rises up which I feel as a tingling on my skin.

Jane was the aspect of control in this house. You could feel it present at all times in the air. The appetites were kept in check. She represented balance and things in their place. Conditions were always being brought back from the brink of disorder and uncleanliness. At night, I would never miss hearing the dishwasher thrumming through the walls, the steady pulse of restoration. If Jane were still here, Karen would not be on the couch; she would be upstairs in the bed for which she was intended. And I would be in mine. Jane was the vital engine of the home, the automatic computer. Doug has no idea the amount of energy that is necessary. One look in the early dawn shows how the house is swinging wildly without the interference of Jane. Even the almost-perfect rhythm of the homey clock seems troubled, sprung—the spaces between the ticks being either fractions short or long. Control has been surrendered.

In my own house, my father and mother battled over which of them should be the one to exercise the all-important decisions of command over life. My mother didn't want these duties, but my father was seldom there to relieve her, and so she determined to do them badly or cruelly instead of simply not doing them at all. I was her harshest critic and also bore the brunt of her bitterness. But where Neil forgave her almost anything, I would stare at her, summoning depths of coldness that reached out and chilled her. Then, when she was up in her room rubbing her pink, fresh-bathed body with creams, I was going out the back door to be missing for hours into parts of Spokane that were mysterious to everyone but me. I was the force whose sympathies my mother could not command. I learned how close to the surface the reservoirs of coldness are; and I was not afraid to draw from them. I believed that she invited this. I never knew a moment of remorse.

My father, returning to Spokane for twenty-four or forty-eight hours, reclaimed command from my mother and used it hardly at all. My mother would sit without her power and watch the power of the house lie wreathed around my father, and him not using it.

She hated him for this. I watched her cloudy eyes. She sat quietly and did the crosswords. Then one night he died in the cellar and left her with everything she wanted, and everything she didn't.

"It's better to be alone in absolute fact than simply alone in practice," she said to Neil one night at dinner, pouring him wine in a jelly glass. She stared at my father's empty seat. I can't remember whether this was before or after he died.

"You know exactly where you stand," she said. "You can look ahead and see how life will be. In plain truth, it will be yours."

In her sleep Karen scratches at herself. I hear the brittle sanding of her nails against her blue jeans. I look at my watch. It is 5:44. I stretch and stand, and go upstairs to take my morning shower. Passing Doug's room, I hear the drawers opening, closing.

I stand beside Doug in the post office. He has brought me coffee and a cakelike donut flavored with bits of blueberry. He tries to be the Doug of before Jane died, but something has deserted him. There was a certainty once in his character and the way people always regarded him as a pleasant, easygoing man. Now he is hardly spoken to. His fellow workers lower their eyes when they pass or when he passes them, or else they stare at him curiously when he is not looking. This isn't surprising. Who knows how to deal with a tragedy? It is a learned skill. I had a third-grade classmate who jumped in an arc from the swings and landed on his back, becoming paralyzed. I could never speak to him again. When the rest of us would be racing around outside, climbing and chasing, he sat in the sun in his wheelchair, reading, a blanket across his lap. A girl brought him water in a Dixie cup. Another boy had weed killer forced down his throat by an older boy. His stomach was pumped in time, and he survived. But he became changed and deeply nervous. One day he offered me grapes, and I turned them down. His hands were shaking badly.

Doug is now transformed in ways he won't admit. I take the donut and coffee from him. His flesh is gray, and his eyes are ringed in red. The grief and guilt have shrunk him. I rise up inside myself in judgment, thinking that a crime too large to be survived has been committed by someone much too small.

He misses the wife he killed.

I sip the coffee and eat the donut. The blueberry flavor is overpowering and odd.

"This is good," I say.

Doug smiles and nods.

I develop the theory that there is too much noise in life. It swells and fades, but there is always too much. Even the least of it is loud. At times I feel the need of silence. I walk past St. Stephen's and am jarred by the tower bells, which make my organs tremble. They play a little song at the quarter hours, a flying up and down, up and down, as though small children were swinging at the ends of the ropes—happy weights.

With Joe LaMoine's bag on my shoulder, I find myself going up the steps to the big oak doors of the church. The ringing stops. I go inside. The door falls shut behind me. I blink to adjust my eyes to the sudden dark. The silence buzzes. The town of Bledsoe disappears. The streets of Joe LaMoine's old route fog over; the names and addresses drop from my mind—the yards and fences and porches and doors. I step across the echoing gray slate tiles and through the carved archway into the aisle at the back of the church. I am ready for something new and great to sweep into my heart and possess me fully.

Three rows in front of me the head of a kneeling woman is thrown forward on her fists. I hear her softly whispering, whispering, but the words are indistinct. Her lips move relentlessly, with an incredible speed. She raises her head off her fists, and her eyes are shut tight the way a child's would be, the skin around them crinkled and the nose squeezed upward. She continues whispering while reaching up with one still-balled fist to rub a still-shut eye. Then her head drops down again, guided by the fist, still rubbing.

I walk on past her, all the way up the aisle to the front of the church. Then I turn left, and left again, by memory, and go down the side to the curtained booth. I go inside and sit. A small slot of a window slides open.

"Father, forgive me, for I have sinned," I say.

"When was your last confession?" says the voice.

"Six months," I say.

"I will hear your confession," says the voice, and begins to wait. I sit in the dark and hear the breathing beyond the screen, on the other side of the box.

"Father, forgive me," I say. "I have taken a woman in adultery."

"You cannot control yourself?"

"No," I say. "I can't. I surrender to a power greater than mine."

"What you're talking about is not a power outside you, but just the animal within. Sin and Satan speak through this beast, entering the soles of the feet from deep in the earth. The truly greater power would never lead you into sin, and it is not of this Earth."

"I believe things happen for no good reason," I say. "Life rolls you over like a wave."

"That's a lie, and a sin to believe that way. We are more than a hunk of seaweed. We are given the choice to control ourselves. God gives us the strength to choose wisely."

"Forgive me, father."

"How long has this sin been carried forward?"

"For many years."

"When will it stop?"

"I don't know."

The priest sighs. "You can give yourself up to your desires, son, or you can join the family of the faith. We are already a large family, but there is always room for more at the table. We will help you learn to choose to be more than an animal that never grows beyond what it wants. To help you begin to learn, say ten Hail Marys and ten Our Fathers and perform seven acts of contrition, one every day for a week."

"Thank you, father."

I stare at the leather bag between my feet. I reach down into it and get the mail for the rectory, counting out the letters and bills and wrapping them with the two supermarket circulars. I slide them slowly through the slot and hear them fall not as far as the floor, but perhaps as far as the gowned lap of the priest.

"I absolve you in the name of the Father, the Son and the Holy Spirit," says the priest. I feel the air moving through the screen from the act of his crossing himself. I cross myself. I get up and leave the box.

I am struck by the cool freshness of the air outside the confessional. The woman is gone. The church is empty. I go straight ahead into the nearest pew and kneel on the cushioned rest. I close my eyes and lay my forehead on my fists. The silence surges around me, filling the stone immensity of the church. I begin to speak the ten Hail Marys, slowly at first, moving my lips to form the words exactly. Then, by the end of the third, the trance of Mary is invoked and the words are spilling out in a kind of thoughtless pleasure, the whispering flooding up around my head with a sweetness, touching my cheeks and nose and eyes. Neil was the first to name this pleasure. He used to tell me he could get an erection in church, saying the soft Hail Marys.

"For it to work," he said, "you have to whisper."

Soon I am through with Mary and whispering the ten Our Fathers. They collide like boxcars coupling in a cool railyard. My lips move faster and faster. By the finish my forehead sweats and slides on top of my fists, and I am almost breathless. In a silence as loud as the loudest noise, I stand and leave the church.

Out on the route I notice several cars that do not behave in a normal way. They pass me slowly and continue out of sight, and later I see them parked with their engines running. Plain cars, cream or brown or blue sedans. Inside of them are men who are shaking maps or newspapers up around their faces, which I cannot see.

I form the opinion that they are mine. Around and above me I feel a personal jet stream shifting its path, refining and refining itself to be smaller and sharper, a wind that concentrates to the width of a hairlike beam and slices through, showing hardly a sign of having entered. And yet it would be inside me, passing back to front, front to back, piercing the organs, refracting in a beautiful burst of color that lights the inner cavity and exposes a faraway piece of film. The science of detection. The beam leaves only tiny bruises on the outside that I might later notice and think nothing of.

I experience the loose attention of these cars. I climb the long flights of stairs that rise to distant porches, and behind me I feel the dull sedans moving in a slow dance directed through softly hissing radios.

What is anyone thinking about me? I have fallen, like everyone else, for the overpowering noise of the Little and Dean cases, and I have forgotten about my own. Suddenly, I greet the possibility that great strides are being made in the case of the seemingly random poisonings. What else explains these cars? Why, otherwise, would they be deployed along my route, behaving with almost an indifference to my discovering their interest in me. If, like a satellite dish, I could capture all of the floating data that concerns my case, what would I then do? Would I flee immediately?

At 44 Sutter Street a toy truck has been left on one of the top steps. I pick it up and examine it in a showy way that someone in a car might observe and be moved to think: He has this sensitivity to toys. I smile and set the truck down with a gentleness. I feel the slender, invisible beam brightening my interior. I slide the mail through the slot and descend. A car pulls up in front of number 48. A man in a Red Sox jacket gets out and opens the trunk. He puts the top half of his body deep into the cavity and appears to be searching for something, a tool. Sounds of rummaging. I walk past. My knees ache. I believe I hear a radio squawk and hiss. I believe I hear an answering voice.

Behind me the trunk slams shut. I resist the urge to turn and look. I begin to climb the steps to 48.

"I'll save you the trip," says a voice from below.

The man in the Red Sox jacket is climbing right behind me. He smiles and holds out his hand. He could be the same man who looked at my truck. But, just as easily, he could be different.

"Okay," I say. I give him the mail, three envelopes, two circulars, a postcard.

"I don't know how you guys get used to all the climbing," he says. "I live here three years, and still I hate it."

"Thanks," I say. "It's just part of the job."

He climbs in a way completely different from me, taking the steps two at a time, athletically. I have learned to climb at a steady pace, a trudge, letting the toe strike the step and slide forward to grip. Then the rising up, and repeating with the other foot. A rhythm geared to last the day.

"No problem," says the man. He puts a key in the lock. A pair of vise grips juts out of his back pocket. He goes inside.

Maybe I am mistaken. Maybe the cruising cars have a purpose unrelated to me. They are out delivering new telephone books or political fliers. And they don't care who I am, except in some innocent statistical way. Trying out this new, unvigilant idea, I expect that instantly I will cease to notice the dull sedans, as though they have disappeared from the streets in a wink. But they remain, they are persistent in my sight. They bracket the streets. Barely visible exhaust billows from the tailpipes. The two ideas—*mine* and *not mine*—take turns prevailing in my thoughts. I walk the route confused, losing time, loading the wrong street into Joe LaMoine's bag at the wrong time and having to go two blocks away to deliver it out of order.

It is inevitable that I will be shaken from time to time by the flow of surplus adrenaline. This will happen until they actually do come forward and put their hands on me and read me the rights and tighten the bracelets on my wrists behind my back. I have prepared for this my entire life. I have waited to be acutely observed. I have known what it would feel like. The personal jet stream splays and cavorts inside me. This is the message I have long expected. Things come down to a point. And now I have the decision to make.

On the third floor of the Deans' house I begin to pack. This consists of deciding whether to leave anything behind. I sit in the comfortable chair and think it through. I close my eyes and place my fingertips on my temples. My decision is this: nothing. I will leave not a trace. Quickly I fill my bags and boxes. I collect them in the middle of the floor. Then I begin to clean the rooms. I go downstairs and get the Deans' old brown Hoover from the hall closet. I vacuum myself from every corner. The bag fills and groans inside the machine. I imagine a cell of my own dead skin beneath an atomic microscope in the FBI lab in Quantico, Virginia, and someone staring down the high-powered tubes at the truth of all my thoughts and deeds. He presses a button and the images are captured somewhere, indexed and cross-referenced; reels of tape spin and back.

I believe that you can be seen inside of. The simple technology exists in laboratories to explode the facts of a long life out of the tiny bits of shed dust a person leaves behind. Strange men in space suits come in and collect everything in plastic baggies: a moment of unhappiness in 1956; a death; two deaths; twenty deaths; reaching up a week ago to touch the warm, candlelit shadows of Ferrin's neck; a broken ankle playing football in 1969; vomiting after eating grapes with almonds stuffed inside. These are all in the dust, collectible. A computer program rages through the photographs of tinctured slides and compiles scenarios that accumulate on stacks of folding paper. The detectives read through the stacks and gain insight into where to look and what to look for—methods, patterns, inclinations.

The Hoover emits the stale smells of old pipe smoke and possibly a long-dead Dean family dog whose hair and cells have forever tainted the inside of the bag. I open the windows. Outside it is sunny but cool. The air floods in and scrubs the smell away. I spin around with my arms outstretched like fan blades, spreading and mixing the new air. I begin to disappear from the rooms as though the wand of the vacuum cleaner reaches back and erases me from the floor up; only the one arm and shoulder and head and neck remain.

Karen walks in the door, stares at me, at the packed boxes, the clothing folded and in piles on the floor and chairs.

"What's going on?" she says. I read her lips, her voice getting lost in the sound of the vacuum cleaner. I turn it off.

"I knocked, but you didn't hear me," she says, pointing back at the door.

"Just cleaning," I say. "Spring cleaning."

She nods.

"A little early. You have to pack to do this?"

"You have to get everything out of the way."

"That's pretty thorough."

I look at the room and see that it appears as if someone is packing to leave.

"Also, I might be leaving," I say.

"Makes sense to me," she says. "Who'd want to stay?"

She goes to the edge of the small, tight fortress of belongings piled in the middle of the room. She looks down upon the boxes and bags as if there is some obvious cause for sadness contained within or around them. She shakes her head.

"What?" I ask her.

"Nothing," she says, still shaking. "Never mind."

She is a strange girl, just like her father said. There is always something she isn't telling you. Or else she is telling you too much. I stare at the side of her face. I see tears beginning to form. They roll out. She probably is thinking about her mother.

"I have a gun downstairs," she says.

"You do?"

"Yes, I do."

"What for?"

"I'm not really sure yet," she says. "But I feel good having it. It's just there if I think of something. If I have a reason for it. That's the point of having a gun around, I think—it's there just in case the need arises."

"Sure," I say.

She wipes her eyes and cheeks with her curled knuckles. I can picture her ready with the gun, crouching in the dark hallway, crying silently. Doug comes up the stairs with a glass of bourbon in his hand. The sound of the gunshot wakes me up. It comes straight at me out of my sleep, like a huge bird of prey in a nightmare. I can't figure out if the sound is real or not; is it just the breaking of some barrier in sleep? But carefully I go down into the hallway, where one of them is dead. (I can always sense it— the cooling, the changing.)

"I won't do anything crazy," she says. "I just have it."

"That's good," I say.

She smiles. "Don't worry," she says.

"Okay."

"But I'm glad I told you," she says.

"Me, too."

She turns around and leaves. She pulls the door shut behind her.

I hear the click, the feet on the stairs. I stand in the silence and wait, listening for whatever comes next. The silence stretches on without conclusion. Finally I turn the vacuum cleaner on again.

At the post office the next morning, I am standing next to Doug, who has brought me a donut and coffee and is watching my face for a sign that I like the flavor of the donut, which has a lemony glaze and bits of cherry embedded in the cake.

"This is good," I say. "Thanks."

He is suddenly stooped and crotchety, and looks twenty, maybe thirty, years older than he really is. He nods his head rapidly and grins when I tell him I like the donut. He looks crazy. As the nodding slows, I thank him again, which causes his head to accelerate.

I am watching Doug's wet and jittery eyes when the room grows unnaturally quiet. The noise of everyone preparing their routes dips down to nothing. Doug and I turn at the precise same instant and see two men approaching.

"Cops," I whisper to myself.

I have never seen these two before. They are not Doug's—Pate and whatsisname—and I feel a sudden frost spreading throughout my deep interior.

The men take forever to get to me. I rehearse the lines I will say when they make the arrest: "What's this all about? This must be some kind of mistake." Twisting and trotting as I am pushed in front of them with my hands in cuffs behind my back.

I think about running. I turn to see what is happening out by the loading dock. The blue lights of cruisers flash in the scratched plastic windows.

Then I realize that they are not mine. I see their eyes fixed on Doug like the eyes of pitiless killers closing in on a certain death. I turn and look at him. He sweats and shakes. He knows. They are his.

"Douglas Dean?" says one of them, five feet away.

"Yes," says Doug.

"We have here a warrant for your arrest in the murder of Jane Cathcart Dean."

"Jesus," he says.

"Turn around, please," says the cop. Doug turns, and the second cop sweeps Doug's right arm back and cuffs it, then joins it with the left. While this is going on the first cop recites the required warning of rights. Doug hangs his head.

"I feel dead," he says to me sideways. One of the cops gently pushes me away from Doug and aims him in a new direction.

People stand like statues throughout the room. Doug is danced toward the door and out. The door closes softly, hissing. It seems like a long time after he's gone before anyone speaks again. But no one says very much—a few words, a single word, a question that hangs unanswered. There's a fear in the air. We stand here dressed alike. We have the closed-off feeling of a tribe. We look tenderly at each other's eyes. We listen carefully when anyone says anything. Then we shake our heads and look down at the trays of mail. We continue to go about our business. There is no substitute for getting ready.

For the first time I do the route perfectly, racing through the friendly flats and climbing the high stairs of the hills without my legs tiring or my lungs running short of breath. The mail flows out of the trays and into the bag, out of the bag and through the brass slots or into the black or silver boxes with a slick whisper. My fingertips have the right degree of moisture; paper slides without slipping, and yet also without sticking. Any carrier will tell you: It doesn't often happen this way. In fact, today there is a pleasing harmonization of my every movement with the work environment. The air is clear; the day is sunny; the temperature is in the mid to upper fifties.

There can be nothing better.

On Sutter and Spruance streets someone has ripped the police sketches off the telephone poles. I see small scabs of paper pinned beneath the remaining staples. Does this mean that people have taken them in to study them more closely? Does it mean that someone else believes himself to be resembled by the sketch?

There are countless possibilities among which I cannot know the true answer.

I have made my decision, which nothing can change.

Karen meets me at the back door and asks for a ride to the airport.

"Reporters have been here," she says. "I have to leave town. They stand outside and film the house. They don't even come up and ring the bell. I kept waiting for it. I crawled on my hands and knees and peeked over the window sills. It was nuts. They just stand outside and fucking drink coffee."

I go in through the kitchen and creep to the front. The street appears empty. Then I hear a rustling sound in the nearest bushes outside the window, and I fall backwards, startled, onto the dining room rug.

I hear Karen calling the police.

"This is Karen Dean calling. At Nineteen Hobart Street? There are television reporters here trespassing. Can you do something?"

I go upstairs. The doors are all open. The beds are unmade, pillows thrown on the floor. The disorder is impressive, thorough. I feel my face in a squint. It is hard to tell if this is the usual level of recent household neglect or if the police have been here executing a warrant. Or both. I go into the bathroom and stare down into the toilet. It hasn't been flushed and is full of everything, like on a bus. I flush it. The water rushes in and swirls; I close my eyes and listen to the sound, hearing the insistent voice that water sometimes presents to me. The voice whispers: "It's time, it's time, it's time, it's time," slowly deepening, falling, coughing, becoming still.

Karen stands in the bathroom doorway and says, "They won't do anything. They're fucking scum."

"Help me carry my stuff down," I say.

"Okay," she says.

We load the truck. Even taking everything, there isn't that much. Karen's two small suitcases go on last. We stretch the black tarp across and fasten the eyelets over the toggle clips, making it snug.

"Where you going?" I say.

"Back to school."

"South Carolina?"

"Yeah."

"I'll drive you there," I say. "I'm heading south."

"That's nice," she says. "But no. I've got an open ticket that's already paid for. I just want to get there fast."

I take a last walk through my rooms. I cherish their emptiness. They have a nothing kind of smell that I never noticed when all my possessions were in them. My nostrils are amazed to search and not find. They widen and try again and again.

"What are you smelling?" says Karen.

"Nothing," I say.

I deliberately try to find a sign of myself. I look in the corners. I run my finger along the top of the baseboard. Nothing. I stand on a chair and look in the top of the closet. Nothing.

"It doesn't matter," she says. "You always leave *something*."

I go in the bathroom and flush the toilet. I run hot water in the sink. I open the medicine cabinet and see the emptiness, the tiny spots of rust on the white enamel. I close it and see Karen in the mirror, curious.

We drive up to Boston in silence. Karen stares out the window. Just south of the city the moon rises behind and between huge gas tanks.

"Look at that," she says.

Soon we go through a tunnel under the harbor. Tiles are missing from the dirty white walls, and the ceiling in places is tattered and water-damaged.

"The last time I was here, my mother drove me," says Karen.

"I know," I say.

"I've tried to miss her, but I don't," she says. "I don't miss her, and I don't care what they do to him. I swear, if a reporter asked me I might say that. Wouldn't that scare everyone?"

We come out of the tunnel into darkness and a sharp right curve.

"Show me where they discovered her," she says.

"I don't know where it was." I tell her. "I wouldn't even be able to find my way."

I keep driving toward the green airport sign, hugging the curve. But in actuality I believe that I could somehow find it, that I could follow a signal still dimly beckoning outward from the spot, the neighborhood air now fully inhabiting the space where the dark trunk of the Deans' Chevrolet once hung. On a street whose name I have now forgotten, if ever I knew it. I believe that I could find it.

"Falcon Street," says Karen.

I ignore her. We are in the airport environment.

"Okay," she says. "Never mind."

Huge signs span the roadway giving the names of airlines and the letters of terminals.

"Which one?"

"USAir," she says. "It's B."

I am already coming to be someplace else. The airport is a good transition, being no place in particular. It produces a stinging sensation in my eyes, the slow circling, the bright, odd-shaped shuttles, the rising and falling pitch of jet engines, the sweet smell of their fuel. I squint. Cars and cabs and buses float left and right across the lanes, merging, close to touching. I look for the letter *B*.

"Departures," Karen says.

The roadway splits. I ascend to the level of the gates.

"USAir," I say, threading in among double- and triple-parked unloaders. The brakes squeal. She opens the door and jumps out. A chill sweeps in. She slams the door on the chill, which buffets me. I get out and go to the back of the truck, leaving the door open. She stands there staring dumbly at the tailgate. I unfasten some clips and throw back the tarp. I take out her two bags. I put them at her feet, the new lower spot where her eyes are aimed. She reaches down and takes the handles.

"So long," I say.

"Good luck," she says, looking up quickly to try and catch me in some expression.

Nothing else happens. She turns and walks, becoming vapor, distance, emptiness. It could almost be that I never knew a Karen Dean. Doors open and close automatically. The hair at the back of my neck stands up, and a shake goes through me. I stretch the tarp down over the toggle clips and make the truck secure.

I am ready to go, and I don't know where. But once I have pulled the door shut behind me, no one will ever see me again in Massachusetts. I won't come back. As I stand here thinking of what I will do, someone honks. I turn and wave, smiling into the many possibilities of bright headlights, smiling and waving at nothing. I reach for the handle of the door.

The truck rides smoothly, floating as though the stubborn roads have softened to a skin that yields obligingly to tires. There are no bumps or jolts, only a hum—a harmony. This is how a departure should always feel, with no troubling difficulties cropping up to throw the move into question. I am on the Massachusetts Turnpike headed west, the fingertips of two hands resting lightly on the steering wheel, in the manner of my father, feeling the contact with the road flow into me, up the arms and through the chest, completing a circuit. I am almost alone on the road. My headlights shoot ahead and capture nothing, and for long stretches no other headlights appear behind me. I have passed the Worcester exits and am waiting for the road that goes south. I have begun to promise the South to myself, the several states clustering downward into Florida. These are places I have never been and yet deep inside of which I envision something for me, an emptiness that I can fill.

Everything always turns out to be a preparation for something else. But not until you encounter that something else does the meaning of the preparation come clear. Neil went alone to Mexico the summer after he graduated from high school. I stood at a window and watched him walk out to the car, a used blue Chevy Impala convertible with a ripped and faded black top. My mother was outside with him, squinting in the bright sun, reaching into the backseat to arrange his two bags just so. Neil watched this arranging activity of hers go on for quite a while. Then he performed a gesture that marked him for me as a newly grown man: He turned our mother by the shoulders and kissed her on the cheek, then pointed her back toward the house, launching her gently up the flagstone walk. With her head down she took a few steps and stopped, looking back at Neil over her shoulder. I saw his lips move: Good-bye, Mother. Then he smiled and got into the car and drove away with an absolute suddenness that shocked me. My mother stood motionless on the sidewalk for the longest time, staring at the empty street. And I stood at the window watching her, feeling the silence of the house, the absence of Neil, waiting for her to move again toward the front door, to fill the house back up to some degree, to help me begin my summer alone with her.

Then, when at last she started moving up the walk, I suddenly turned from the window and went quickly to the kitchen and out the back door, letting it bang. I hurried down the steps and around the corner of the house and walked away through the neighborhood, away and into downtown Spokane, where I spent the afternoon in a cool, dark, nearly empty theater watching the same thing two and a half times but paying almost no attention to it. It was better than having to be at home to comfort my grieving mother.

Neil came back two days later, surprising us at dinner. At the first distant sound of the throaty engine, my mother looked up from her plate, alert as a dog.

"Do you hear it?" she said. "It's your brother." We went to the window and watched the car pull up.

He had gone only as far as San Francisco before deciding to turn around. I tried to think up excuses for his return, and asked him leading questions that invited a variety of explanations of something bad that had happened having to do with money or the car. But he just shook his head.

"No," he said peacefully. "I just decided I wanted to come home." Then he smiled that same grown-up smile he had given my mother upon leaving, and I stared at him as if he had slipped forever into some unreachable, faraway zone. He sat in our father's old chair and balanced a beer on his knee.

"Why?" I said.

He shrugged. "I guess I just stopped and asked myself what I was doing. And I decided the only reason I was going away was just to be able to say I'd done it. But I wasn't having any real fun being off by myself. I didn't know anybody in Mexico, or anyplace else along the way. And I started thinking about all the money I could make this summer and save for college. And I thought about leaving the two of you here all alone. It felt really selfish. I don't know . . . It was a lot of things."

"I'm so proud of you," my mother said, coming in from the kitchen with an amber drink in one hand and a tea towel in the other. Neil looked at her.

"I mean it," she said. She raised the glass in salute.

Neil nodded and joggled the cold neck of the beer bottle between his fingers. Our mother sat down beside me on the couch and slapped me happily on the thigh.

"Neil's back!" she said. Neil stared at me, and I saw that he knew I had his number. Underneath all his grown-up thoughtfulness was the fear of just being out there alone. He tried, but he couldn't do it.

"He sure is," I said.

I think of Neil when I am setting out by myself for someplace new, someplace where I have never been, where I don't know a single soul, and where I can't predict exactly what will happen. This is how Neil and I were always different. Nothing tugs me back. I feel so perfectly normal now. In fact, the urge is absolutely still. I have gone for days without a flare-up. I am just a lone man traveling in his truck. And I ask myself: What if the urge has finally been outlived? I have sometimes thought that this was possible, that the urge would simply stop of its own accord and I could go on and live without it. And everything else that comes after will turn out to be the life that the urge prepared me for and left me ready to make my peace with. A new journey is a fresh opportunity to have a better life and leave something worse behind. So I make this pact with myself: If I can get to where I am going without the urge reappearing, I will launch the silver canister high over some body of water—an ocean or a lake, whichever is handy—and I will watch it spin like a spaceship in the moonlight, falling forever. And then I will go to a church and make my apologies.

I see up ahead the green sign for the interstate highway that will begin to take me south. It has the number 86, which is the designation of anything that has vanished. I am vanishing from Massachusetts. I am prepared for whatever comes next.

Behind me bright headlights are coming up fast, at a rate of speed that I have always associated with police. The car comes closer and closer to me and then shoots past with a whoosh. Not police. But abruptly it slows in the left lane and lets me float up right beside it. We are side by side, like horses. Suddenly I feel a light on my face. I turn to this light and see that it is a flashlight beam, incredibly bright, shining on me through the closed window of the other car and the closed window of my truck. The beam holds steady, shimmering. I turn my full face away from the light and give it only profile. I tap on the brakes to slow the truck. The car slows too, the light unwavering.

Then the exit for route 86 approaches and I turn my blinker on and move to the right. The flashlight switches off and leaves me in the dark. The car surges on ahead, past the exit, disappearing, floating, looking for someone.